OF 22 THE
SHIELD
HERO

Aneko Yusagi

Natalia

Filolia

Mamoru Shirono

THE RISING OF 22 THE SHIELD HERO

Ren Amaki

Naofumi Iwatani

Raphtalia

"Filolia," Mamoru said. There was no reply. The girl floated in the culture tank, eyes closed, saying nothing.

Table of Contents

Prologue: The Reticent Blacksmith

Ren was blacksmithing in the village. He lifted a piece of softened, red-hot metal from the blazing forge, placed it down on the anvil, and started to hammer it. There was a clanging sound as sparks scattered. He worked the metal gradually into the shape of a weapon.

I was watching him work as I made accessories alongside my fellow accessory-making student, Imiya. Ren continued to swing his hammer with intense concentration, completely absorbed in making more weapons.

"Shield Hero?" Imiya asked me.

"Huh? Right, sorry, I'm here," I replied. I decided to stop looking over at Ren and get back to work.

My name is Naofumi Iwatani. I was once a regular university student until I read a book in the library called *The Records of the Four Holy Weapons*. Before I knew it, I'd been summoned to a completely different, fantasy world. I was summoned to play the role of one of the characters from the book, the holy Shield Hero. The world I was summoned to was at risk from a series of disasters known as the "waves." I was summoned to help fight off that destruction, but that proved to only be the start of my troubles.

First, I was framed for rape. That was bad. Even after I cleared my name, there were all sorts of other issues. I was still seeking the one who framed me, a woman now named "Bitch," but she continued to elude justice. I wanted to put her to the sword as quickly as possible, but while she kept on showing up in the places we visited, she always managed to get away—often with the help of her mysterious allies.

In any case, suffice it to say that it had been one thing after another since the day I was summoned here.

It had first seemed to be simply about surviving the waves and restoring peace to the world, but all sorts of other information had come to light in the time since my arrival. We'd recently learned that the waves were being caused by an advanced civilization from yet another world. They were called "the ones who assume the name of god." They had a habit of turning other worlds into their playthings. If nothing were done about the waves, they would cause different worlds to merge. And if too many worlds merged in a single place, they would all be wiped out.

This made the ones who assume the name of god our enemies, and they weren't taking our resistance lying down. One ploy they were using to try and stop us was to pick megalomaniacal losers out from other worlds and send them to ours as the "resurrected," with orders to kill the heroes (the heroes were the ones who could combat the waves) and destroy information and records from the past, as well as all sorts of other convenient gear. It had already taken us a long time to learn just this much, and we'd been through all sorts of battles along the way. I'd even traveled to yet another different world, where I made friends with a girl called Kizuna Kazayama, the Hunting Tool Hero.

We had received word from Kizuna that she and her allies were on the ropes, hounded by more resurrected sent by the ones who assume the name of god. We'd headed back to her world to help out, but this had placed us on the radar of the sworn enemies of S'yne, a girl joining us from a world already wiped out by the waves. This unwanted attention ultimately resulted in me and a group of my allies being sent back into the past of the world I had been first summoned to.

That was the tip of the iceberg in terms of the shit I'd had to wade through since arriving here—and now we were stuck in the past.

However, more recently, things had taken a turn for the better. We had succeeded in killing one of those who assume the name of god—one of those causing the waves. He had been hosting what seemed to be some kind of wave death game, and we'd managed to catch him off guard and kill him.

We'd learned some more things during that battle too. For a start, none of the most powerful weapons we heroes could wield were able to hurt the ones who assume the name of god.

The 0 series of weapons, however, had proven most effective. I had obtained the 0 series by placing a drop from a red potion into my shield, which we found in some ruins back in the time period I was originally summoned to. As the name suggested, the 0 series was a very risky-looking set of weapons that had zeros across the board for all stats, including attack and defense. It was most ironic that these hunks of junk were effective against the ones who assume the name of god, those wielders of seemingly infinite power.

Based on the vague information we had received from those same ruins, it sounded like the role of the four holy heroes was to buy the worlds some time until those who could actually drive off the ones who assume the name of god could arrive . . . a group now being called the God Hunters. The 0 series had likely been left in this world by the God Hunters in the period between when we were in the past and when we can come from in the future. That was why we had managed to kill that one who assumes the name of god.

Our current goal at the moment, however, was to find a way back to the future we had come from. We hadn't completely defeated the ones who assume the name of god, but finding a way home was important too, so we'd just have to do both of those things for a while.

That was the situation.

In that exact moment, we were making new weapons and

armor for the sake of the village and villagers who had been sent back into the past along with us. We could expect more fighting in this time period. We had a forge in the village, and all sorts of materials at our disposal, so if we threw in some crafty people, we could make some good stuff.

I was leaving weapons and armor to Ren Amaki, the Sword Hero. He had been apprenticed to the weapons old guy—one of my staunchest allies—back in our time and learned plenty of forging techniques from him. Meanwhile, Imiya and I—both students of accessory making—were helping out by making accessories. Taking advantage of the blessings and techniques provided to us by the four holy weapons, we could turn out gear that was better than gear made by a lot of so-called professionals.

"Shield Hero, what do you think about this stone here?" Imiya asked me.

"Let's have a look." I lifted the stone to the light and peered into it. "No translucency problems, that's for sure." I could check the quality of materials just using the skills provided by my shield, but sometimes they could still be cloudy or flawed in minor ways even after I used the skill, so it wasn't one hundred percent accurate.

"We need to heat-treat it, don't we?" Imiya said.

"That will really bring out the color," I agreed. "But go too hard and you'll crack it. Imiya, I'll leave that side of things up to you."

This world was a lot like a video game. Equipping accessories provided bonuses to stats. The accessory dealer who taught me the craft was actually one of the most skilled creators in the world, and in turn, I could now make pretty good products myself.

I also knew of at least one other person who had stepped on the path of accessory making—a guy called L'Arc. But Imiya was a lumo therianthrope—a mole girl, basically—who was one of the slaves in my village. Her real name was too long for me to remember. Her skills with her hands had allowed her to apprentice with me under the accessory dealer. I watched her use earth magic to shape the stone she was holding in her hands. She could even alter things like its density. All very useful tricks to have.

"I think this stone can be used now," Imiya said.

"Okay. We'll get it heat-treated. What about the design?" I asked.

"We're mainly making accessories for the Sword Hero, correct?" Imiya confirmed with me.

"That's right," I replied. "I was thinking of making a scabbard, but Ren asked for something else. He wants to remove the hassle of even having to sheathe his sword." Attaching accessories to a hero's weapon could provide all sorts of additional effects. Sometimes they just provided a pure stat boost, but they could also change skills or do other stuff. Some effects could only be applied to a sword through the use of a scabbard, but in that case the sword had to be sheathed in order to gain those benefits. The results of doing so could be quite dramat- ic—Raphtalia, the Katana Hero and my right hand, could attack at an even faster speed than normal by drawing her blade from her scabbard. This time, though, I was going to make some- thing that could be attached to the pommel of the sword—like a key holder, basically. "I'm also hoping we get lucky and make an accessory that gives float skills an auto-tracking function," I said. Trying to work that out would be completely trial and error. Ren wasn't all that great at using the Float Sword skill, but he also seemed strangely obsessed with getting better with it.

The one who assumes the name of god had used a similar method to attack us. It was a convenient feather to have in your cap, even just from the perspective of increasing your number of attacks.

Even if we didn't bag something related to the float skill, there were other appealing skills we might get our hands on. Key-holder-type accessories could also be passed on to Raphta- lia and other party members.

"I think the Sword Hero would like this kind of design," Imiya said, quickly sketching out some lines. Even just a rough image could help to give the desired item form. I drew my own design for a gemstone-like key holder. It was nothing too large, easy to use, added a little accent when equipped, and was something Raphtalia and the others could also use easily. I also made some that looked like bird wings and some like those long-range weapons from that one famous robot anime. They basically looked like onions, unless you knew what you were looking at. People who hadn't seen any of that anime would be super puzzled by it.

Then I looked over at Imiya's design, and it made me furrow my brow. It looked like something a middle-school kid would like—a magic circle with a silver cross and a gemstone in the middle. The whole thing was set up to look like an eye. It was pretty twisted.

"Tell me about that," I asked her carefully.

"What about it? I'm sure the Sword Hero will love this kind of design," she replied. She was right; Ren probably would love it. He'd once tried to pull off the whole too-cool-for-school thing. But he'd probably be too embarrassed to take this if he was offered it directly; like even if you had a collection of porn, you wouldn't admit it to a family member.

"Sure, why not?" I eventually conceded. "If he doesn't want it, we can give it to someone else. I can try it out too." Either way, I wanted to see his reaction.

It might not have much of an effect as an accessory for me, but it could be cool to just wear it for decorative purposes. It could fit around the gemstone part of my shield, like a cap. That might be cool.

"What do you think for materials?" Imiya asked. "I'm still trying to decide my overall approach . . ."

"How about using some Glawick ore? That will give it floating properties and might draw out the desired effect—or at least raise speed," I pondered.

"Okay. I'll try that," she agreed. It was easy chatting with Imiya because she possessed the same skills as I did and understood where I was coming from.

We made a mold, melted down the metal, and poured it in. As I checked the metal as it melted in the forge, a string of different accessories started to take shape. Even as we worked, the sounds of Ren's hammer provided metallic percussion in the background. He was so focused on his work that he didn't seem bothered by us bustling around him. That intense focus was one of his best qualities, but it was also a weakness—when he concentrated too hard, he lost all awareness of things around him. I peeked over at what he was making . . . It looked like a katana. Both Ren and Raphtalia could use a katana, so it would be useful.

He placed the hot katana into water. Maybe he was finished. I tilted my head when I noticed that the water was swirling around.

"Phew!" Ren wiped the sweat from his brow and looked up, then turned around when he realized I was behind him. "Hey, Naofumi."

"You were pretty deep in the forest, huh?" I said.

"Yeah, I guess so," he replied.

"How's the finished product? Any good?" I asked. He pulled the weapon from the water and looked it over. It wasn't completely finished yet, and the blade itself was still dull, but it still looked like there was some kind of vortex of air swirling around it. "Looks good to me. A nice new weapon. Like a wind katana or something?" An elemental weapon. I'd seen them somewhere before.

"Huh . . . to be honest, this isn't going to be close to what my master can make," Ren admitted.

"Really?" I asked. The appraisal technique offered by my shield indicated that he was maintaining a high level of quality, even if he wasn't finished yet. The rules of this world allowed an energy called life force to be imbued into things to increase their quality. Adding life force to food, for example, would make it taste super delicious. I often used this technique myself when I was making accessories. It was no exaggeration to say that simply being aware of this technique, and being able to apply it, would make a decisive difference to the quality of the item you were making.

On the other hand, while it was enough to make you *almost* as good as a specialist craftsman, it still wasn't quite enough to allow you to compete with them. Of course, *I* intended to compete . . . eventually.

"Yeah. If Master was making this, he would be finished by now, and it would be better than mine," Ren said. Ren's master was a terrible womanizer—a lot like the Spear Hero Motoyasu had been before his complete break with reality. Internally, I called the old goat "Motoyasu II." He was a great blacksmith though; I wasn't doubting that. He just wouldn't make any weapons for me. "This just makes me feel—again—that I really can't compete with him," Ren admitted.

"Don't beat yourself up too badly, okay? This intense concentration is all very well, but you need to make sure to get some rest," I told him. While I was away in Kizuna's world, Ren had been left in charge of the village—and the sense of responsibility that had created had left him immobilized. He had been looking out for the villagers, dealing with Motoyasu and his rampages, and also training hard—that was a lot to take on. I'd known about all that stuff, but it seemed he'd been forging weapons as well. That was a schedule so packed I was left wondering if he got any sleep at all. Maybe he had been hoping to work himself to death.

"I will," he replied. "What about you, Naofumi?"

"Just need to piece these together and buff them up a bit. Right, Imiya?" I said.

"That's right! We've finished a few of them already!" Imiya said brightly, lifting up some of the accessories for Ren to see.

"Take a break later and go test these out, okay?" I said to Ren.

"Okay. I'll let you know what effects I find. I'm also making a shield for you to use, Naofumi, so that's something for you to look forward to," Ren replied, showing me the work-in-progress shield. He was using the materials from the Phoenix we had defeated a while back, and it looked red and warm to the touch already.

"Looks like a hot one," I commented.

"That's due to the materials," Ren replied. "Master says they'll split apart if the temperature isn't carefully controlled." The Spirit Tortoise materials had been hard to handle too, and it had taken the weapons old guy a decent chunk of time to complete my Spirit Tortoise Carapace Shield—which was now the shield I used the most. From that perspective, Ren was probably doing well just to keep the shield in a cohesive shape. He must have been instructed in how to handle these materials, or this would surely have taken him even longer to pull off. "I can't match my master—or the old guy—and I don't quite have a handle on these materials either, so it could be a pretty rough job . . . but it might produce some skills you can use. Look forward to it," Ren said.

"You bet," I replied. Ren already had his own sword made from Phoenix materials, a weapon he had received from his master. It was called a "Scissors Sword," able to split into two blades or be used as one big one.

Ren was looking at the katana he made, sighing to himself.

"You got a problem there?" I asked.

"What makes you think that?" he replied.

"The way you're acting, it would be strange to think otherwise," I stated. From what I had seen, it looked like a pretty solid weapon. He'd mixed in some of Filo's feathers she had shed. That was likely to make Motoyasu jealous, if he heard about it. Filo had recently become "Filo of the Wind," one of the four heavenly kings, in Kizuna's world. That made her well suited to providing materials. It was impressive that she was still helping out, back here in the past. Maybe I should have Ren use the remaining feathers to make a staff for Melty.

"It's just . . . whatever I make, it feels like I hit a wall. I can't match my master in anything, let alone quality. Master said my work is too bland, that I'm just doing what I'm told—what I think he wants—and I need to put more of myself into my work . . . but I don't really know what that means," Ren said. In this new light, I looked at the katana, shield, and other practice pieces that Ren had made. I saw it immediately.

"Yeah, bland. That really is the word," I commented.

"Shield Hero, I don't think you should . . ." Imiya said, stunned at how blunt I was. I loved getting that kind of response from her—like I did with Raphtalia. The banter would have proceeded even more smoothly if she finished her sentence and pushed me a little harder.

At that moment, Raphtalia herself was off with Eclair—a

knight from Melromarc, who was Ren's guardian. They were helping out with our trading. The two of them had been training too. They got along pretty well.

"What I mean is they're balanced but average . . . no outstanding strengths, but no staggering flaws either," I said. They would be easy to use, for sure. I didn't hate that. But they could be a little more . . . stimulating too.

"Hurts my ears to hear it," Ren admitted. "That's exactly what Master said to me—that I'm not working a production line here. Can you tell me what I should be doing instead, Naofumi?" I wasn't sure I should tell him anything. Keeping quiet might be better for Ren's own personal development. One could often improve at something by simply doing it repeatedly. Even before we started training, I was using my free time to make accessories and medicine. Making medicine had been pretty easy, especially with my cooking experience.

I showed Ren the designs that Imiya and I had just come up with.

"This is the answer here," I said.

"That looks pretty nice," he said, but also furrowed his brow a little. Then he looked at the one Imiya created and didn't seem sure what to say. It was written on his face though; he wanted to use it.

"We designed this to add an auto-tracking feature to your float weapons. Hopefully it will work," I told him.

"You did?" he replied. "Okay then . . ."

"We'll make it using materials suited to that purpose," I assured him. I seemed to remember not only the accessory dealer but also Motoyasu II telling me that a deep understanding of materials was vital for accessory work. He only mentioned it once, so I've pretty much forgotten about it.

Ren had a bigger problem than that, anyway.

"Ren, you need to stop holding yourself back. That's why you keep choosing these plain, unremarkable forms. You need to bring your adolescent semi-goth, death-metal sensibilities to the fore! Let your freak flag fly!" I told him. As soon as I said it, I knew it was a terrible line. So cheesy and bad. I would never have gone for that myself, if someone said that to me.

"What the hell? What are you talking about? I'm not into that stuff!" Ren shouted, shaking a little woodenly and averting his gaze. This was exactly what I'd been thinking about before—he understood the truth, deep inside, but was too embarrassed to admit it.

"You were a jerk when we first got here," I told him, keeping the blunt streak going, "but I think you would have been better suited to this kind of work. You need that kind of confidence! Let Motoyasu work with Filo's materials and I'm sure he'd make something better than this!" Motoyasu had already been making clothing for the filolials by hand. His skills with needle and thread were so impressive the Sewing Kit Hero

S'yne considered him a rival. The source of that power was his insane—almost sick—love for Filo. If I asked him to make clothing that would allow Filo to shine even brighter, and that used Filo's materials . . . the results would be so epic I almost considered doing it. Of course, Filo was highly unlikely to wear anything Motoyasu made.

"You think that's all I need to do?" Ren asked.

"That's how this world works. Makes me sick to say it," I told him. The student from the bottom of the barrel has more room to grow than the perfectly sculpted honor student. It sounded like the main character from some pulpy novel, and I could kind of understand his desire to deny it. "What I want to say is you need to push down your reason a little and work based on instinct. Presupposing you have the skills required for the task, of course." He was able to blend Filo's feathers into metal, so he had to be pretty good at this. I might be able to use a Filo feather as an additional little decoration, but I couldn't hope to mix them with metal. The two hardly seemed compatible to me. Being able to pull that off told me that Ren's forging skills were already pretty advanced. What he needed was to break free of the internal limitations he placed on himself. If he continued to be reticent, taking the bland and safe path, he would never be able to bring out the true potential hidden in these materials.

The weapons old guy and Motoyasu II had cautioned

him on this point too. Back then he had been trying to make a sword, but it had turned into a katana. They had told him to listen to the voice of the materials and then bend them to his will, but Ren clearly hadn't made it to the "bending" part yet.

"Start by using life force as you work. That should provide you with some kind of image; make what you see," I suggested.

"Ah. Master said something like that. I think I get what you mean," Ren replied.

"So go get good at it," I told him. I'd never heard the "voice" of ingredients when I was cooking. That annoying rotund noble had gone on about the ingredients being happy, but who cared about him? No one, I was hoping.

It almost made it sound like I was bending the ingredients to my absolute will. That wasn't the case. I was just cooking them based on my culinary experience. I wondered if that was the "voice of the ingredients." Nope, I was pretty sure it wasn't. I'd been working within the realm of home-cooked foods, basically, but recently my confidence in that area had taken a drop. I'd been called things with a kitchen theme too, like the "Pot Lid Hero." I still hadn't forgiven the one responsible for that, and never would.

"I get it, but . . . easier said than done," Ren admitted.

"Let your embarrassment go. No one makes the perfect product their first time out. Honing yourself a little at a time is how you get better at things like this," I reassured him.

"Okay. Can you watch me for a while? If you think I'm holding myself back, let me know," Ren suggested.

"I might break your concentration, but okay," I agreed. Ren nodded and then started preparing the katana for another forging. "We'll keep going with our accessories too. Don't worry, I'm watching," I said. Imiya and I started working on our accessories again, a short distance from Ren. Keeping focused on providing the assistance to float skills for Ren, I took a Glawick ingot created from Glawick ore and started my work. I'd need to add some gemstones too.

I nodded when I saw that Imiya had selected a gem shaped like a cat's eye. It had a vertical line running through it, and it was aptly called a "green cat's eye." Adding an eye gem to the eye design for an accessory, in hopes of adding a tracking effect, made sense. I'd been planning on making a similar choice, so we were able to proceed without even having to talk to each other. I had to melt the ingot, pour it into the mold, cool it, then buff it up. Imiya was already cutting the green cat's eye. The work proceeded smoothly, and each time I had a spare moment, I looked over at Ren.

With more clanging, his hammer was beating on the heated katana, further working it into shape. At a glance it didn't seem much different than before, but then I noticed the top was thicker . . . it was taking on a design like a bird. Then Ren started to rework that, trying to return it to normal. I tapped him on the shoulder and wordlessly signaled for him to leave it. He snapped back to himself with a nod and then restored that thickness.

I wasn't sure myself, but this did look like the right shape for a weapon using Filo's feathers. It had a bird-based feel now and looked like it would move pretty fast—but it didn't look like the easiest weapon to wield either.

Imiya and I continued our work, watching Ren while making our own accessories. Watching mine cool, picking my moment, I proceeded with the buffing and discussed the plating and other techniques to use with Imiya. Eventually we were finished.

Glawick Ingeye
quality: excellent

Cross Glawick Third Eye
quality: excellent

"Next, magic imbuing," I said. "First we should try them out and confirm their effects."

"Okay. Just adjusting the output during magic imbuing can create all sorts of changes. This really is a deep and complex subject," Imiya replied. Imbuing an accessory with magic could provide additional effects, but we had discovered that using a hero's weapon could noticeably change the effects from before and after the imbuing. If the effect we wanted was already there, it wasn't worth the risk of losing it.

That was good enough for the prototypes, anyway. We moved on to making multiples of the same accessories in order to increase our chances of creating desirable effects. As we went about our work, a wind suddenly whipped up inside the forge. I looked in the direction it was blowing from to see the katana that Ren was shaping taking on even more wind than before.

"Looks like it's working," I commented dryly.

"Try to calm down!" Ren shouted at the blade, not at me. All that wind gusting around made it look pretty hard to hold onto. "I haven't even sharpened you yet!" He had a frustrated look on his face. The wind continued to whirl around the weapon. It was like the blade was out of control; that sounded pretty rock 'n' roll to me. The wind katana continued to blow up a storm, completely ignoring the commands from the one who had created it. I checked it over and saw that it had definitely changed to a better product overall—just one that seemed even harder to handle. Failing to listen to anything people said sounded a lot like the one who had contributed her feathers to this endeavor. That would make sense. In which case, I had to calm it down. I moved my face closer to the weapon.

"If you don't quit right now, I'll have you reforged as a naginata and give you to . . . Motoyasu," I murmured. The weapon seemed to shake on the spot, and the wind immediately dissipated.

It was like Filo herself had become the weapon.

"Wow. That seems to have totally changed its attitude," Ren said.

"I only tried it because you said you used Filo's materials. I didn't really expect it to work," I replied.

"That's a big help, anyway. If I can follow through on this, it should be the best weapon I've ever made," Ren said.

"Good luck," I told him. He replied with a firm nod.

It didn't take long after that for Ren to finish his katana made from Filo's materials.

Heavenly Wind King Katana
quality: excellent
imbued effects: Demon Dragon's protection, power of the four heavenly kings, filolial blessing, agility increase, wind blades, quick charge

I was lucky that appraisal worked on it, maybe because of Filo's feathers. It also seemed Filo's new role as the heavenly wind king was superseding her role as a filolial. "Wind Blades" apparently allowed blades of wind to be fired off just by swinging the weapon around, while "Quick Charge" allowed the user to charge up power more quickly.

"Looks like a pretty good katana to me," I said. "What about the stats on it?"

"Not quite at the same level as the weapons Master made from the Spirit Tortoise or Phoenix," Ren admitted. With the Demon Dragon blessing and by channeling my rage through the Demon Dragon and Filo, I might be able to push them a little higher. That wasn't bad.

"Go ahead and weapon copy it, Ren. Then we can give it to Raphtalia and see what kind of abilities it gives her," I said.

"I've copied it already," he told me. He changed his sword to the Heavenly Wind King Katana. The original had a strange shape, but for some reason, his had turned into a far simpler blade. "The equip effect allows for the use of wind magic. It has haikuikku too."

"That's all Filo stuff," I said. When Ren had this sword equipped, it would expand the range of magic he could use. As it was an equip effect, he wouldn't be able to use it with anything other than the Heavenly Wing King Katana, but it was still a super high-spec weapon.

"The techniques inside . . . it has charge reduction and a bonus to agility when leveling up," Ren reported. The focus of the weapon was definitely placed on speed. "There's also a skill called Wind Cutter Whistle."

"What does that do?" I asked.

"I'm not sure. It doesn't sound like anything I know from

Brave Star Online. I'll just have to give it a try," he said. A new and powerful skill at this point would make things a lot easier in the battles ahead. My expectations were rising a little. We left the forge and Ren unleashed the skill in a spot with no one else around.

"Wind Cutter Whistle!" Ren shouted. His sword started to glow faintly. Maybe he had applied some kind of element to his weapon. Ren could already use Magic Sword, so this probably wasn't going to be all that useful after all. Ren proceeded to gingerly swing the sword, and we heard a high-pitched whistling noise.

That was when the filolials passed the forge, chattering happily about feeding time. There was a strange atmosphere in the air . . . like something surreal. The voices of the filolials almost started to sound like crows.

"Any effect?" I asked. He swung it a few more times, and I could tell the sound was changing. "I bet Itsuki could use that to cast magic just by swinging it," I commented. Once he had played music on a leaf to cast magic. Maybe a weapon like this could trigger his sound magic.

"Sorry. I don't get along well with instruments," Ren replied.

"This could just be a dead skill," I said. But it might also turn out good for something. At least Ren was making good progress as a blacksmith. "Let's check the accessories we made," I suggested. We spent the rest of the day conducting tests around the forge. I also had Raphtalia copy the Heavenly Wind King Katana, and she ended up with pretty much the same stats as Ren. She also got a skill called "Wind Wing Cutter," which was a quick draw skill to be unleashed in the air. The blade took on a winged shape and launched a powerful vacuum blade in a straight line—a perfect re-creation of one of the heavenly wind king's moves. I could see Filo throwing a typical hissy fit if she saw this, like she was being told she was no longer needed. Now Raphtalia could do the same things as she could. Her dissatisfaction at being made one of the four kings were already hard enough to deal with.

Chapter One: The Progenitor

It was the day after working with Ren and Imiya at the forge. We put the testing of the rest of the accessories on hold and headed to the castle in Siltran for a meeting. The situation was changing again, and we needed to discuss how we were going to handle it all.

Having overcome the recent battle, Siltran really seemed to be coming back to life. I'd been making those accessories with Imiya in order to sell the ones we didn't need to Siltran's rich folks to make us a bit more money to help with recovery.

"How are things looking?" I asked Melty. She was the queen of Melromarc and had also been unlucky enough to get caught up in the village being transported into the past.

"We've received emissaries from the other nations, each trying to gauge our circumstances for themselves," she replied.

"That's not the issue though," Mamoru took over, muttering to himself, head in his hands. Mamoru Shirono was apparently my predecessor as Shield Hero. He was also the one leading the nation of Siltran, which would eventually become Siltvelt. After we had been shot back here into the past, Mamoru—the Shield Hero from this time—had been the first person we met. Through that piece of good fortune, we had obtained the cooperation of the country he was leading—Siltran, which in our time would become the demi-human therianthrope nation of Siltvelt. Even here in the past there were ambitious enemies who had to be thwarted, like the massive nation of Piensa, who was leading others in the world to try and occupy Siltran. We had worked with Siltran to stop one such attempted Piensa invasion, but it had turned out that Mamoru had some secrets he couldn't share with other people.

One of these secrets was that the four ruling races of Siltvelt in the future, which seemed to be based on the four divine beasts, had been created by Mamoru here in the past by modifying orphans under his care.

But there was more. Here in the past they had also fought the guardian beasts, just like we had in the future—beasts that sought to protect the world by creating a barrier fueled by human souls. During one of those battles, Mamoru's girlfriend had been killed by Suzaku, a guardian beast, and her soul was partly absorbed. But he was now trying to bring her back to life.

Only some of those who had come to the past with me knew these facts. I was going to have to fill everyone in soon. Mamoru was still clutching his head, but he didn't look worried about his secrets getting out. His issue was more likely something else.

"They're trying to work out what we're planning, right?" I said.

"That's right," Mamoru replied.

"I've seen that look before on the generals when I was in Q'ten Lo," Ruft commented. He had been the Heavenly Emperor of Q'ten Lo, so I wasn't surprised he had experience in such matters. I'd received my own reports of more outsiders visiting the village recently. Some were trying to bring us into the fold, others trying to hold us back, while they were all conducting their own surveys to see how best to act next. Luckily, we had plenty of high-level individuals in the village, and the Raph species could spot anyone trying to come in and poke around while concealed. We also had the filolials and monsters on watch, making it pretty hard to sneak around us. That was probably why they were approaching Mamoru, trying to forge some kind of connection and see what was going on inside our nation.

They also probably wanted to know where we had even come from.

These were common tactics even in the history of the Earth I came from. A missionary would visit to spread their religion but really investigate the military strength of a nation and then report back to their homeland. If a decision was made the nation could be defeated, the invasion would follow quickly. Even if our visitors didn't have such aggressive plans, they were likely checking to make sure we weren't a threat to their own nation. Wanting to find out the truth behind warriors capable of defeating one of those who assume the name of god or making sure their own nation wasn't at risk . . . there were multiple reasons. It wasn't difficult to give them the boot, after all. But either way, I wanted to avoid a situation with emissaries coming to the village at every hour of the day or night.

Another issue was that our village had arrived close to Siltran's border. It wasn't exactly the best location. Defeating the ones behind the waves was important, but getting back to our own time was important too. However, if we could defeat all of the ones who assume the name of god in this time period, maybe it would bring peace to the future. We could hope. There were also S'yne's sworn enemies, the force that Bitch had aligned herself with and that had been pulling the strings of the chaos in Kizuna's world. They seemed to be an extension of the forces of the ones who assume the name of god, and so changing history might wipe them out completely—not that I was counting on such a simple solution to our problems.

In any case, we needed to find a way back home. That was something we weren't having much luck with, and under those circumstances, it was foolish to worry too much about keeping nosy visitors happy when we had no real idea what they wanted.

"Queen Melty is a political animal," I said. "We should probably leave this kind of stuff to her." Melty had spent most of her life observing the complicated political dealings of a massive nation back in our own time period, so she should be able to bring those skills to bear here. It was a stroke of luck that we had the perfect person for the job here with us.

"You know how to put me to work, Naofumi," Melty moaned.

"We can handle any fighting that breaks out, but when it comes to political stuff, that's your arena," I responded.

"I guess you're right. I don't think we have to worry about them now, anyway. Just let them do their thing. In fact, we should probably be putting on a show of force for them—even more than we have already," Melty suggested.

"Should we avoid revealing too much about the ongoing recovery, then?" I asked. The nation was still in tatters after the war and the Suzaku attack. The lumo we had in the village were all good with their hands, and we had them helping out with the repairs. Things were proceeding well, but the cracks still showed, if you looked hard enough.

"No need to hide that stuff. They know the extent of that already. The bigger threat at the moment are those of us from the future, Naofumi," Melty said with a serious expression on her face. "We're going to start facing all sorts of plans and attacks to try and steal us away. We need not only the trading parties but everyone in the village to be strong enough to defend themselves from whatever might come."

"Sounds like some more level grinding ahead," I said. It wasn't a bad idea to enhance our forces. In this world, killing monsters allowed for experience points to be gained, represented as a numerical value. Once a certain amount of them were accrued, you could level up and become stronger. I recalled the battle with S'yne's sister. Based on our struggles in that conflict, it was clear that even we heroes needed more levels.

Each of the weapons a hero held had a power-up method inside, and from among these methods there was one that allowed the basic quality—the foundation abilities that would become future strength—to be enhanced via the consumption of levels. We were making use of it ourselves. But based on what we had seen in battle with S'yne's sister—who also possessed a hero weapon herself, as did others in the force she belonged to—she was clearly enhancing herself in the same kind of way. That meant there was a gap in our abilities that was difficult to pinpoint based purely on level number. Even if on the surface we appeared to be the same—say level 80—if the accumulated enhancement actually created a 100-level gap, then in reality we wouldn't stand a chance.

The waves had also led to monsters rampaging across the world, causing all sorts of damage. Cleaning up some of those monsters would help keep the peace, and the enhancement received from it would also be useful once we got back home.

"Good idea. We need to show them that they'll get a fight if they come for us. What we really need to watch for, though, is the possibility of attempts to obtain sensitive information from people other than the heroes," Melty warned.

"I think all the villagers are on the ball when it comes to that. We should be fine," I said, a little offhandedly. Many of the people in the village I had restored came from the same nation as Raphtalia, and almost all of them were former slaves. They were generally a lighthearted and cheerful bunch, but they had all been through the wringer in various ways and knew how harsh the world could be. That said, some of them weren't that smart. We did need to be careful. "I guess a potential issue would be that yappy puppy, the filolials, and Keel," I pondered.

"You just said Keel twice," Raphtalia noted archly.

"She's so dumb. That's my concern. Even if it isn't for some totally nefarious scheme, she could easily fall for some legit-looking spy and start giving stuff away," I said.

"That's . . . actually quite possible," Raphtalia admitted.

"I have to question you questioning the filolials so casually. Why did you ignore that part, Raphtalia?" Melty cut in.

"Ah, I'm sorry," Raphtalia replied.

"I'm just telling the truth," I defended myself.

"That's right," Ruft backed me up. "There's nothing scarier than a flock of filolials."

"You need to stop giving all your favors to the Raph species and start getting along with the filolials too," Melty chided him.

"I don't think that's going to happen," he replied.

"I simply can't believe you were once such a filolial fan," Melty said, putting a hand to her forehead at Ruft's response.

"Filolials are violent beasts, after all. There are still some who come after Keel and Imiya, seeing them as prey. Ruft has his head on straight in this matter," I said. The filolials we were talking about were avian monsters large enough to pull a wagon. They developed in unique ways if they were raised by a hero. They were generally easygoing and loved to eat, but they could turn violent.

"I'm not sure how I should respond to this exchange," Mamoru said from the sidelines, evidently unsure what expression to make. We had recently discovered that the filolials were probably creatures originally created by Holn, the Whip Hero in this time. There were all sorts of secrets concealed back here in the past, meaning we had to stay alert even though we knew the future. There could be any number of pitfalls waiting around each corner.

"What about your girlfriend? Overcome her little problem yet?" I asked him. I was talking about the self-named Filolia, the Claw Hero and seemingly the origin of the filolials. When I said "little problem," I was actually talking about her death in battle. Mamoru was desperately trying to bring her back to life. We had been party to a recent experiment to do so, and I was subtly asking about how it was going.

"You have a girlfriend?" Melty asked, picking up on something and looking over at Mamoru.

"It's going well. You and your friends have really helped the situation, Naofumi. But there's no need to hide any of this here, is there?" he asked.

"I already know you're keeping secrets. Isn't it about time you let me in on them?" Melty asked. She was of royal blood, after all. She could pick up on someone hiding something but continue to ignore it on purpose, if it so suited the situation. It was the mark of a ruler. If she couldn't play these kinds of games, she wouldn't be fit to lead the largest nation in the future.

"Okay. We can let you know now," Mamoru said. "All thanks to you, Naofumi. But . . . I would rather Natalia doesn't hear about this," he confessed with a wry smile. Then Mamoru started to explain to Melty all the secrets he had been keeping.

Our discovery of all this had come on the night before we defeated one of the ones who assume the name of god. Cian, one of the kids Mamoru looked after, had led us into a hidden research base located beneath Siltran castle. There we had uncovered his experiments to restore his girlfriend Filolia to life and his modification of kids into the future representative races of Siltvelt. We'd had a bit of a scuffle, but they had proven unable to match us. Cian and I managed to talk Mamoru down, and after accepting defeat, he had explained the situation. We had gone on to pretty much resolve it for him.

"I don't think that's especially pleasant research," Melty admitted, "but considering what we're facing, maybe we should accept it as a necessary evil." After what we had seen during the last wave, it wasn't surprising that she might think this way. We'd been lucky enough to have a weapon that proved effective in the battle; if we'd been left to our regular means, we wouldn't have stood a chance.

We still didn't know what path the past was going to take, but at some point after this, the filolials would be created.

"I see," Melty finally said. "I had no idea the origin of the filolials concealed such a sad secret."

"You can accept this, Melty? You too, Ruft?" Raphtalia asked.

"Making a fuss about it now won't change anything. It sounds like Naofumi has already negotiated this out," Melty replied pragmatically.

"How is this different from what happened with Mikey?" Ruft said, also totally casual about the whole thing. "The Raph species were created in a slightly different way, perhaps, but isn't it the same kind of thing in the end?" Ruft hung out in his Raph species-like therianthrope form most of the time—Keel could even take notes. He was in his demi-human form right then, and Raphtalia gave him a strange look. I guessed it was because he looked so much like her own father. That made me wonder which of his forms caused her less mental distress. Both of them were hard on her, just in different ways.

"Of course," Raphtalia finally said, with a twist of her mouth. "You've already undergone human experimentation yourself, haven't you, Ruft? I chose the wrong place to look for sympathy."

"I look pretty great for it too, don't I?" Ruft said, showing off the results. Raphtalia did not reply.

"Just take a look at Naofumi's village!" Melty chipped in. "He's in no position to talk about any kind of moral code."

"That's true," Raphtalia said. "The Raph species, and Ruft, and then Ruft again. Naofumi even said he wants me to become like Ruft." She was still carrying that around.

"Sounds like you're pretty much the same as me," Mamoru said with a laugh. "That certainly makes this easier."

"Still, this isn't information we want our enemies to know. It's probably better to hide it from Natalia if we can," Melty agreed.

"I guess so," I pondered. "The worry there is that if hiding it fails, Natalia might turn on Mamoru in anger, and our alliance with her would fall apart."

"I'm asking you to do this with a full understanding of the high risk of failure. I won't hold it against you if things do fail . . . and Filolia has regained consciousness now anyway, so there's no need to even worry about it," Mamoru revealed. His eyes went over to the doorway even as he spoke. He had been wishing for this reunion with his girlfriend for so long; he must have wanted to be with her really badly.

"Oh? She's awake?" Melty asked.

"Yes. She should be able to come out soon," Mamoru said happily. Things seemed to be proceeding even more smoothly than I'd imagined. "She's awake and talking. I've explained everything about you and the others, Naofumi. I'd like to introduce you, if you have some time now?"

"Sure, okay. If she melts away the moment she comes out of that thing, don't blame us," I said.

"Why do you have to say such horrible things?" Melty chided me.

"If that did happen, I'd also be at fault. We've taken every step we can to make sure this will work," Mamoru said confidently. "No need to worry on that score." The meeting kind of fizzled out at that point, and we headed to Mamoru's previously secret underground facility.

We headed down the stairs beneath Siltran castle. Along the way we encountered one of Mamoru's familiars standing guard in front of the lab. It was the one called Fitoria. She raised a hand and gave us a casual greeting. At a glance she looked younger than the Fitoria we knew and seemed far less emotional. She wasn't exactly a doll, but it did feel like she only moved according to orders.

"Hey, Naofumi," Melty asked, tugging on my sleeve. "She looks a little younger, but is that . . . Fitoria?"

"Maybe, but I don't yet think she's the Fitoria that we know," I replied.

"I understood everything you told me back there, but after seeing Fitoria, I actually believe it," Melty mused.

"I guess we can consider her a prototype Fitoria," I said.

"Are you trying to sound cool?" Melty asked snidely.

"Not really. She's very different from the Fitoria we know. There's a chance she's a different person with the same name. Holn said she was still being worked on," I replied. It might be this one is just the shell for now, with the contents to be added later. She did have certain aspects that were the same as the Fitoria we knew . . . but there were clearly things that were different too. This prototype Fitoria was lacking something . . . something soul-related. That much was clear to me.

"Okay then. But she really does look like her. I can feel the reality of everything you told me," Melty stated. We headed into Mamoru's lab as we talked. Only about half of the tanks were occupied, as the kids Mamoru took care of had already finished their treatments and were now resting around the castle. The remaining tanks contained experimental clones of Filolia . . . those that would presumably become the filolials. Further in the back there was another girl floating in a final tank, her chest more prominent than last time. She had a face that was like a mixture of Fitoria and R'yne, a girl with long hair. She had red wings on her back, which had apparently come from the application of a Suzaku gene.

"Ah, you finally decided to show up," Holn, the Whip Hero

from this time, said. She was there in the lab to greet us. She called herself an evil alchemist and was apparently Ratotille's ancestor, the alchemist who took care of the monsters in my village. Holn was a researcher who used the power of the Whip seven star weapon to conduct all sorts of experiments. She was also Mamoru's collaborator and was closely tied to the current incident. The one who ultimately created the filolials was more likely Holn than it was Mamoru. The filolials' hatred of dragons was connected to Holn too.

It seemed Holn had a whole thing against dragons being the most powerful monsters. That idea seemed to have been passed down to her descendant, Rat.

"Does this mean you are finally letting little old Filolia out? Everything is ready," Holn said.

"Thanks, Holn," Mamoru replied.

"Where's R'yne? Won't she want to see this?" I asked. I was pretty sure she was training with S'yne again today.

"She was here talking with Filolia until a moment ago. But she upset her and got chased out," Holn explained.

"Stuck her nose in the wrong place again, did she?" I said. R'yne was the Sewing Kit Hero from another world and seemed to be S'yne's ancestor and Filolia's sister. She never took anything especially seriously, no matter the situation. She'd met up with Mamoru and his allies when she came here looking for her own sister, who had been summoned to another world as the Claw Hero. She was also the one who had suggested to me that my inability to attack would mean sex with me wouldn't hurt either. I hadn't forgiven her for that, and I never would. I could use a knife when cooking and chopping things up just fine! There was no basis for her hypothesis . . . or so I liked to believe.

I started down that path for a moment—during cooking, I was actually cutting with the attack power of the knife, while sex would be considered something I did with my own bare hands—but then shook it off. She was always running her mouth. That was the point I was trying to make, and so she must have said something to piss her sister off.

"They seemed to be getting along well," Holn said. "But then Filolia chased her off for some reason."

"Okay, whatever," I said. What a failure as a sister to get chased off just when her sibling was about to come out of this tank. I didn't really care and looked idly over at the doorway to see it open and Cian peering inside.

"Ah, are you about to let Filolia out?" Cian asked us after looking around.

"Seems like it," I replied.

"Where's Fohl?" Cian asked.

"He's back in the village," I replied.

"Really? Why?" Cian inquired.

"We just ended up here after the meeting, and he's not involved in meetings," I explained.

"Okay," Cian said. She was one of the orphans, a cat demi-human, and seemingly the ancestor of the hakuko, which was Fohl's race. We'd discovered a whole bunch of ancestors, basically. Cian was very open with Fohl as a result, interacting with him with all her barriers down. She acted differently from how she did with Mamoru or me . . . like a big sister ordering her brother around. Fohl didn't seem especially comfortable around Cian, and personally I thought we should keep them apart unless it was really required. This feeling probably stemmed from the fact Cian felt a bit like Atla.

"Filolia," Mamoru said. There was no reply. The girl floated in the culture tank, eyes closed, saying nothing. She looked exactly as she did when I saw her before—no changes at all. We were faced with the fact that the situation might be very different from what Mamoru had been expecting. The atmosphere around us was taking a nasty turn—I had to wonder if things really were okay. "Filolia? Hey, are you okay?" Mamoru continued, checking the vital signs displayed on the terminal. Nothing seemed to be out of place. Filolia's eyes seemed to have fluttered a little.

Mamoru seemed to be struggling a little too, sounding concerned and sighing with a furrowed brow over the text on the terminal. He continued to try to operate it, but to no noticeable avail. Concern grew on his face with each attempt, and he scratched his head and tried again. Eventually it looked like he had given up completely, and he looked despondent.

"That's enough! Everything is ready! Return to life! The most ultimate and powerful life-form that I have ever created!" Mamoru said. I was a bit surprised by this outburst, and then he hit a button on the terminal. The liquid inside the tank started to bubble and drain away. With a hissing sound, smoke whipped up around the tank and then the sealing popped open.

"I awaken from my long slumber!" the girl from inside shouted, appearing amid the lingering smoke in a pose with her left hand covering her right eye. "Filolia returns beautifully to life!" I was left speechless. "Thank you all for participating in my awakening! Your names shall go down in the Chronicles of the Dark Hero, the Maniacal Brave, as chronicled by the great chronicler of the Crimson Evil Flicker, Red Shadow Wing! Bring all of your strength to bear!" She held the same pose, an expression of pure confidence on her face.

No one else was speaking. Silence stifled the lab for a moment.

Her real name was apparently L'yne. She had used being summoned to another world as an excuse to change her name to Filolia. That had been a bit of a red flag for me already.

"Mamoru, sorry to be the one to say this, but it seems the experiment has failed. We woke her up too quickly, and she seems to be suffering from . . . mental defects. We should dispose of this failure at once," I suggested.

"Hey! Hold on!" Filolia said. She seemed shocked by my words.

"I warned you," Mamoru said to her, looking exhausted by the entire thing. "Naofumi isn't the kind of person to go for that kind of joke."

"I'm not joking around! I'm the Dark Hero, the Maniacal Brave! I'm cool!" she retorted. Mamoru and the girl calling herself Filolia started to argue with each other.

"Filolia seems the same as always. I'm glad," Cian commented.

"That's a success?" I said.

"Yeah," Cian nodded. She actually nodded. I wasn't sure what to do with this information. "High maintenance" did not seem apt enough for what a girl like that would put you through. I suddenly had no idea about Mamoru's tastes at all. When he told us about her, he had made her sound like she had her head in the right place. She was the one, he had told us, who said it was strange for Siltran to rely purely on the heroes to fight the waves. From the exchange I had just seen, she looked like a moron, nothing more. "She always jokes around like that," Cian explained, "but when things get serious, you'll want her around."

"Okay . . . a shame she can't be serious all the time," I commented.

"I agree," Cian said simply.

"I wonder if you shouldn't have made some modifications before releasing her from the tube?" I said.

"That wouldn't be reviving little old Filolia, now would it? It wouldn't be the Filolia that Mamoru so wants to see again," Holn replied.

"It would probably be better than this," I stated.

"Just let them have their fun. She'll be serious when we need her," Holn responded. There were all sorts of reasons why I didn't want to give this new nutcase the time of day.

"It sounds like everything you told me was legit," Melty said.

"Why are you okay with this?" Raphtalia asked. Ruft and I seemed to have the same question.

"Haven't you ever seen this, Naofumi? Raphtalia? Sometimes there are filolials who act like that," Melty said.

"Okay. I've never seen that and don't want to," I told her. All the filolials I knew were airheaded gluttons. I'd never encountered one with an extreme case of chuunibyou.

"If the others talk with one like that for too long, the same tendencies get transferred over to them," Melty continued. It was like some kind of sickness. I definitely didn't want to catch that.

"Any way to fix it?" I asked.

"Filo and Chick tend to keep them under control, which stops it from getting too bad. But they can't do anything to stop the original spreader," Melty explained.

"Sounds hopeless," I replied.

"Just think of it as her personality and let it go," Raphtalia suggested.

"The only monsters we need in the village are the Raph species," I asserted.

"You said it!" Ruft agreed.

"Please don't reduce this issue down to that," Raphtalia said. "Now can we please introduce ourselves?"

"Yeah, I guess we should . . ." I looked over at the two of them again. Filolia was waving her arms up and down at Mamoru, like a child, trying to convince him she wasn't wrong. I decided to just go ahead. "I'm Naofumi Iwatani. I'm the Shield Hero from the future. Mamoru has been helping me and my friends out. Nice to meet you," I managed. The girl calling herself Filolia turned to look at me. She did have a Filo vibe about her. I could understand if this was the progenitor of the filolials.

I held out some candy, which I'd picked up as a treat to take back for Keel and the others.

"Oh, thanks!" Filolia cried, reaching out for it at once and then starting to lick it happily. "So sweet! Delicious!" she exclaimed. It was starting to feel exactly like interacting with a filolial. I was confronted by the power of genetics.

"There, there," I said, putting a hand on Filolia's head and patting her.

"Naofumi?!" Mamoru exclaimed. Filolia gave a happy titter for a moment.

"Hold on!" Then she snapped back to herself. "How dare you touch the Maniacal Brave, the Claw Hero, also known as Brave Claws!" She tried to knock my hand away but was met with a solid wall of resistance, which she also started to complain about. "So hard! This guy is like a rock! I can't move his hand at all!" I wondered how long this comedy routine was going to continue for. Maybe I could just laugh it all off, but I wasn't sure that was the best idea. "Mamoru!" she said and proceeded to jump onto Mamoru. I was starting to worry about all the fresh crap it looked like we needed to deal with.

Mamoru, for his part, seemed nothing more than Filolia's guardian. Right then, he was holding Filolia, stroking her head to soothe her.

"Look, you see. If you act normally with Naofumi, he'll answer you back normally. If you joke around, then Naofumi will treat you like a child," Mamoru explained.

"Boo . . . okay," Filolia said. For a moment I seriously considered calling her Filo II. She felt like Melty and Filo combined together, with some of the old Ren mixed in.

"I'm Filolia, the Claw Hero and ally to Mamoru. You've come from the future? How lovely!" she said.

"Lovely, is it?" I muttered. I was getting more and more suspicious. I really didn't want to get involved with her, but I continued the conversation. "And do you understand the situation you're in?"

"Yes. Look at the forbidden arts you have dabbled with in order to revive me. I knew this was a profession that demands all forms of malevolence, but then I'm at fault for having been killed so easily . . . I'm ready to join you in working to atone for our sins and wish to bring an end to the waves alongside you," Filolia stated. She seemed to like to say things in a roundabout way. Talking to her was wearing me out.

"Filolia. Your words, your words," Mamoru chided her.

"I'm not enamored with everything you've done, but this is the situation we're in now, so I'll do my best," Filolia said. It had taken all this time just to impart this simple information. This really was going to be a pain.

In any case, I seemed to have no choice but to accept her as both S'yne's ancestor and one of the filolials.

"Okay. Then we'll ask for your help . . . I guess. If you understand the situation, then you know what we're trying to do, right?" I asked.

"Yeah. You've been helping Mamoru and my friends, so I'll help you too. Whatever I can do to help you get back to the future, count me in," Filolia said, giving another bow. "I can deploy these as my new optical wings. Some aspect of the Suzaku." Filolia raised her claws as she spoke. The seven star weapons were the vassal weapons of the four holy heroes . . .

the holy weapons. I wondered if the claws were a vassal of the shield. I didn't have anyone using them in my party.

Chapter Two:
Claws and Hammer Power-Up Methods

"Back in our time, the claw seven star weapon has fallen into the hands of the enemy, so we don't know what its power-up method is. Can you explain it to us?" I asked.

"What?" Mamoru said in surprise. "You're that strong . . . without the claw power-up method?"

"What's wrong with that?" I said defensively. "The claws won't play ball."

"No, it's just . . . you told me you could use the power-up methods from the world of the sword holy weapon, after the fusing, so I was kind of taking the others for granted," Mamoru admitted.

"Didn't I explain that?" I asked. "We can't use those since coming to this time." The reasons were still unclear, but we had lost about half our power-up methods since our arrival. Ren and I worked out a rough idea of how through our many discussions. From the power-ups from the four holy weapons, I could only use the shield and bow, and Ren could only use the sword and spear. We'd been working together to cover this gap in battle, using life force along with our attacks and applying buffs. It had worked out so far because the whip power-up method was so powerful. I could also apply the mirror power-up method, which provided me with some boosts. That was why we needed to know the claw and hammer power-up methods as quickly as possible.

We really should have asked Mamoru about this sooner.

"I can't believe you're that strong without even using it . . . That's terrifying," Mamoru breathed. Filolia gave an evil chuckle as she looked over at me intently. Then she twitched and straightened.

"The claw power-up method provides a mastery level for skills. Using the same skill over and over increases its level and enhances the abilities of that skill," Filolia explained. "It can reduce the required SP, change the effects of the skill, increase its damage, or reduce the cooldown time."

I looked at the skills I could use, and now—holding a firm awareness of the claw power-up method—I saw gauges appear on each one. It seemed to make sense. The more you used a skill, the easier it became to use. Even better, the mastery levels I had theoretically earned so far were now reflected. The Air Strike Shield branch and Shooting Star Shield master were high because I used them so often, but all my skills had received a boost in some fashion from this. It would be worth going through them all and seeing what had changed. I always popped off things like Float Shield when something kicked off, so those kinds of skills had earned a lot of experience.

The issue was, among the heroes we had here in this world, I was probably the only one for whom these changes had been reflected. The power-up method Ren needed to learn was the axe, maybe.

"Do you know the hammer power-up method?" I asked.

"Legend says it is the fusing of weapons," Mamoru replied. We certainly didn't have "legends" about power-up methods back in our time, but if that provided the details, then so be it. I took a moment to think about weapon fusing. I had an idea what it would mean. "You can take the most characteristic equip effect from one weapon tree and apply it to another weapon," Mamoru continued. I decided to try it with the Spirit Tortoise Carapace Shield, which had been enhanced a lot already.

Spirit Tortoise Carapace Shield 100/100
<abilities locked> equip bonus: skills: S Float Shield, Reflect Shield
special effects: gravity field, C soul recovery, C magic snatch, C gravity shot, vitality boost, magic defense (large), lightning resistance, nullify SP drain, magic assistance, spell support, growth power
special equip effect: Shooting Star Shield (Spirit Tortoise)
Item enchant level 10, defense 15% up

There were some new circular icons down at the bottom too. Those had to indicate the hammer power-up method. Then

I looked at using the Shield of Compassion from the Bless Series, just to make sure its effects were a different category of power-up from weapon fusion. The Bless Series couldn't be directly enhanced. It worked by being mixed with a normal shield. It didn't matter how weak the other shield was; it would get a real boost from the Shield of Compassion.

I decided to try adding the Soul Eater Shield to the Spirit Tortoise one. I recalled that the Shield of Compassion also had the equip effect "spell support," which acted in the same way as Trash's staff to make casting magic easier. Combined with the support of the copy of the Demon Dragon, I could cast Liberation in half the time it took anyone else.

I was getting off track, anyway. Soul Eater Shield weapon fusion!

Spirit Tortoise Carapace Shield 100/100
<abilities locked> equip bonus: skills: S Float Shield, Reflect Shield
    special effects: gravity field, C soul recovery, C magic snatch, C gravity shot, vitality boost, magic defense (large), lightning resistance, nullify SP drain, magic assistance, spell support, growth power
    special equip effect: Shooting Star Shield (Spirit Tortoise)
        Item enchant level 10, defense 15% up
                Soul Eat

I immediately noticed that all enhancements to the Soul Eater Shield had been reset. I tried further fusion with other enhanced shields, but it seemed there was an upper limit for increases, depending on the strength of the weapon. So this system wasn't going to be a walk in the park either. I took a look at the Reflect Shield . . . to see I hadn't used it at all. It allowed the counterattack effect from any shield to be temporarily added to a shield that didn't have one of its own. There just weren't many chances to use it, with the Spirit Tortoise Carapace and True Demon Dragon Shield already having their own powerful counters. I had been using the Shield of Wrath recently, but that caused quite a drop in my defense. Basically, reflect was becoming a dead skill that I couldn't use. It couldn't even be applied at the same time as other skills.

In any case, my counterattacks were weaker than those from Raphtalia and Ren. Maybe they could be used when trying to cause status effects, but pretty much anything of any significance that we fought was ready for it. Taking attacks on Shooting Star Shield didn't trigger it either.

I wondered if the mirror vassal weapon was still attached to me and providing support for the shield. The mirror did keep popping up on its own. It wasn't completely clear, but the enhancements I had performed with the mirror still seemed to be working and were reflected in my stats. It was higher than the stats that Ren, Raphtalia, and Fohl had told me about.

If Itsuki was here, maybe we could have verified all of this.

Raphtalia had access to the power-up methods from the hunting tool, jewels, katana, mirror, harpoon, and book. She couldn't use the ofuda power-up method, which was similar to the whip. Luckily, all her training and the whip playing along—for the time being—allowed her access to that, although Raphtalia had complained to me about the enhancement ratio.

I'd need to give the hammer power-up method some thought. It looked like the enhancements could be removed afterward. The Soul Eater Shield was also displaying a remainder. It looked like three was the maximum. I wondered what would happen when they were all used up.

"Mamoru, I've got some kind of remaining number displayed?" I asked him.

"That's right. Once you use all of those up, you can't make any more changes. Obtaining those materials again will replenish the number," Mamoru explained. That was pretty much what I'd been expecting. "There are also weapons you can only obtain through fusing. It's a pretty deep system." It reminded me of a weapon from that famous Roguelike game that could be obtained by giving a fully enhanced katana to the blacksmith. Maybe using a specific, special fusion method could create the ultimate sword. If I could use this method at the moment, though, it meant Ren probably couldn't.

"Maybe if you fill in the weight category, you'll stop getting hungry?" I pondered.

"What are you talking about now?" Mamoru asked. "Some game thing again?"

I ignored the minus effect of equipping any other shield that would make your stomach super small.

"Yeah, something like that," I said. This provided the potential for something other than using grow up—like the bow power-up method. You could use materials to enhance a weapon to the maximum and evolve it into a new one. Filolia looked pretty pleased with herself, for some reason, and switched her claws to weapons that looked like dragon heads.

"I mixed in some claws that were effective against dragons with my regular claws and obtained new, more powerful claws." Filolia chuckled maniacally. "Further power only increases the darkness inside me!"

"Sure, whatever," I said. Being able to combine some shields together and create something totally new did sound promising.

"That's all you've got to say?" Filolia replied, a little disappointed.

"Filolia, you can't expect to get a reaction from Naofumi. His ultimate ability is to ignore other people trying to make a joke," Mamoru told her. Raphtalia was the one who responded to attempts at comedy. If Filolia wanted a reaction, she should direct her comments at Raphtalia. With that thought, I glanced over at her.

"Mr. Naofumi, please don't look at me," Raphtalia said quickly. This whole thing was such a pain, but at least it had also provided some fresh information. I'd just collect what we could and move on.

The hammer was a vassal weapon with forging elements. At least that was easy to understand. The issue was which combination of shields to use. I tried combining wrath and mercy together, but no dice there. I couldn't combine the 0 series either. Special shields clearly couldn't be fused. For the foreseeable future, I'd work with fusing the Spirit Tortoise Carapace Shield and True Demon Dragon Shield. I'd use the Spirit Tortoise Carapace Shield as the base. It still annoyed me that combining materials from the four benevolent animals was likely to create the ultimate shield. The only way to get the dragon ones would be having Gaelion turn into it, and that would also mean having to fight him. I wondered if maybe we could use one of his scales instead. I remembered the Demon Dragon saying he had a seal similar to one of the benevolent animals. It sounded like there was something there to explore.

At least I could use the shields from the Spirit Tortoise and Phoenix materials. It wasn't worth worrying too much about. I mixed in the True Demon Dragon Shield and got Dragon Scale and a counterattack effect added. I couldn't activate them all at the same time, so choosing the right thing for the right situation was going to become more important in combat.

There was a lot to be said for the past, at least in this regard. I was honestly thrilled to have these lost power-up methods restored to us so easily.

"What are the remaining vassal weapons?" I asked. We had Holn's whip, Filolia's claws, and the hammer taken care of.

"I think . . . probably the carriage?" Mamoru replied.

"Okay. The carriage." I shook my head. So that was a thing. I'd seen Fitoria with something that definitely fit the bill. I wondered why she hadn't said anything about it to us. That was harder to understand. "What's the power-up method?"

"There haven't been enough holders for us to know that. The holders have tended to be so . . . unique, shall we say. Even the pacifiers have trouble handling them," Mamoru explained. It had only been a few moments and I was already feeling like taking back my thoughts on how great the past was. Maybe we were dealing with a spirit as stubborn as the person I suspected of holding the vassal weapon in the future. Once we got back to our time, we'd have to get her to talk. "We can't afford to rely on you guys forever, Naofumi. We need to find someone worthy to carry the hammer."

"I'm going to use my new powers for the good of those goals! Let's go say hi to everyone!" Filolia spread her arms at her sides like airplane wings and dashed away. She reminded me of Filo more and more.

"Can we introduce ourselves to you first?" Melty asked.

"Oh! Of course you can!" Filolia proceeded to shake hands with everyone and complete the introductions with my party. That marked the revival of Filolia, the girl who was basically a filolial.

We emerged from the underground facility, and the kids Mamoru looked after all mobbed Filolia.

"Filolia! You're back!" one cried.

"Filolia returns!" Filolia replied. I hoped she wasn't going to refer to herself in the third person too much. "Have you all been good kids?"

"You bet!" another said with a sniff.

"No lying! I'm not blind, you know!" Filolia adopted another strange pose as she chided the kids before she rushed over to them.

"What? Filolia sounds mad!" a third kid shouted. All of them turned their backs on her and ran for it. Filolia glared at them, fixing them in place. She still didn't look especially angry to me. She took a deep breath, putting her hands down on a couple of kids' heads.

"I understand why you did it, but you need to stop Mamoru if he goes out of control, okay?" she told them. Her expression was gentle but her words were sharp.

"We just wanted to help him," one of the kids replied.

"Like I said, I understand, but I'm also not happy about

everything that he's done to your bodies. There's no taking it back now, anyway, so that's the end of it," Filolia said. The kids shuffled their feet. "I know who is to blame here, don't worry. This all might even have been required for the development of Siltran. But it isn't a good thing. You shouldn't feel proud about it, okay?"

"Okay," the kids finally managed. Filolia gave a smile and then petted them all in turn.

"I'm back now, anyway! Let's use our new powers to take over the world!" Filolia shouted. The kids all gave shouts of agreement. I wondered if this was okay. She seemed to have a moral compass and her act together, but then she also seemed to be an empty-headed imbecile. She contradicted herself. Maybe she was like Sadeena—a bit hard to get a handle on.

As this reunion unfolded, R'yne and S'yne came in from the castle garden.

"I thought I heard a commotion. They finally let you out, huh?" R'yne said.

"Ah, R'yne, so nice to see you," Filolia replied, suddenly calm again, as though formally greeting a guest. There was some tension in her forehead, suggesting she had difficulty with R'yne.

"That's a bit stiff, talking to your flesh-and-blood sister!" R'yne replied, grabbing Filolia up in a hug that ended with Filolia's face buried in R'yne's chest.

"Stop it!" Filolia roared, only somewhat theatrically. "You big-breasted witch!" I hadn't noticed R'yne's chest being that large. She seemed in the same ballpark as Raphtalia and Sadeena, but I wasn't exactly taking measurements. She was big compared to Filo or Melty. I mean, she wasn't a washboard.

Taking a moment to consider it, I realized that Raphtalia actually had quite a nice-sized rack. Then I quickly backed away from that kind of thinking. Who cared about breasts, honestly?

As these thoughts ran through my head, Filolia broke free from R'yne's hold on her and put some distance between them.

"You almost sent me back to the underworld! Evil hero from another world!" Filolia declared. I was seriously going to have to ask Mamoru what he saw in this flake.

"It's nice to see you the same as ever, but do you have to be so hyper?" R'yne said, shaking her head. Filolia gave a cough.

"Why don't you just go off back home, R'yne?" she suggested.

"And why do you treat your flesh and blood so coldly?" R'yne asked again. She tried to grab Filolia again, but Filolia used her arms to block her. Then they both had their arms up, looking for an opening to strike the other. I wondered if this was what two bears looked like, circling each other, trying to get the other to back down.

"This is the home of my heart," Filolia said. "I don't need any annoyances getting in the way." I could tell she didn't get along that well with her sister. I didn't want to deal with R'yne myself—mainly because she was so rude to me all the time. She must have had her fun with Filolia before she was summoned to this world. I was starting to understand how Shildina and S'yne felt. I wondered if big sisters were always problematic for their siblings. I still wanted to believe it was just these three.

"That's enough, Filolia. R'yne was super worried about you too, so maybe don't treat her quite so harshly?" Mamoru said. Filolia didn't look happy about it, but she did lower her arms.

"Okay. I'm sorry," Filolia said.

"I'm just glad you understand," R'yne said. "It looks like you were talking to the kids."

"Yeah, just giving them a bit of a lecture. I'm not completely happy with everything that's been going on while I was away," she said.

"Everyone here was involved. You're not going to get us to regret these results either," R'yne stated.

"That's settled now, anyway. Who's this here?" Filolia asked.

"Her name is S'yne. She's from our world but came here with Naofumi. It sounds like our world has been destroyed in the future," R'yne explained. S'yne was watching their exchange with a frown, but after her introduction, she showed off the sewing kit, then extended her hand.

"I'm the Maniacal Brave, the Claw Hero, also known as Brave Claws Filolia. Nice to meet you," Filolia said. S'yne didn't really seem to know what to say to that. She looked over at me. I signaled with my eyes for her to just play along.

"I'm S'yne. The Sewing Kit Hero from the future—but I recently haven't been getting any respect as a hero," S'yne said. The one who assumes the name of god that we fought against hadn't included her among the heroes at all. The reason lay with her vassal weapon, which was losing its strength due to her world having been destroyed. At least the translation function that caused her speech to skip seemed to have been resolved.

"The techniques R'yne can use have all been lost in S'yne's time. R'yne has been training her," I explained. Filolia moved her face closer to S'yne and spoke quietly.

"Huh? Are you okay, spending so much time with her? Doesn't she wear you down with all that chatter?" she asked. I almost did a double take—of all people, asking that question. S'yne just looked puzzled and tilted her head, unsure of what was going on.

"S'yne is very chatty too, I'll have you know. She talks a lot with me," R'yne said. That was true. Once S'yne got started, she could ramble on a bit. Both of them having come from the same world probably gave them plenty to talk about.

"Is that true? I want to chat with you too! I'm super interested in the future . . . and I'd love to hear some prophecies from the heroes coming from there!" Filolia said. I was a little concerned about the second part there, but she could do whatever she liked so long as it didn't interfere with me.

"L'yne, you have some knowledge of magic, correct?" R'yne said. "Could you help with the teaching? I'm having trouble imparting how to deploy her optical wings."

"Stop calling me by that fake name! Who'd have thought Dark Brave herself would have to suffer under such a burdensome sister?! But very well. It can't hurt for her to learn these things," Filolia said. It sounded like she could teach the magic from her world. That could mean a power-up for S'yne. "Shall we get into this right away?"

"No, hold on. I think we need to go to Naofumi's village and say hello to Natalia first," R'yne said.

"It's past lunch . . . We'll take Keel and the others back too, get some food, and make the introductions," I suggested. We headed to the town below the castle, met up with Keel and the other villagers working there, and then all returned together to the village.

Chapter Three: Holn's Research Weapon

After returning to the village, I gave Keel and the others orders to disperse before heading over to where Fohl, Ren, Eclair and the others were training. Natalia was there with them too. We arrived at the training ground to hear—

"Hah! Eight Trigrams—" It was Natalia, swinging a hammer with all her might.

"Dafu!" said Dafu-chan, otherwise known as Raph-chan II, and the intended target of Natalia's attack. Dafu-chan dodged easily to the side and then countered by whacking Natalia on the head with a mallet.

"Bah! What is this creature?! I can't believe how capably it evades my attacks!" Natalia fumed.

"Because you still overcompensate for everything . . . but that doesn't seem to matter in this case," the Water Dragon admitted with a sigh. "I'm willing to state that this creature is more powerful even than your own father."

"Dafu!" said Dafu-chan. I took in the whole scene. Dafu-chan was clearly having fun toying with Natalia.

"Raph!" said Raph-chan, noticing our arrival and rushing over to me.

"We're back," I said.

"Welcome back," Ren said, noticing us, stopping the training, and coming over. "You've got quite the party together. Any reason?"

"A few things did come up," I replied.

"What's this?" Natalia came over. "Surprised to see me losing?"

"Not really," I replied. "I don't even know how strong you actually are." Mamoru and his allies seemed pretty concerned about her, so she had to be pretty powerful, but with Dafu-chan giving her the runaround so easily, she probably wasn't all that strong.

"Dafu!" said Dafu-chan.

"There's something with this little critter! It's like she can read every move I make!" Natalia complained.

"I mean, I'm not surprised," I said with a shake of my head. Dafu-chan was powerful enough to take Sadeena on and beat her too. If she got totally serious, there were only a handful of us who could hope to match her technically. Raphtalia had been hard-pressed to land a single blow, and that was when Dafu-chan had been holding back. Shildina had had trouble too. That's how strong she was. In her Raph species form, she faced no impediments. She was really something.

"Dafu!" said Dafu-chan. I didn't see any reason to hide it. But Dafu-chan was hopping about, making it clear she didn't want me to let the cat out of the bag. I wasn't sure why.

It seemed pretty unfair for Natalia. There was a whole load of stuff she didn't know now, including all of Mamoru's secrets.

"It wouldn't surprise me if this creature had some Q'ten Lo technology embedded inside it. Like a Dragon Emperor core, perhaps," the Water Dragon hypothesized. Close, but no cigar. "It sounds like there is all sorts of strange technology sealed away in the future. Q'ten Lo must be secure, if they have access to it. It's certainly running rings around you."

"I don't think we need the extra hassle of Natalia getting any stronger," Mamoru muttered, mainly to himself. It would be a bit of an issue if she got any stronger. It hadn't looked like she was holding back when fighting Dafu-chan.

"This seems like an opportunity for you to learn some new tricks," the Water Dragon suggested.

"I don't especially like it, but very well. I might pick up something useful. Before we start that though . . ." Natalia said and looked over at Filolia. "Didn't you die in battle? How can you be here now, and with a strange pair of wings?"

"Me? Die in battle?" Filolia retorted with a cackle. "That was all misinformation, pacifier who espouses justice!" Her tone was full of life, and she struck the same kind of pose as when she introduced herself to me, the one with her hand covering one of her eyes. "I fight while feeding on the power of evil, but sometimes it resists and weakens me. Expecting just such a situation, I worked with Brave Whip to create a dummy that could fight in my place. That dummy is all that was destroyed, nothing more!" She had probably worked out this explanation with Mamoru ahead of time.

"I see," Natalia replied, looking highly suspicious but seemingly letting it slide for now. Natalia probably found dealing with Filolia a pain too.

"As for these wings, pacifier, do you know everything about my race? One of the secrets of my race is being able to absorb the strength of a particularly compatible enemy! This is the power of Suzaku itself! Watch my future ass-kicking and despair!" Filolia crowed.

"So you're telling me you have the power of Suzaku in your body now. Okay then. I'm hardly an expert on races from other worlds. I will admit that," Natalia conceded. It wasn't such a crazy story as to clearly be a lie, after all. There was no way Natalia could know much about Filolia's race. To top it off, Filolia was hyperactive and a pain to interact with. It was like trying to handle a child looking for some attention, and so she always spouted stuff that might be true but also might just be made up. "Did you need me for something?" Natalia asked. It looked like she had given up on getting to the bottom of Filolia's return already. I understood that feeling. I wanted as little to do with her as possible myself.

"Do you know anything about the hammer vassal weapon? Mamoru is looking to boost his fighting strength," I explained.

"The hammer is a vassal weapon of the shield holy weapon. It plays a role in activities like forging and also in providing advice to the shield. Think for a moment about what would happen if someone with a shield fought someone with a hammer," Natalia quizzed us. "You can consider the compatibility of claws and hammer at the same time." I took a moment to consider how someone equipped with a regular shield, rather than myself as Shield Hero, would approach that situation. A hammer would likely be used as a blunt, smashing weapon. I considered what it would be like using a shield to defend against a hammer and against claws. Claws mainly dealt with slashing attacks. Punching would be more the role of gauntlets. Scratching attacks could be effectively deflected with a wide-surfaced shield, making it easy to repel and withstand them.

A hammer, meanwhile, would employ hitting attacks. Even if the shield or armor being struck could take the hit, the impact would still be imparted into the hand or body behind them. That suggested a shield-bearer would have trouble fighting someone with a hammer. If there wasn't someone around who could use it, we needed to find someone and fill that spot.

"Enhancing your fighting strength. I see where you are going with this," Natalia said, nodding as I pondered the problem she had presented. "The hammer vassal weapon's whereabouts are currently unknown. It apparently departed after the previous holder was killed. This might be a good time to look for it."

"You can track it down?" I asked.

"Within certain limits, yes," Natalia replied. So she had that kind of ability too. I would very much like Raphtalia and Ruft to learn a bit of that. With that thought, I looked over at the pair of them. They seemed to have read my mind, because Raphtalia gave an understanding nod, and Ruft's eyes were sparkling. "I will need a little time, but I will start at once." Natalia moved to leave, and then Holn—who had been silent until that moment—stepped forward.

"Wait a moment. If a pacifier affiliated with the force who defeated one who assumes the name of god starts making some big moves, we don't know what kind of trouble it could stir up," Holn said, voicing her concerns.

"I can handle any trouble I might 'stir up,' I promise," Natalia shot back immediately. She really didn't like Holn.

"Oh really? I only have the best intentions, and you don't even want to look at what I've invented?" Holn replied, one eyebrow raised.

"What have you done now? You don't give up, do you?!" Natalia said, exasperated.

"This is little old me you're talking to here! This isn't going to be bad for you, I promise. If you're heading out anyway, just swing by and take a look. No hassle for you at all," Holn taunted provocatively. Natalia gave a sigh.

"If you insist. Just because I'm going out anyway. Tell me,

what is this fresh madness?" Natalia asked, still with some trepidation.

"That's for me to know and you to find out! Which means Mamoru, Naofumi, Filolia, and the Heavenly Emperors need to join us in heading right back to Siltran," Holn stated.

"I might need to do some cooking first," I commented. Natalia frowned over at me—and then noticed the villagers and the expectation in their eyes.

"I'm not one to tear people away from their plates! My inventions aren't going anywhere either—and maybe the food will lure out my descendant, letting me drag her along too!" Holn said. It was therefore decided that I'd make some food right away, and we'd set out after eating. Natalia seemed to enjoy eating together with everyone in the village.

"Hmmm, this is so delicious I'm not sure I could go back to Q'ten Lo cooking," Natalia told me.

"If we catch some fish, I could prepare some seafood dishes. I spent quite a while in your country. It was just in the future," I told her.

"That sounds like an excellent plan. Don't you think so?" the Water Dragon said and was chowing down pretty impressively. I wondered why all the dragons around me seemed so similar. They all loved to eat so much. The same went for the filolials—and everyone else in the village.

"How close do you think you could get?" Natalia asked,

sounding interested in my idea. If she had been away for a long time, maybe she wanted a taste of the flavors of home.

"Q'ten Lo dishes made by the Shield Hero? We had some effwah recently. It was pretty much the best I've ever tasted, just sublime," Ruft cut in, jumping at the chance to bring up the names of food from home. This one was like a fluffy dish made from eggs, which dated back to the Edo period in Japan. When prepared at home, it could end up being a little bland. You needed to be careful of various aspects when preparing it, such as the stock and the state of the eggs, but it was essentially a pretty easy dish to make, involving simply warming the stock in a pan, whipping the eggs a little, and then pouring them in and hardening them up. Altering the stock that was used allowed for various different flavors to be enjoyed. Of course, if I mixed in some life force when preparing it—a little culinary doping—I could create something on a completely different level. "His sashimi was delicious too. It dances on your tongue. It's so flavorful." Ruft was giving Natalia a rundown of my entire repertoire. Natalia did not reply.

"Natalia?" Raphtalia asked, making the Heavenly Emperor's ears prick up.

"Yes, sorry?" Natalia replied.

"I'm glad you seem to be enjoying Mr. Naofumi's cooking," Raphtalia commented.

"That's not really my point . . . I think I'm just missing Q'ten Lo flavors," Natalia said.

"I think I prefer the food that the Shield Hero makes for me. It's nicer than the food I was served when I was Heavenly Emperor," Ruft continued.

"You don't sugarcoat things, do you, Ruft?" Raphtalia commented. "I feel sorry for the people in the castle who made your meals."

"Maybe . . . but Shildina told me the people in the castle all learned from the Shield Hero anyway," Ruft replied.

"We do get a lot of cooks coming to poach Mr. Naofumi's cooking techniques," Raphtalia admitted. "He even spent some time as a cooking-specialist Mirror Hero in another world, where he stuffed enemies and allies alike." That sounded bad, but I was only doing it to enhance my allies.

"The more I see, the more dangerous that sounds," Natalia admitted.

"Another talent of the Shield Hero, surely," the Water Dragon said, trying to quell Natalia's unrest. "Sharing meals together is one way to earn the trust of allies." Everything seemed suspicious if you started looking for trouble.

"Mamoru! The food on my plate vanished in front of my eyes! What happened to it?" Filolia suddenly squawked.

"You just scoffed it down!" Mamoru replied. "Don't you even remember?"

"What? I don't remember a thing! It was delicious!" Filolia replied, instantly contradicting herself. She must have eaten it without thinking.

"You got so carried away you don't even remember! Your appetite is definitely intact," Holn commented. The three of them almost looked like a happy, smiling family. Over to the side of them I spotted Fohl and Cian eating more quietly.

"You're pretty lucky, Fohl, getting to eat like this every day," Cian commented.

"I guess so. No one can really beat Brother's skills in the kitchen. He re-created a dish my dear mother used to make, just from me describing it," Fohl said.

"Food from your homeland, Fohl? I'd love to try it. Will you make it for me?" Cian asked.

"Ah, no . . . you should ask Brother to do that," he replied.

"I could do that, but would you be okay with it?" Cian queried.

"Let me think about it," Fohl finally managed.

The lively village banter continued until we were all done eating. Keel and her cronies got up to their usual antics, of course. I was getting pretty sick of them by now.

"I can't believe how incredible that food was! I almost want to start research into how you can make it taste so good," Holn commented. We had finished our meal and returned to Siltran castle.

"Mamoru," Filolia groaned, "I think I might throw up I'm so full!"

"Just don't do it here," Mamoru warned her. I thought maybe S'yne, R'yne, and Filolia ate the most. Maybe that was some characteristic of their race—like these people called sky-wings from a different world were unable to control the pace at which they ate. It was like starting to see the roots of where the filolials got their appetites from.

"Was this invitation just to pick up some cooking tips?" Rat asked, a little pointedly. She seemed to have trouble dealing with Holn. She still hadn't forgiven everything Holn had done to her precious Mikey.

"Do the monsters like the food?" Holn asked. So we were still on that topic.

"Lots of them want to eat the Duke's food, that's true," Rat admitted.

"I don't feed it to them all that often," I added. Those monsters that could turn into a humanoid form, such as the pesky filolials, sometimes launched a raid on the refectory, but I rarely went out of my way to cook for the other monsters. They mainly ate things like bioplant vegetables. But I was inclined to give the Raph species some treats on the side. Rat's precious Mikey had even tried some recently, perhaps after hearing all the talk about my culinary skills. I'm sure he was just trying to express how much he loved it by using his body. But I had mixed feelings about him choosing to melt. I didn't need to see the Raph species melting before my eyes; it wasn't good for me.

"We're here to show the pacifier my latest inventions. I want you to get your opinion on them too, descendant, that's all," Holn said innocently.

"Okay then. I guess I can help with that," Rat replied cordially.

"Where exactly are you taking me?" Natalia piped up.

"Right here," Holn said. With that, she led Holn down into Mamoru's underground laboratory. After all the effort taken to hide it, she let her in pretty easily. If they just called it "Holn's lab," then Natalia probably wouldn't get suspicious. Holn was a cunning one. They'd been keeping their dangerous research completely hidden for days now. The path Holn was leading us down was different from the one into Mamoru's lab. Raphtalia had a worried expression on her face. But it was nothing serious enough to tip Natalia off.

"Raph!" said Raph-chan.

"Dafu!" added Dafu-chan. The two of them were up on Raphtalia's shoulders, looking around. They were so cute! I was holding hands with Ruft.

"I already knew this about you, but you really do like your secret labs," Natalia commented wryly.

"Every evil alchemist should have at least one or two!" Holn cackled, puffing herself up.

"That's nothing to boast about," Natalia shot back, exasperation in her voice. Holn had made one secret base underneath

our village already. Kyo had done something similar. I wondered if Holn was right. Maybe it was something alchemists felt
compelled to do. "You do seem keen to show me something,"
Natalia continued. "What exactly have you got in store for me?"

"You'll find out soon. This is the room," Holn reported.
She opened a door located deep in the facility and ushered us
inside. At a glance, the room we came into looked a lot like
the one in the facility under our village where she had been
planning to modify Keel. There was a cultivation tank at the
back of the room, which had a hammer floating inside it. That
definitely caught my attention.

"Daful!" said Dafu-chan, as surprised by the hammer as
I was. I looked at it more closely. I was pretty sure I'd seen it
somewhere before.

"What is this? Some kind of modification of the old weapons we found in the filolial sanctuary that you took from our
village?" I asked.

"Nope, this is something completely different," Holn replied. "This one isn't even finished yet." I gingerly moved over
to the hammer and checked it out.

Hammer of—
quality: ?
Imbued effects: ?

"It certainly looks unfinished to me. I thought you were more the type to keep things secret until they're complete," I commented.

"What is it?" Natalia asked, a frown on her face.

"There's certainly something strange about it. All these surprises are getting to be a bit much," the Water Dragon said. I didn't have a clue what it was either.

"I'm not a fan of explaining things by starting with the conclusion, but okay. I was wondering about making something like this, thinking about future generations and filling in the gaps left by losses in battle," Holn started to explain.

"I think I understand," Rat said. She seemed to have worked out what was going on. "You just keep on making incredible things, don't you!"

"You are my descendant, after all. I thought you'd understand what this is," Holn replied.

"I've seen others making similar pieces. There are always alchemists and blacksmiths who seek to make weapons equal to those made famous by legends," Rat said.

"And this is one of those? Equal to what, one of the holy weapons?" I asked. I wouldn't say no to having a powerful new weapon at our disposal, but Holn had said it was incomplete. It felt strange that Holn, an alchemist, was making weapons. She wasn't a blacksmith. Then there was the fact that repairing ancient weapons fell under modification, not invention.

"That's almost the correct answer, but not quite," Holn replied.

"R'yne mentioned that prior to coming here she visited a world where weapons could take on human form. Are you trying to re-create that?" Mamoru asked.

"That was very interesting too, but also not the correct answer," Holn stated. That sounded like a crazy place. Of course, there were worlds where gemstones turned into people. Therese was one such person. What a big universe. So many strange races in all these other worlds.

An unfinished weapon that was a hammer, the same as Natalia's weapon. She was a pacifier, not a hero, and used techniques unique to Q'ten Lo. Then there was Holn, an alchemist with skills that would be impressive even in the future. This hammer being based in alchemy suggested an emphasis on more than pure function as a weapon.

I was still thinking about that world where people could turn into weapons. I wondered what might happen if a gemstone like Therese was polished up and placed in the middle of such a weapon. Weapons that could become people meant weapons that had minds of their own. I looked again at the weapon floating in the cultivation tank. It reminded me of an old game I played once.

"Hey, Shield Hero. This looks like the hammer Shildina used," Ruft said.

"Now that you mention it . . ." His comment reminded me of where I'd seen this hammer before. It was the hammer the past Heavenly Emperor had been using! Shildina had used its latent memories to trace the awareness of its owner. If this weapon was completed and then ended up in Q'ten Lo . . .

"What would the term for this be? Personality transcription?" I asked.

"Bingo! You hit the nail on the head, future Shield Hero! This invention of mine can transcribe the personality of those with skilled techniques into the weapon and then re-create their moves," Holn revealed. That would definitely re-create powerful residual memories, especially if they were there from the start.

"I thought as much," Rat said. "But even if you have the technology to give life, is such a thing as 'personality transcription' really possible?"

"Turning the impossible into the possible is what I was born to do," Holn said, being as humble as ever. Pretty much none of her work had made it to our time—likely due to interference from the ones who assume the name of god. But she was going to follow up on Mamoru's research and create the filolials as a result, so it seemed safe to expect big things from her.

"It should turn out to be a pretty powerful weapon, capable of copying techniques and reducing magic casting time.

Unlike my other work, this isn't a living creature that looks like a weapon," Holn said.

"I get what you're trying to say . . ." I trailed off. The difference there was difficult to pin down. Kyo had made some pretty suspicious weapons too. I wondered if the only difference was whether they were alive or dead. If it allowed access to the techniques and magic of the person it was modeled on, that was something different, but I wasn't ready to simply accept that and move on. "If you're going to perform this personality transcription, whose personality are you planning on putting in there?" I asked. I certainly didn't want it to be me. I'd rather die than have a copy of my personality going around in a weapon.

"If I'd never bumped into you guys from the future, I was planning on having the pacifier help me out. Q'ten Lo already has this kind of technique, I believe, so it should match well with her, and she'd definitely make a good copy," Holn said. She was talking about the oracle powers that Shildina had used— the ability to draw the intent out of something and trace it.

"You must be joking!" Natalia raged. She gave Raphtalia a run for her money when she got mad. Her hair and her miko priestess outfit were rippling with magic.

"Human curiosity is an incredible thing," the Water Dragon said. "I'm a dragon, a creature formed from a core, and this is still amazing to me." He certainly sounded intrigued, but I wondered if that wasn't dangerous too. Natalia, meanwhile, was swinging her hammer and closing in on Holn.

"Oh boy! Mamoru, are you going to let this happen?" Filolia asked.

"I'm sure Holn has something up her sleeve," Mamoru stammered back. He seemed willing to just let Holn handle everything rather than get involved and maybe blow things up.

"Why do I have to take part in this experiment?" Natalia asked. If Holn said the wrong thing here, she was going to get hammered into a stain on the floor—if not by the authority of the Heavenly Emperor, most definitely by Natalia's personal indignation.

"The future Shield Hero and his buddies drove off the ones who assume the name of god for us, for the time being, but what if they go back to where they came from? Mamoru and little old me have had our hands full simply dealing with Piensa," Holn reminded her.

"Which means what?" Natalia retorted.

"Are you really going to stand by while a hero is pushed further into the corner? If we could copy the techniques of a pacifier, one so skilled in combat, and then give that weapon to someone with plenty of potential but still lacking in technique . . . can you think of any greater boon?" Holn asked.

"That's all you've got to say?" Natalia replied. She looked ready to execute Holn on the spot, but Holn just smiled as she delivered the final blow.

"The world is in crisis! Does a pacifier incapable of

self-sacrifice really have the right to punish a hero in such times?" Holn jibed. Silence fell around us. I was amazed she could just come out with something so incendiary, but she was right. An observer who did nothing for the world and simply punished heroes as she saw fit was nothing but an inconvenience. Keeping to the rules didn't matter if it meant the end of the world.

To top it off, the Whip Spirit seemed to have taken a liking to Holn and removed her from being a target for possible punishment. If Natalia ignored such comments coming from a hero like Holn who was fighting on the front lines, then her own position as a pacifier could be in jeopardy. Just forcing the elimination of Holn here would go against that role and her position as protector of the world.

"She got the better of you there. Give it up, Heavenly Emperor," the Water Dragon said, cautioning Natalia with his chin on his dragon paws.

"I'm still not sure . . ." Natalia persisted.

"We need to be focused on maintaining the existence of this world," the Water Dragon cut her off. "This is about more than just punishing a foolish hero or two." Natalia sounded disappointed as she lowered her hammer and backed away from Holn. This seemed to happen with her a lot. "A pacifier must sometimes punish a hero, but also sometimes provide guidance. We can't rely on these heroes from the future forever. It's worth our time to help out with this kind of experiment," the Water Dragon told her.

"Easy for you to say, water snake! You might feel differently if you were the one being copied!" Natalia raged.

"I'm no snake, and it isn't easy for me to say either! You know what kind of creature a dragon is," the Water Dragon reminded her. They did live a long time, that was true—especially when it came to a Dragon Emperor. It looked like the Water Dragon himself was still alive in our time. That was mind-bending, when you thought about it.

"She will create something with a copy of your personality as a friend for the Water Dragon," I prompted.

"I'm not sure I want a friend like that," the Water Dragon added, destroying my attempt at persuasion. We didn't need to make Natalia's standing any worse. If we cornered her completely, there was no telling what she might do.

"That's my line! Am I forced to put up with your supercilious ways even after I'm dead?" Natalia retorted.

"Dafu, dafu!" said Dafu-chan, suddenly getting angry about something.

"So then, Heavenly Emperor, you're going to help with my transcription experiment, correct?" Holn confirmed.

"I really don't want to, but okay. I'll take your word that this is all for the sake of our world. But if you waste my goodwill here, I will kill you!" Natalia shouted.

"Excellent. This is still a prototype, so I don't expect it to go smoothly. I'll need to keep making little adjustments," Holn explained. She took out a strange-looking helmet and put it on Natalia, then had her sit in a chair. If Ren was here, he'd probably make a comment about diving into the world of a VRMMO. I'd bring him along later to take a look. We could have Holn make a sword and transcribe Ren's personality into it.

Holn fiddled with the peculiar helmet for a while and then flipped a switch on the wall and started the experiment. There was a throbbing noise. Then light started to flow from the cables connected to the helmet and to the cables connected to the cultivation tank.

"What if it sucks out her soul or her consciousness and puts them in the hammer?" I joked.

"Mr. Naofumi!" Raphtalia exclaimed. Natalia also jumped as soon as I spoke.

"I'd never fail in such spectacular fashion! You don't believe me?" Holn asked innocently.

"I don't want to," Natalia said stubbornly.

"And yet our first experiment is already finished," Holn replied. Natalia sounded surprised as Holn clicked the switch off. The water gurgled away in the tank and the case containing the cultivation vanished into the floor. Holn touched the hammer, thought for a moment, and then handed it to Natalia.

"I can hear your thoughts when I touch it. You sound pretty stressed," Holn said.

"Uh . . . I hear it too," Natalia replied.

"Looks like this is working. Keep hold of that for a while, as a prototype. The transcription should gradually transfer over," Holn said.

"Now I'm interested. What kind of voice do you hear?" I asked, reaching over to touch the hammer. But Natalia pulled back and resisted me. Her reaction was a lot like the first time I tried to touch Raphtalia's tail.

"I'm not letting anyone else touch this! Maybe I should just break it right now!" Natalia said.

"That won't change anything, I'm afraid," Holn replied. Natalia sighed. She didn't quite seem to know what to do with this troublesome new item.

"I understand how you feel, Natalia," Raphtalia offered, placing a hand on her shoulder. I wondered where that was coming from. First Natalia had a look like Raphtalia couldn't possibly understand, but then she followed Raphtalia's eyes and her expression changed to one of sympathy.

"Yes, I see. I think we're quite similar," Natalia agreed.

"We both just have to do our best," Raphtalia replied.

"Huh? Why are those two suddenly getting closer together?" I asked Ruft.

"No idea, but this was a lot of fun, Shield Hero," Ruft said.

"Raph!" said Raph-chan. As Ruft, Raph-chan, and I each voiced our bemusement, the others around us looked even more assured in whatever it was they were thinking. I still had no idea what it was.

"You just wanted to boast to me that you made this?" Rat asked after watching our discussion.

"Not quite. I want you to help out. Another pair of hands would be a big help right now," Holn admitted.

"If you say so . . . I think Mikey could help out as well," Rat pondered.

"I knew you'd get it," Holn replied. The two of them started swapping ideas. I decided there wasn't anything else we could do and signaled a retreat for the rest of us. Natalia followed along behind, clutching her new hammer and muttering about never letting anyone else touch it. She had a suffering expression on her face. The Water Dragon watched her and then gave a sigh.

"I'm going to go and look for the hammer vassal weapon," Natalia said. "By which I mean I'm going to lay low for a while."

"That's quite a slip of the tongue," the Water Dragon cautioned her. "But it does seem important for our future. It should only take us a few days to find it." With that, Natalia and the Water Dragon left Siltran Castle behind—or, perhaps to put it more aptly, ran for the hills. Mamoru sent them off to the same country where we first met them, which was also where she sensed the hammer the strongest. I decided to give it a few days and just see what happened.

Chapter Four: Quality Check of Heroes

It was the next day. After all our research into accessories, Ren, Imiya, and I were showing off our work, and with Raphtalia and Fohl joining the party, we were trying some of them out to test their effects. Mamoru, Filolia, and Holn were taking part too. The idea of including R'yne and S'yne had sounded too troublesome to Filolia, so they would be testing things later. S'yne had placed a pin on me, and R'yne the same on Mamoru; it was for the purpose of watching over us, but that also meant they heard everything we were saying.

This was a good chance for heroes from both sides to get better acquainted while trying out some items that might help us in our struggles ahead. Melty was still in Siltran Castle, while Ruft and that sheep therianthrope who worked with Mamoru were off acting as envoys to other nations. Mamoru had told me that not showing his face too easily was one method he used to place pressure on the opposite side when negotiating. Eclair had also gone along to keep them safe, but I was a little worried about whether they'd be okay.

"You guys make all sorts of accessories, don't you, Naofumi?" Mamoru commented. He was doing the same thing I was—trying all sorts of different prototypes on his shield.

"I guess we do," I agreed.

"Oh, this is a good one. It gives a massive boost to the power and range of Shield Boomerang." Mamoru proceeded to throw his shield, which flew a long distance at considerable speed. I squinted as it went, noting that the shield was spinning in the air and surrounded by blades of light. It was going faster than before and looked more potent. I was jealous, I had to admit.

"That one's really for Ren," I told him. I'd designed it hoping to provide that auto-tracking effect to float skills. I didn't even have the skill Shield Boomerang. Mamoru had told me that he'd learned it from the Frisbee Shield—a shield that I'd also copied; I didn't learn any such skill. We were both the Shield Hero, so these differences between us were starting to piss me off.

He also had a skill called Shield Chain, which he could unleash as a follow-up to Shield Bash. I had Shield Bash, but I didn't have Shield Chain. But I did have Chain Shield. With just a little swapping of the words, the effect was totally different. The fact he could attack at all made me so jealous. Even though we were both the Shield Hero, there were so many differences between us it offered almost no points of reference at all.

"I like this one!" Filolia exclaimed. "Imiya, was it? You have some real skill! You've caught the eye of the Maniacal Brave! Can I place a custom order?"

"I'm sorry, what?" Imiya asked, flustered and looking in our direction as Filolia closed in. She was holding the Cross Glawick Third Eye in her hands.

"That was made for Ren," I told her. It was the one with the eyeball and magic circle motif. The special effect Ren had applied when he equipped it had been to increase the accuracy of his Hundred Swords. He had explained that the skill was the same as Motoyasu's Aiming Lancer and Itsuki's Arrow Rain. He said it also offered an effect predicting incoming magical arcs—the weapon allowed you to see, to some extent, the trajectory of incoming magic—and had also speeded up the activation of his magic a little. Maybe it was the eye motif that had created this focus on accuracy and eye-based effects. From the perspective of wanting to add a homing effect to float weapons, it was a failure. On the other hand, offering three effects at once was pretty incredible.

"The effect will probably change if you imbue some magic," I said. This was one that Raphtalia, Fohl, and I had all tried first to be on the safe side.

"This is all very interesting," Holn said. "Can I get involved?"

"I can see you making a load of half-animal accessories," I commented. "Like those plants from before." Holn had created the leaves for the Raph species. I would have preferred for her to research the accessories that could bind the holy or vassal weapons and find a way to break their hold more easily.

"In a certain light, those could maybe become accessories," Holn pondered.

"I'm sure they could, but that's a bit outside my expertise," I replied. I worked with accessories by processing gemstones and metal; creating them using alchemy was something I had zero experience with. I was interested in finding out what would happen if you crushed a gemstone into powder and turned it into an accessory though, like when making medicine. "If that hammer you gave Natalia works out, maybe you can apply the same kind of techniques."

"An interesting proposition," Holn mused.

"Accessories, huh," Fohl muttered, looking at the one in his hand.

"In your case, Fohl, I think some additional adornment might be better than something like a key holder," I suggested. Something like metal spikes to wind around his gauntlets. His weapon was not dissimilar to the claws, but it involved more impact, after all. That said, there were some sharp gauntlets available, and the weapon operated differently from the claws Filolia used. "If you'd like to place a request, I'll do my best to fill it," I told him.

"I'm not sure how to respond to that . . . It's clearly better to have something, but I'm not sure what. I haven't learned float weapon skills like the Sword Hero yet, and the basic nature of the gauntlets means both of my hands are always full," Fohl explained. It sounded like he didn't really know what kind of effect would be useful for him. It wasn't like he really had a go-to skill.

"What about if we connected the two gauntlets together by a chain or rope?" I suggested. It might make them look like handcuffs, at a glance, but I'd be interested to see what kind of effects they would have.

"I think attaching something like your shield, Brother, would probably offer better effects," Fohl replied. The original use of a gauntlet was for defense, that was true. Fohl was using them as impact weapons, but they had a defensive side. There were things like bucklers, which I could copy as well. I wondered if it would count as a copy or an accessory for Fohl. It might be worth trying to attach a small shield as an accessory. I wasn't sure what judgment my weapon would finally make, but if it increased my pool of weapons, then that suited me. Making the distinction between accessory or armor, though, that was something else—and whether it would count as blacksmithing or not was something else too. I'd have to talk to Ren about it later.

"What kind of accessory is Ren looking for, anyway?" Mamoru asked. He knew that all of these had primarily been created for Ren to use, but he didn't know the reason why.

"He's trying to improve his abilities with float skills.

We're really looking for an accessory that will work as an aid for him," I explained.

"Float skills are convenient, I'll give you that," Mamoru replied. Both he and I popped out our own Float Shields. It was like having extra arms, making defense a lot easier to pull off.

"You have a pet Dragon Emperor, correct? Why not get him to donate a fragment or two and turn those into accessories? That might provide a different means to control weapons," Holn suggested. She hated dragons, but she didn't seem averse to making use of them. That made me think of the Demon Dragon, who at the moment was nothing more to me than a voice that murmured in my mind when I incanted magic. The reduction in casting time was great, but she could be obnoxious.

"In that case, the Water Dragon might be our only option," I stated. Gaelion was still in the future, and the actual Demon Dragon was in another world completely. Raising a new dragon in this time would be a pain in the ass—and the last thing we needed was more of them.

"I do understand how the Sword Hero feels," Filolia said, cackling to herself. "A floating sword is a beautiful thing to behold." She definitely shared the same adolescent tendencies. "Ren, is it? Filolia, the Maniacal Dark Brave, can understand where you're coming from! Let us both descend into this darkness together!"

"Naofumi!" Ren looked at me, a pleading expression on his face as Filolia closed in. She had a hand covering one side of her face again, her visible eye twinkling, like a hopped-up goth teenager. Ren wanted to move on from this aspect of himself—perhaps seal all memories of it away forever—but circumstances around him were not allowing that to happen. I almost felt sorry for him. He might be in a similar position as me and my rage, wanting to move past it but also still needing to make use of it.

"Okay, I know. Try and use that to help with your forging. I bet you'll be able to make good stuff even when I'm not around. Think of it as trying to master your own past, okay?" I told him.

"That's just mixing words! You're still asking me to dig up my own dark history!" Ren replied. He looked mortified almost as soon as he said it. He'd been keeping his outbursts under control recently, but I'd probably also been mocking him a little too much. He couldn't stay quiet forever. The whole business with that out-of-control sword had been pretty embarrassing for him. There was only so much a person could take.

"You have to believe that your adolescent angst can save the world!" I replied.

"Brother takes a big swing!" Fohl chipped in. I would've preferred he stayed silent.

"Mr. Naofumi, you said something similar to Kizuna, didn't you?" Raphtalia recalled. "About believing that laziness could save the world. Have you taken a liking to saying things like that?"

"It could also be considered just passing the buck," I said.

"I don't think that's something you should admit to so openly," Raphtalia chided.

"Please!" Ren extended a hand toward me. I dodged out of the way, while Filolia closed in. "Why can't I escape my past!" Ren lamented.

"That kind of line is exactly the angst we're talking about," I commented. I shook my head but decided to help Ren out. I pointed at Filolia's keeper, Mamoru, indicating he should do something about his ward—while making sure Ren also saw the gesture.

"Hey, Filolia. Give the guy a break, okay?" Mamoru said.

"Why?" Filolia objected. "If he joins me in working hard at this, he'll only get stronger too!"

"Sure, but look at him. We guys can be sensitive about stuff like this," Mamoru told her.

"Seriously? You can't be a hero if stuff like this makes you embarrassed," she retorted.

"What's so embarrassing about being a hero?" I asked.

"You stand out, for one thing! You need to be cool so that others will follow you! You won't get anywhere if you're always shy and embarrassed!" Filolia opined. Both Mamoru and I were giving her disapproving looks. But I had to admit, I'd heard making people look cooler with things like military uniforms would boost morale. "This is the time for the darkness inside Ren to awaken!"

"Naofumi . . ." Ren pleaded again, seriously coming to me for aid. Filolia wasn't listening to anything Mamoru had to say on the subject. I decided to try something else.

"Ren, what do you think of this accessory?" I asked him. I showed him the Cross Glawick Third Eye that Imiya had made.

"Huh? What's this got to do with anything?" Ren asked, puzzled.

"The design looked kind of embarrassing, maybe, but once it's actually fabricated and attached to a weapon, see? It doesn't look all that bad, does it?" I replied. Ren didn't say anything, just looked at the Cross Glawick Third Eye. "Even if it's embarrassing for the one making it, when considered objectively, it's not that bad," I told him. Imiya's work was impeccable, that was for sure. The fact the design was right up Ren's alley—and yet once it was finished, it didn't look that adolescent at all—spoke volumes about Imiya's skills. When it came to embarrassing articles . . . those lures that Kizuna had made were far worse.

"I'm not sure," Ren said, unconvinced.

"When you consider the production process, it might seem like a joke, but the finished product looks fine. It doesn't matter how embarrassing something looks—if it works, no one's going to complain," I assured him.

"Still not sure," Ren said, sticking to his guns.

"Okay. How about the weapons old guy? That gruff muscle-head made a costume for Filo to wear," I told him. There was indeed a costume for Filo that the weapons old guy had made. That was his own dark history. I had often wondered what he felt about making it, but I'd never worked up the guts to ask him.

"Huh? I caught a glimpse of that once. He made that?" Ren asked.

"More accurately, he created it through repeated modifications," I replied. "Would you like to know more?" After additional work, Melty was now using it as sleepwear.

"No, I'm fine," Ren said, backing down.

"You get my point," I said.

"It feels like you really brought that one home," Raphtalia commented from the sidelines, as sharp as ever. I was currently in the process of negotiating with S'yne—without Raphtalia's knowledge—for the creation of my own Raph-chan sleepwear. She was busy with her own training, of course, so I had no idea when it would finally be made.

"Hey, Naofumi. What about Mamoru's special shields? Can you use those?" Filolia asked.

"Special shields?" I asked with some trepidation. Hopefully she was just talking about that shield that looked suspiciously like it came from a certain legendary kingdom.

"Filolia, you're not talking about the shields I think you are . . . are you?" Mamoru asked. They sounded like something Filolia had been involved with and that Mamoru didn't want to see the light of day. Mamoru had his fingers cocked like he was shooting a gun—at least one of these shields was clearly so bizarre that just a hand signal was enough to identify it.

"That's right. A bit of this, a bit of that," Filolia said, raising both her arms and then swinging them down in a chopping motion. I was getting even more concerned that something I wouldn't be able to scrub from my memory was about to appear. Sensing danger, I moved to depart, but Raphtalia—and then Ren too—both grabbed onto me.

"What betrayal is this?!" I seethed dramatically.

"There's no escape for you. You treat us like your playthings all the time," Ren said.

"That's right. Now it's your turn to take one for the team and give us all a laugh. It will only make you stronger!" Raphtalia added. I grunted. I'd only been offering Ren some friendly advice on his forging! As for Raphtalia, I had no regrets there. The filolials should be replaced by the Raph species. We didn't need that high-strung flock of greedy feather faces for anything.

"Even if Naofumi can copy them, I bet he won't be able to use them," Ren said tauntingly. "But I guess more shields are better than nothing."

"Could you bring them out for us to take a look at?"

Raphtalia asked sweetly. Ren and Raphtalia both had their best salesman smiles on, their faces practically sparkling.

"Yeah, okay. R'yne, if you're hearing all this, can you bring them over?" Mamoru said, addressing thin air, assuming that R'yne was listening. A few moments later, R'yne and S'yne popped in.

"Hey, everyone! I've got what you asked for right here!" R'yne said brightly.

"You dare show your face, harlot who spreads filth on the ears of anyone who'll listen!" Filolia cried out, her adolescent angst at her sister exploding immediately. "Once you've delivered what you came for, be gone, sexy strumpet! Go back to the castle and study your magic!"

"Being called 'strumpet' almost makes me want to stick around," R'yne joked.

"Me too," S'yne said with a nod, but she was probably only agreeing with the part about sticking around.

"Hey, R'yne. Do you think you could take this one off our hands?" Ren asked, indicating Filolia.

"What?! Brave Sword has already fallen under the control of my sex-craving sister? Do I smell a payoff?" Filolia exclaimed as Ren tried to palm her off onto R'yne. Ren clearly wanted as little to do with her as possible.

"Nothing like that! I don't do that kind of thing . . . anymore," Ren said defensively.

"Oh really? You've taken a step back from that life. Is that what you're trying to say?" Filolia said with a chuckle. "I see the thoughts in your heart and how they differ from your words! Join me on the side of right and put this sex-starved nympho into the ground!" Filolia wasn't giving up either. Maybe because she'd found someone like herself. We didn't need the filolials getting infected with this madness. We would have to be careful.

"Someone, please stop her," Ren pleaded. He was having a tough time, but mainly due to our own deeds.

"No need to get too riled up," Mamoru cut in. "R'yne and S'yne have their own accessory-testing planned for later, so if you could just wait until then . . ." he asked, throwing a lifeline to Ren and Filolia.

"You want to swap them out with Filolia?" I confirmed with him.

"Sounds about right. You invited us to do this, after all," Mamoru replied. There was a lot going on among his allies. Keeping Filolia and R'yne in check looked like a nightmare. The nightmare that we had to deal with—Motoyasu—was still in the future. I was glad that Filo wasn't a hero. If she had been, we might have needed to swap them around like this as well.

"We can watch though, can't we? I'm going to casually chat with S'yne and watch you go at it. L'yne—I mean, Filolia— don't cause too much trouble," R'yne said.

"You don't need to tell me that! I'm only trying to awaken

the power hidden inside the Brave Sword!" Filolia protested.

"Please, enough," Ren begged. I personally couldn't pick which of these sisters was more annoying, the sex-obsessed older one or the angsty and dark younger one. Not a choice I would relish being faced with. I had a lot of sympathy for Mamoru.

I was reminded for a moment of another pair of sisters, one older and hard to get a handle on and one younger who loved card games and was a bit ditzy. All you had to do was keep them liquored up and things never got too bad. That did give me an idea. I could drink these two under the table and take them off the board for a while.

"Mamoru, why don't we teach these two the joys of drinking (until they pass out)?" I suggested.

"Did I hear some extra words on the end there?" Raphtalia cut in, always the spoilsport. We understood each other so well now that it was like she could read my mind just by meeting my eyes.

"You two need to rein it in a little or you're going to make Mamoru collapse. Have a little more awareness of what you're doing. Otherwise, you'll pass out like Ren did! Like Ren did!" I said.

"No need to emphasize that part," Ren said forlornly.

"Oh my. Did your poor sword go all floppy?" R'yne jibed. "I'm the big sister, so I'll be the adult. For Mamoru's sake, I'll leave you to get on with things."

"Now you play the responsible adult card!" Filolia raged. "I'll never forgive you for giving Mamoru permission to have his way with me!" There was literal fire coming off her wings as she shouted this. It sounded like R'yne had always been hard to deal with. I could see why her younger sister might hate her. When I thought about S'yne putting up with all of this, it really made me appreciate how incredible she was. Incredibly tolerant, maybe. R'yne was a lot like her own sister, however, so I hoped S'yne was keeping her guard up a little.

"Whatever. See you later!" R'yne handed over the items Mamoru had asked for and then left again.

"These are your strange shields?" I asked Mamoru. I lifted one of the items, which was wrapped up, and started to check it out. As soon as I touched it, I knew it was a shield, just from the shape. But one side of it was larger than the other. It had a silhouette almost like a surfboard.

"Yes. Take a look inside," Mamoru prompted me.

"Thinking about it now," I said wryly after sitting through all that banter, "it might have been better for you to just change to the shield and show it to me."

"I considered it, but I think getting your hands on the actual thing is best," Mamoru replied. He obviously wanted to try and surprise me with whatever this was. I wondered what kind of crazy shield I was going to be looking at, either made for or by Mamoru. I took off the wrapping to answer that question and found a round shield with a hole in the center . . . and a gun attached. This was what they called a "shield pistol," if I recalled correctly. The shield could be taken on and off like a kind of attachment. Maybe a crossbow could be attached too.

"This is definitely a strange weapon," I said. Mamoru seemed to be conducting some serious research into all sorts of potential shields. I relied entirely on the weapons old guy, meaning I'd never had a chance to use something like this. "What happens when you use this?" I asked him.

"Exactly what you'd expect. I can attack by pulling the trigger. I made it as an experiment, so it only fires one shot," Mamoru explained.

"Okay. You didn't try using a more powerful gun, like a rifle, or try to increase the rate of fire?" I asked him.

"If you take things too far, it won't recognize it as a shield anymore. The gun becomes the main part of it. I switched the gun for a crossbow and I couldn't copy that either." With heroes being summoned here from various other worlds, weapons such as guns did exist. However, even firearms were affected by the status of the user, meaning at a low level they were far weaker than one would expect. I would have liked to make a shield machine gun and give it to Itsuki to copy. Most likely it would register as either a gun or shield, and neither of us would be able to copy it. I gave the shield pistol a try.

Weapon copied!

Conditions for the Iron Shield Pistol have been unlocked.

Iron Shield Pistol
<abilities locked> equip bonus: accuracy + 2
equip effects: magic bullet, shield transparency

Stats-wise, it was really crappy from my current position. But I had been able to copy it. I switched to the Iron Shield Pistol to try it out.

"You managed to copy it, Naofumi," Mamoru said.

"Barely," I replied. Mamoru changed to the Iron Shield Pistol as well. He pointed over at a nearby rock, then took aim and pulled the trigger. There was a light-sounding pop and a shot was fired from the shield, flying over and hitting the rock dead-on.

"There you go. The main issue is that it's not even as strong as Shield Boomerang or Shield Bash," Mamoru revealed. He had the advantage over me in that he was a Shield Hero who could actually fight back. This might be a useful means of attack. I hoped the bullet damage was fixed; that would mean I'd be able to injure assailants regardless of my own status. While mulling these things over, I pulled the trigger myself to hear a far less exciting sound than when Mamoru did it. My shot hit the rock at a lethargic speed.

I had nothing to say. The rock didn't move at all. No one else had anything to say either. My lack of attack power was being reflected after all, just as I'd expected. The awkward expressions of the others only made me feel worse. This was why I had wanted to run away!

"What was . . . Hey, try not to feel too bad, okay?" Filolia gave up her normal chuunibyou act and tried to console me. That only made it worse! I didn't want their pity! I didn't need salt in my wounds!

"That's all I can do? Even with the 'magic bullet' equip effect?" I bemoaned.

"Huh?" Mamoru raised an eyebrow. "It has that effect for you? It's called 'single shot' for me." It sounded like the same shield could have different equip effects, depending on the user. That seemed worth investigating. I imbued some magic into the shield—this was a "magic" bullet we were talking about—and pulled the trigger again. It made the same clicking sound, but nothing else happened. It didn't look like simply providing some magic was enough to make fresh ammo. My first shot hadn't consumed anything either. Maybe I needed to add some actual magic. I decided to try with some simple magic . . . and at that thought, the Demon Dragon infesting my mind popped up.

"My time to shine!" she quipped. "First Heal!" That was minor enough that the effect wouldn't really change whether I incanted or not. I felt the sensation of the magic being transmitted into the center of the shield. I decided to give it a try and found myself pointing the shield at Fohl. The resulting sound was far more promising this time and my magic bullet was fired off toward Fohl. I thought I heard a very quiet voice say, "Experiment time!"

Fohl gave a shout as magical light scattered over him. The shot was fired too close for him to avoid it. He didn't seem to have suffered any damage, but that was probably a given since the "attack" had come from me. It seemed more likely that he had been hit by First Heal.

"It looks like a shield that can turn magic into bullets and then fire them off," I surmised.

"You didn't hesitate to shoot me, did you, Brother?!" Fohl complained.

"I actually didn't pull the trigger," I replied.

"Maybe it was Atla playing a prank," Raphtalia suggested.

"I think . . . I'd quite like that," Fohl said. His feelings were definitely complex when it came to Atla! I couldn't say outright that it hadn't been her. I even heard that unexpected voice. I had to wonder about a sister who would just shoot her brother without any hesitation at all.

"Turning magic into bullets and firing them around. That's pretty impressive," Mamoru said.

"The issue there is that I can only use healing and support or buff magic," I said.

"I can't see much need to turn those into bullets and shoot them—at least not in this little old time period," Holn said, providing analysis already. Healing magic in this world could be activated by selecting a target and incanting; so long as they were within range, you didn't have to be able to see them for the magic to still work. It wasn't like attack magic, which you needed to actually aim with.

"I guess not. There might be ways to use it, but I doubt situations quite so specific will ever come up," I said. I recalled working with the Demon Dragon to turn some support magic into a ball that we bounced off my mirrors before activation. There might be some applications like that, but they would also be a pain to set up. Ren provided more powerful support magic than me. My own enhancements weren't reflected in my magic at the moment. It wasn't even really a candidate for weapon fusion—too finicky to use.

"Can you have someone else charge it with magic and then use it yourself when you need it?" Mamoru suggested.

"Let me give that a try," Ren said. He reached toward my shield with one hand and incanted some magic. It didn't feel like it loaded into the chamber like before.

"Doesn't look like it," I said.

"It's never been the easiest shield to use," Mamoru replied, exasperated. I wondered if we could make a few modifications to it ourselves. When I saw the Shield Spirit again, I was definitely going to complain about Mamoru being able to attack when I couldn't.

"Best just not to worry about it, Mr. Naofumi," Raphtalia suggested.

"I guess. Let's check the next shield," I said. I unwrapped the second shield that Mamoru had got R'yne to bring over. I could tell this was a big one even when it was still covered up. But once revealed, it really demonstrated Mamoru's hard work. The big shield had three swords attached to the top and bottom, a weapon known as a "sword shield." It was used by swinging it around and mashing it into enemies. It could be used defensively too, of course, but it was mainly about bashing stuff. Filolia picked it up in both hands and started swinging it around.

"This should count as a shield," Mamoru commented.

"I think I saw one like it in Siltvelt," I replied. I hadn't copied it—to be more precise, it had been so decorative that I hadn't been able to. The one in Siltvelt had been used more as a kind of riff on the idea of a national flag. I picked up this new one and checked it out.

Conditions for the Iron Sword Shield have been unlocked.

Iron Sword Shield
<abilities locked> equip bonus: defense + 2, strength + 2
equip effects: enhance Shield Bash, Wild Swing, reduce impact

The equip effects seemed good, but I wasn't sold overall. It might give the shields the old guy had on display in his store a run for their money, but that was about it. No matter the enhancements, it wouldn't be worthy of any of my current shields. Equipping it didn't even change my attack, meaning I could swing it around all I liked but I wouldn't be doing any damage other than to my pride. Just to make sure, I used some iron ore to enhance it via the bow power-up method. It had an upper limit but couldn't fail. And as expected, that increased defense but not attack power. That was to be my lot in life.

"My attack power isn't increasing," I reported. I changed to the shield and swung it around a bit. I focused on Wild Swing and it did feel like a skill with the motion appearing in my head. I gave it a try, but my pathetic attempt to attack just sliced through the air. It was so big I needed to hold it with both hands, which was a pain. Also, Wild Swing—as the name suggested—left the user completely exposed. I liked the enhancement to Shield Bash, but when I used that skill, I could only stun for a brief moment. It might be worth using if it boosted the length of that stun. Some weapon fusing might eventually make it useable, but I doubted the effect would be that great even then. Yeah, I didn't need this either. It was going to just bolster my stats and that was it. "Based on the shape, I might make use of it as a surfboard or canoe," I joked sardonically.

"I hate to say it, but you're not wrong," Mamoru admitted—and this was the guy who made the thing, not to mention a Shield Hero who could actually attack.

"It's just bizarre, that's what it is," I said.

"It increases your attack quite a bit, right, Mamoru?" Filolia confirmed. "You relied on it a lot when we were starting out." I bit my lip in frustration. Mamoru and his balanced approach to combat pissed me off! I was so focused on defense I couldn't do anything alone! I blamed the shield too. Why did it allow Mamoru to attack but not me?

"Well, Raphtalia? Ren? Are you happy now?" I gave my best unhinged laugh.

"You sound so sad . . ." Raphtalia sympathized.

"I'm feeling a little bad about it," Ren admitted.

"Being unable to attack has allowed you to defend us from all sorts of things, Mr. Naofumi," Raphtalia reminded me.

"That's right! The very fact you can't attack is what makes you the toughest! You're more durable than Mamoru too, right?" Ren said, picking up from Raphtalia.

"I'm jealous of that myself, it's true . . . but still . . ." Mamoru stopped for a moment. "No, that's enough about this. Saying anything more will have the opposite effect, so I'll keep my mouth shut." His consideration of me actually only pushed me further into the corner. I knew all too well that everyone pitied me for being unable to attack! I didn't need their sympathy!

"You two had better remember this!" I warned Raphtalia and Ren.

"I was starting to regret forcing this on you, but that threat has removed those feelings," Raphtalia said pointedly.

"You mess with us all the time! This makes us even," Ren added.

"I'm not sure we should be fighting among ourselves," Holn said, watching our exchange with a sigh.

"I think this is how they show their affection for each other," Mamoru told her.

"A bond of trust, yet constantly picking at each other at all times . . . I like it," Filolia said.

"I guess we do tussle like this quite a lot," Fohl admitted.

"Everyone, I'm sorry to interrupt, but what about the accessories?" Imiya had been quiet up until now, but she tried to get things back on track—as much for my sake as anything.

"You're my only ally, Imiya," I said. I hugged her from behind and stroked her head. She moaned uncomfortably and stiffened up in my arms, embarrassed. It might be worth calling in Raph-chan and Ruft to bolster my forces. If I toyed with Raphtalia too much, she might turn against me.

"Mr. Naofumi, please don't make too much trouble for Imiya," Raphtalia said. But I decided to ignore her calmly delivered request.

"You've always got a quick retort, Raphtalia," I bemoaned. "I miss the time you were more like sweet little Imiya here." I continue to stroke her.

"I'm sorry . . . I went too far," Raphtalia said, backing down. It was all the stuff with the Raph species that had made her more prickly toward me. Before that, Raphtalia had been better at matching the general atmosphere and was more conscientious in her replies.

"Please, Raphtalia," said Imiya, still moaning.

"I'm not angry, don't worry," Raphtalia replied. "Mr. Naofumi, please stop causing trouble for Imiya," she said to me again after taking a calming breath. Imiya did seem close to passing out. She was very shy about pretty much everything. Raphtalia wouldn't be jealous of Imiya over just this. If she was willing to compromise, so be it. Our Raph species research would continue.

I stopped stroking Imiya and checked the accessories. We'd found some good ones. I was pulling my weight.

"Okay, everyone. Can you split the accessories up into those you want to keep and those you don't need? I'll try reworking the ones we don't need and see if I can bring out a different effect," I said.

"Understood," Raphtalia replied.

"Hey, could you make a special accessory exclusively for me?" Filolia asked Imiya, her eyes sparkling. Accessories were always very sought after in video games.

"Ah, I'm not sure . . ." Imiya said.

"What do you mean by exclusive, anyway?" I asked. Since I was an accessory maker myself, that seemed like a legit question. In games there were accessories that only specific characters could equip, but I had no idea what an exclusive accessory would look like in real life. Exclusive to a profession, maybe—or to a weapon. For my shield, that could be a cap to cover the crystal on the shield, but with a little work, it could be a hilt for a sword too.

"I mean . . . make it knowing that I'm going to be the one using it!" Filolia replied.

"That's one way of doing things," I admitted. "That could be an exclusive accessory. But you could only make such a thing with a good understanding of the person you're making it for." Imiya or I probably didn't know enough about Filolia to pull that off. To me, she was just a chuunibyou bundle of mouthy angst. "You might get an equip effect from a wedding ring, if Mamoru made one for you," I suggested. Filolia's face turned bright red instantly, and she started to stammer. Mamoru was looking embarrassed too. Two twittering lovebirds. Holn was fanning herself with an annoyed look on her face. "Exclusive equipment though. That might be quite a thing," I pondered. The leaf that Holn had given me felt like an exclusive accessory. It was something easy for all the Raph species to use. I remembered Raph-chan using it like a throwing star. She played by tossing multiple leaves around. It had been made using the bioplants and sakura lumina. I had no idea how it worked, but somehow it could multiply. There was a main leaf, the actual accessory, but that could multiply, allowing you to throw the extra leaves like ninja stars or ofuda. The clones would wither away after a while, but they kept their shape until they hit a target.

Others from the Raph species had borrowed it from Raph-chan and played around with it themselves. Some of the tricks had been fun to watch, like turning the leaf into a fireball in midflight. Raphtalia hadn't been so impressed. When I suggested using it like an ofuda to see if it might be able to activate the magic of Kizuna's world—the world her katana vassal weapon came from—she had made a strange face. That was what you called "exclusive equipment." So we had a template.

I immediately found myself fantasizing about exclusive equipment for Raph-chan. Raph-chan was very tanuki-like— just like her origin, Raphtalia. Thinking of a tanuki turning into a human made me think of fairy tales and the kind of items they used there. Mt. Kachikachi wouldn't be any good. Putting her next to Ethnobalt would paint quite the picture, but in that story Raph-chan would be the bad guy, killed by the rabbit. She wasn't a nasty tanuki who caused trouble for nice old people. I thought for a moment longer about other such items from fairy tales.

I took out some paper and started to sketch designs for my next accessory. One looked more like work for a blacksmith. I scratched it away with my pen. I was just getting my ideas down. First, I drew a Raph-chan shape. Then I added a fairy-tale bewitched teakettle and teakettle-style armor. I expanded it from there, working to make it suit Ruft as well. He was big, so I could use a teakettle for his armor. For Raphtalia, meanwhile, the miko priestess outfit suited her so well I made the kettle from wood taken from the sakura lumina.

"Mr. Naofumi? What are you thinking about over there?" Raphtalia asked. I snapped back to myself as Raphtalia placed a hand on my shoulder—a murderous feeling in her hand.

"Exclusive equipment for you and the others, Raphtalia. Something like this," I said.

"I understand you want to make equipment for Raph-chan and the others, but why does it look so strange?!" Raphtalia exclaimed.

"The enchanted teakettle," Ren guessed.

"Yeah, I thought so. From that fairy tale," Mamoru agreed with a nod.

"It might suit Ruft," Ren said, "but it might be going too far for Raphtalia."

"A different tanuki-based spirit that might suit Raphtalia . . . how about the Akadenchu?" I pondered.

"Never heard of that one," Mamoru said. Ren was tilting his head too.

"It comes from around Tokushima. Not especially ghoulish in nature, it's about a tanuki in a red jacket that turns into a little kid and then asks to be piggybacked around. Doing so makes it happy," I explained.

"It doesn't, like . . . get heavy and squash you?" Ren asked.

"Nope," I said. It was just happy at being carried around. Mamoru and Ren didn't seem especially impressed.

"So it doesn't do any harm . . . but not much good either," Ren finally said. I was going to put little red jackets on Raph-chan and the whole tanuki gang. They'd look so cute, I knew it. The perfect piece of fairy-tale lore to apply to Raph-chan. "When you weren't here, Naofumi, Ruft wore something like that when we were going to play in the ocean with Keel," Ren explained. It sounded like Ruft had already worn something like it, but it hadn't been tailored for him. The experiment could go ahead.

"Raphtalia, which do you prefer? The fact our model is wearing nothing but a jacket might cause some titillation," I pondered.

"I don't want any part of any of this," Raphtalia replied. Fair enough. That was exactly the answer I expected.

"Whatever. I'll have S'yne make a simple red jacket . . . No, anyone who can sew could do it. If we choose materials carefully, it could have some good effects. Ren, you handle the teakettle," I said.

"Why? And what do you mean by 'whatever'?" Raphtalia was fighting back hard, her tail big and fluffy. I'd hoped to muscle this through, but maybe not.

"I'm talking about testing some exclusive equipment," I said innocently.

"You can't expect that to work!" Raphtalia shot back.

"Raphtalia, be sensible," I said persuasively, massaging her shoulders. "I won't allow you to give up anything that could make you stronger."

"I'm worried that if I back down here, you'll realize it works on the Raph-chans, and then I won't have any escape," Raphtalia said. She really had grown up so much. I couldn't just steamroll her anymore. She was fighting back with some intense logic. Of course, that didn't mean I was going to back down. I had shouldered an important and mighty purpose—to power up the Raph species. Maybe I didn't have to shoulder it, strictly speaking, but I loved the idea of "exclusive equipment." The experiment would continue!

"You do have it hard, sister," Fohl sympathized.

"You have an outfit from your species, right, Fohl? Does that give you some kind of equip effect?" I asked him.

"Some of them do have effects that only work with haku-ko," he told me, speaking honestly. Of course they did. That had to be a thing. Which meant weapons also had to exist with species-exclusive effects. "Sister, you could obtain something like that from Q'ten Lo, couldn't you?"

"I know we have Natalia here, but we can't borrow things from this time period," I said.

"I'm sure Natalia will happily lend us whatever we need. It's better than running the risk of whatever you might create," Raphtalia said.

"Natalia isn't here right now," I countered. "What you're looking for might not even be in Q'ten Lo in this time period. Rather than waste time finding out, wouldn't it make more sense to just make some new exclusive equipment? Even if you have some for yourself, the Raph-chans have nothing but that leaf," I argued.

"You aren't going to back down, are you, Naofumi?" Ren stated.

"An exclusive ring for me . . ." Filolia said, still looking cowed, face red. This could be a good way to make her shut up in the future.

"Would it still work if you wore the red jacket over the top of your miko priestess garb?" Ren said, proposing a compromise to Raphtalia.

"Hey, I wasn't expecting her to wear nothing but the jacket!" I clarified.

"I would certainly hope not!" Raphtalia shot back. I had meant the jacket over her current outfit from the start! It might be too many layers, but it could work as a jacket. "This entire exchange reminds me of Natalia from the other day."

"I can see that," I agreed.

"Overlaying my interaction with Natalia on this farce is very rude!" Holn interjected. Raphtalia gave a deep sigh.

"Okay, I give my consent," Raphtalia finally said. "Just don't take things too far. I don't want to end up practically naked."

"Of course not. Just what do you take me for?" I said, offended. Certainly not the kind of creep to raise a slave girl and then make her wear nothing but a red jacket. And wasn't that a short and sweet summation of Raphtalia's life!

I took a moment to recall what we had been discussing. Right. Exclusive equipment. We might be able to apply that term if an accessory was made for a particular individual to use. Just keep things simple, then. Put your heart into making something for that person.

Making an accessory for Raphtalia would be great training for me. I counted on her the most out of everyone. That was where the Raph-chans and my love of them came from. That made me think of that arm band I made for Raphtalia. The direction of the piece, as well as how to combine the materials to get the most out of them, was important to consider. Raphtalia might like something decorative, with gemstones, but that didn't suit my image at all.

"Mr. Naofumi?" Raphtalia stammered. I had taken her hand and was checking the size of her wrist. The last time, I'd simply made something I thought she could get the most use out of. I needed to consider a size that would make it easy to use and ensure it wouldn't get in the way in battle. I'd have to choose the materials carefully based on these points. Something with a strong connection to Raphtalia too . . . like a sakura stone of destiny, sakura lumina, or emergency medicine. It felt like my ideas were taking shape. The only issue was I didn't expect it to enhance skills even when it was completed.

"Hey, Raphtalia. What happened to that ball I made from those balloons for you?" I asked.

"That ball? I keep it safe on a shelf in my room," she replied. The memories of when we first met brought a smile to her face.

"And you have some more balloon materials in case it ever needed repairs, right?" I confirmed with her. I knew what a precious treasure that ball was for her. I hadn't given it much thought when I made the gift, but for Raphtalia, it was a super important memory.

"I do," she replied.

"If you have some to spare, could I have them? It should

be auspicious to make use of those materials," I explained. That was exactly what this item was going to need.

"Okay," Raphtalia finally replied.

"I often sympathize with you when Naofumi is giving you the runaround, but I can see how close you really are," Ren said quietly. I considered this to be business as usual.

"It looks like you've had a good idea or two," Holn commented.

"I noticed that too," Imiya added, the pair of them looking at me with smiles on their faces. I just wanted everyone to stop staring at me.

"I'm not going to use the balloon materials to make a thong, if that's what you're thinking," I said.

"And I wouldn't give them to you if you were!" Raphtalia fired back. I wondered how we always got off topic like this. All I wanted to do was practice making some powerful exclusive equipment.

"Finding the right combination of exclusive equipment and weapons could be a lot of work," I stated. I'd practice making exclusive equipment for Raphtalia and the Raph species first and then narrow down the search to something suited to their weapons.

We continued to spend the day testing more accessories. At the end, we had quite the haul. I walked away with enhanced durability for Shooting Star Shield, longer range for Float

Shield, and the ability to choose reflect magic up to Zweite class. I could add some life force to increase the output of the magic reflection, but after too many boosted reflects, the accessory itself would be destroyed. Ren had increased accuracy for Hundred Swords, night vision, and early warning for magic activation. Raphtalia gained additional stars that scattered from her Stardust Blade—swinging her sword, making flower petals appear for slashing follow-up attacks—and a boost to magic. Fohl and Filolia got visible critical points when attacking, easier charging of life force, and increased speed. S'yne and R'yne took home enhanced attack power and tensile strength for their thread attacks and boosted stats for their familiars. Mamoru got enhancements for Shield Boomerang, additional strength for Shield Bash, and auto Shooting Star Shield. Holn got increased length of time for the whip binding skills, a paralysis effect added to her attacks, and a reduction in compounding time.

I was especially impressed with Mamoru and his automatic deployment of Shooting Star Shield on a fixed cycle. I even gave it a try myself, but it didn't work for me like it did for him. I cursed the Shield Spirit again. That annoying ball of light seemed intent on dragging me through the mud. I was seriously thinking about changing full-time to the Mirror Hero.

Mamoru did say he was jealous of my magic reflection, but I wondered how honest he was being. It was probably a case of "the grass is always greener" for both of us. Holn's items were pretty run-of-the-mill, but she seemed to like them. I could easily imagine the kind of things she had in mind to use them for.

Chapter Five:
Gathering the Power of the Raph Species

It was the next day. I decided to practice magic with Raphtalia. She had only been using skills and techniques in our recent battles, and so her magic was falling behind. Raph-chan had various advantages over her in regard to magic already, so she needed some comprehensive training. She was doing all sorts of things to help treat Keel, but I was hoping to up her game when it came to combat. If she could weave in some illusions among her attacks, that would really confuse the enemy. Even if the enemy had some resistance, it would work if she could excel at it.

"Here I come," Raphtalia said.

"I'm ready," I replied.

"As the source of your power, we implore you! Let the true way be revealed once more . . ." Raphtalia started to incant some magic. It was the Way of the Dragon Vein, and I started the reverse analysis.

"My time to shine!" said the Demon Dragon in my head, performing the analysis and completing the nullification formula. The magic this time was a failure for Raphtalia. It wouldn't be this easy to nullify her magic if she was using Liberation class; she was clearly stuck at Drifa.

With the help of the Demon Dragon, Raphtalia had at least learned to use the Way of the Dragon Vein, but she was struggling to actually complete the magic.

"Stop right there," I said.

"Okay . . ." Raphtalia said forlornly.

"You can use the Way of the Dragon Vein, at least a little, so why isn't this going well?" I asked.

"I'm so sorry," Raphtalia replied. She was looking down at the ground, clearly taking it hard.

"No need to worry. Why don't we try practicing some of the magic from Kizuna's world?" I suggested.

"You can do that, Mr. Naofumi?" Raphtalia asked.

"Yeah . . . a little bit. Not any of that music stuff though," I said. Itsuki knew more about that side of things. Filo could trigger it by singing, but I didn't understand how that worked either. "You can use the magic the Demon Dragon used, right?" That was magic that involved requesting power from subordinates and then using their strength as magic. The basic structure was close to the Way of the Dragon Vein. It was magic that allowed access to be established to those you trusted and have them cooperate with you from anywhere. It was probably a lot like making a deal with the devil. The copy of the Demon Dragon that infested my own mind had tried to explain the whole thing to me, and I did recall some of it. However, I couldn't trigger it myself unless I was using the mirror. We needed to work on that.

"Yes, I can use it," Raphtalia said. This was suited to her, I could tell. The more collaborators one had, the shorter incanting would be, and the more powerful the resulting magic. It was like a fusion of the best parts from cooperative magic and the Way of the Dragon Vein. In Kizuna's world it was magic that had been sealed away long ago; using it seemed likely to give us a big boost in battle. But it could only be used by those with weapons affiliated with Kizuna's world and who had also been given the protection of the Demon Dragon.

"Who should I borrow power from? I know you, Mr. Naofumi, and the others will cooperate, but will that be enough?" Raphtalia asked.

"I could lend you mine, sure, but I think your attack power would actually decrease," I said, conflicted. Raphtalia used illusion magic, meaning we weren't completely incompatible, but it would also remove any leeway for me to cast magic myself. She wouldn't get much of a boost just from me either.

"Raph!" said Raph-chan, dashing over to me as I discussed the problem with Raphtalia.

"Good idea. Why don't we have Raph-chan and the other cuties help out?" I suggested.

"Hold on! Mr. Naofumi?" Raphtalia didn't sound as keen as I was on that idea. Raph-chan had originated from Raphtalia's own hair. That meant she was likely a great source of magic for Raphtalia. The source of their magic was the same. They might be able to unleash power equivalent to cooperation magic.

"The four heavenly kings of the Demon Dragon were—from one perspective—created from the accumulation of magic provided by those loyal to the Demon Dragon," I said.

"I remember your comments about Demon King Raphchan, Mr. Naofumi. But in this case, wouldn't that make me the Demon Queen?" Raphtalia queried.

"Demon Queen Raphtalia, huh?" I mused. That was fine too. Some people called me the Shield Demon King.

"Mr. Naofumi!" Raphtalia objected.

"No need to worry," I told her. "If you can gather the power from the Raph species, you'll have a much easier time in battle. Right?"

"I'll give it a try. The Demon Dragon taught me all the basics. I'd rather not use them, but very well," Raphtalia finally conceded. We proceeded swiftly to have Raphtalia try and borrow some power from the Raph species and incant some magic. "I'm ready. Raph-chan, please lend me a hand."

"Raph!" said Raph-chan brightly.

"I'll bring in the Raph species from the village! Raph species, come on!" I shouted. Then I explained the situation to the Raph species who were present in the stables. They all voiced their enthusiastic cooperation.

"Okay then . . . here goes," Raphtalia said, still with some trepidation. She started to focus, lifting her arms and incanting magic. She was wearing her miko priestess outfit, so it was almost like watching Glass dancing. The Demon Dragon magic could use an application of the Way of the Dragon Vein, so the incanting part was easy. All you needed were the basics, and then the Demon Dragon's protection did the rest. Those you were borrowing the power from were required, but the composition of the magic itself was just cooperation magic. Raphtalia had those here that she could borrow from, so I was sure this was going to work. Pretty sure.

"My universal collaborators! Respond to my call and materialize your magic power!" Raphtalia incanted. The Raph species voiced their agreement again and started to provide power in accordance with Raphtalia's request. Raphtalia slumped forward at once, almost toppling over.

"Are you okay?" I asked.

"Yes . . . just . . . not sure what . . ." Raphtalia stammered. Raph-chan suddenly turned into a ball of light, flew up above Raphtalia, and then became a shimmering ceremonial coat and settled around Raphtalia's shoulders. At the same time, a brilliantly glowing tail appeared on Raphtalia. "Oh my . . ." Raphtalia said, looking at the coat and her big shining tail. Then she slashed her hand to the side. Some yin-yang-shaped beads appeared, rotated around, and then three of them fired off. Raphtalia narrowed her eyes and took out her katana, obviously keen to continue the experiment.

"Five Practices Destiny Field Expansion," she said. The magic circle used to launch any of the Heavenly Emperor techniques appeared smoothly at Raphtalia's feet.

"Eight Trigrams . . ." Raphtalia adopted the pose for a big attack, which had always taken her a while to unleash in the past. Then she swung her katana. "Blade of Destiny!" A pretty deadly-looking arc sliced out to the side of her.

"This isn't exactly how the Demon Dragon used it," I commented. "The point is to incant some magic, right? Why are you using techniques?"

"Ah! You're right. I feel a lot of power flowing into me . . . I'm not even sure how I'm launching the magic," Raphtalia admitted. That sounded fine to me. She could use magic without having to incant! I pinched the glowing coat she was wearing between my fingers to check it out. Upon further inspection, it was a hoodie, not a coat—and the hood had a design like Raph-chan's face. I spread the hood out and put it over Raphtalia's head.

"That you, Raph-chan?" I asked. It felt like my eyes met with those on the hood for a moment. Raph-chan had all sorts of tricks up her little sleeve! I had no idea she could pull off such fashionable garments. As for the tail—it felt a bit weird. It was like the air had hardened. It was a feeling of intensely concentrated magic.

"Try using some magic. You can target me," I told her.

Raphtalia agreed and concentrated again, starting to incant some Demon Dragon-style magic.

"This power is a marker for illusions! True magic that lays waste to all, illusions that confound our foes! The Heavenly Emperor orders you! Sink my enemies into an ocean of illusion! Demon Emperor: Illusory Layers!" Raphtalia's magic activated fast, creating multiple black shapes wreathed in mist all around me. I sure hoped they were just illusions. I realized this was actually my first time being on the receiving end of Raphtalia's illusion magic. I'd seen the past Heavenly Emperor fighting with that fox woman, and this felt similar to that, like things from inside my mind were appearing in the mist.

"Raph!" said a horde of Raph-chans, all around me.

"Mr. Naofumi? Are you okay?" There were two Raphtalias too. These were some potent illusions.

"I'm fine. These illusions are powerful, Raphtalia," I told her.

"Sorry, Mr. Naofumi. I'm not over there," Raphtalia replied. I was talking to the illusion Raphtalia. I wondered if these were like the illusions produced by Emptiness is Form, magic I incanted with Raph-chan. I hadn't really given much thought to how I used it, but this could be quite dangerous. "It feels like I can create a large number of illusions with this magic," Raphtalia reported. The mist cleared away and I saw Raphtalia again.

"That's powerful illusory magic," I told her again, this time to her face.

"Yes. Thanks to the power I'm receiving from Raph-chan and the others, I was able to activate some magic at the ritual class with almost no incantation time," Raphtalia explained. That was impressive, even though this was all still practice. "I also understand something else after using that magic." She pointed at the large tail behind her. "It seems this tail can absorb magic. If I flick away magic using it, I can turn some of that into my own magical power."

"Sounds like Motoyasu's Absorb," I commented. The hero-exclusive magic Absorb from Motoyasu allowed his spear to absorb magic and turn it into his own magical power. The difficulty there was that moving around nullified the effect, but Raphtalia was moving about without any problems. The conversion rate looked lower than for Absorb, but when considered as a simplified version offering greater mobility, it could be quite a good means of protection.

"Yes, I think that's close to it. It should have a range of applications. Still, just what do you think this coat and this magic tail are for?" Raphtalia wondered.

"Don't ask me," I replied. I hadn't seen anything like them with the Demon Dragon, but they seemed to be a result of the cooperation of Raph-chan and the others.

"The Raph species were greatly influenced by you, Raphtalia. This is likely a reflection of their power. We should ask Holn and Rat," I suggested.

"I'm not sure I want to know the answer," Raphtalia replied.

"But these powers could be useful in our future battles," I reminded her.

"True enough . . . ah, let me end that magic," she said. The mist instantly faded, and then her coat and tail of light faded away.

"Raph!" said Raph-chan, returning back to her normal self on Raphtalia's shoulder. The other members of the Raph species sounded lethargic. They slumped down on the ground around us.

"They look like Shildina after she possessed Glass," I said.

"This might be a similar thing. It's like I gathered the strength of the Raph species and forcibly summoned it into myself," Raphtalia agreed. Although it was being achieved by proxy, this still looked like a decent boosted state for Raphtalia.

"It looks like borrowing their magic really drains the Raph species," I commented.

"A powerful trump card to play at just the right moment. I'm quite impressed that we found something like this," Raphtalia said.

"Me too. You definitely need to train harder at your magic. If this is what happens when you use the Raph species, next time Ren or I will lend you some magic and you can train with that," I told her.

"Okay," Raphtalia stammered. Then Ruft showed up. I thought he was still with Melty at the castle.

"Did I just hear Raphtalia asking to borrow some of my power?" Ruft said. I'd been expecting this. His connections to the Raph species meant he had heard what we said.

"That's right. We were conducting an experiment with magic from another world," Raphtalia explained.

"And the results were even better than expected," I continued for her. "The Demon Dragon knows about magic. Crappy personality, awesome magic." I explained to Ruft how Raphtalia had achieved her power-up. He nodded along as he listened for a while and then tilted his head.

"Just from hearing you describe it . . . it sounds like Astral Enchant," he commented.

"Hey, yeah. You're right," I replied. Astral Enchant couldn't be used without the blessing of the Heavenly Emperor and a sakura stone of destiny barrier, but it allowed for the temporary boost to a single person. We were heroes, so we couldn't use it, but it was a Q'ten Lo technique that allowed all the levels and strength of allies to be focused on one person. The fact it involved using sakura lumina and the power of the sakura stone of destiny to gather the levels of allies and provide them to one person was very similar to what we were using here.

"Were we able to use this because we're in the village?" I asked Raph-chan.

"Raph?" said Raph-chan, looking puzzled. That didn't help.

"Maybe you should test it in other places too," Ruft suggested.

"Good idea," I replied.

"I understand that you're keen to keep experimenting, but . . ." Raphtalia said, her voice trailing off.

"What's the problem? I doubt anyone else could use it, but it seems like a pretty convenient power for you," I told her.

"I'm having a hard time admitting that I need the Raph species," Raphtalia finally said.

"You're still hung up on that? You do have a stubborn streak, Raphtalia," I told her.

"Mr. Naofumi, of all people, calling me stubborn . . ." Raphtalia lamented, her shoulders slumping.

"Let's give it a try outside the village," Ruft said, keeping things moving along. "Raph species, can we count on you guys?" They replied with general agreement. They seemed to have recovered quite a lot already as they responded favorably to Ruft. We headed out of the village to practice Raphtalia's new power-up and magic. The results were promising—it seemed she could use it anywhere. The main issue was that she couldn't do it without Raph-chan; none of the other Raph species seemed able to play that pivotal role.

"I like that big tail Raphtalia gets," Ruft said.

"Me too," I agreed. "She looks like she's wearing a costume, but you can still see her face."

"I'm not happy about any of this," Raphtalia commented. Having the hood up or down didn't seem to make a difference, so she was doggedly keeping it down. If she wore the hood pulled over her face, she could apparently use the Raph-chan eyes on it to target her magic or perform analysis. She could even see souls like that.

So it turned out to be magic exclusive to Raphtalia and Raph-chan, which the two of them could use anywhere so long as they were together.

Chapter Six: Selecting the Hammer Hero

It was a few days later. Mamoru had received word from the Water Dragon and was leading us to meet up with Natalia. It was all connected to her search for the hammer vassal weapon.

It turned out that the holder of the hammer vassal weapon had been killed by the ones who assume the name of god, and the Hammer Spirit had fled to escape being used for evil. After we killed one of the ones who assume the name of god, the signal from the hammer had increased in strength again, allowing her to locate it. Now Mamoru needed to go check it out, and with as powerful a party as possible. Raphtalia, Ruft, the Raph-chans, and I were tagging along to see how they handled things. We were going to stay completely in the background. We couldn't have one of us being selected as the vassal weapon holder in this time period—the ramifications for the future were insane. It wasn't worth the risk to even experiment with such an idea.

We'd left Ren forging with Filolia. Eclair had informed me that he was complaining a lot, but actually doing some good work. However, he had also started to act a little strangely—a little more like the old Ren. When called out on it, he returned to normal, but he had started saying odd things and striking odd poses. Being around Eclair and Wyndia wasn't a problem for him, but maybe all that teenage angst was getting out of control with Filolia around.

Holn and R'yne weren't with us either. Holn was busy with her research and R'yne was still training S'yne.

"There you are," Natalia said in greeting. We were in the forest of the nation where we had first met Natalia, that nation where that nine-tailed fox monster had been controlling the king. Natalia had killed the fox, but even after the king returned to his senses, he had ordered his men to kill Natalia, leading in turn to the Water Dragon obliterating the ruler.

"You found it faster than expected," I commented.

"Yes. There were already some rumors about it, and a steady stream of people have been coming to try and claim it. But it's in a spot that only those of a certain strength can reach," Natalia explained.

"It wants the future bearer to display their strength," I pondered. "Not suited to performing the ritual for summoning from another world."

"And what if someone from a world already experiencing the waves is called? That's a possibility," Natalia said. That was a good point. If such a thing happened, I could easily imagine the issues that would ensue. Shildina and Filolia were good examples of this. I wondered what I would do myself if these "death games" taking place in other worlds were matched to the world I was born in—like if we were matched with Japan. When I first came here, the answer would have been clear—screw this world over and protect my real home. Luckily for me, there were no waves in Japan.

Shildina had a harsh outlook on the world and so might have done better living in a completely different one. And yet, she had still wanted to go home. That might suggest some changes in her mental makeup—and that her meeting us had been good for her. She seemed closer with Ruft than before. If Sadeena was Raphtalia's "big sister," then Shildina was Ruft's.

Any changes in her personality certainly weren't because she wanted to drink with me.

"Let me show you," Natalia said, leading us to the location of the hammer vassal weapon. We proceeded together through the foggy woodlands. Visibility was poor around us. There was a certain romanticism to the idea of a legendary weapon slumbering in a forest. I also loved the conceit that you needed to be a certain strength to even get there. When the weapon was located in a safer place, like with the gauntlets, there was a constant stream of people trying to get picked, plenty of whom didn't handle rejection well.

We finally came out into a wider space, and I saw a spot ahead with sunlight falling onto it. That was where the hammer vassal weapon was placed. It looked a lot like the gauntlet seven star weapon had, embedded into something like the Rosetta stone but for hammers.

"Okay. We don't have the bow holy weapon holder here, but can I ask the Shield Hero?" Natalia turned to face Mamoru. "Do you want to perform the summoning ritual and call a holder for the weapon or try and see if anyone in your group is suited to using it?" We still needed to meet our original goal of increasing our fighting strength before the ones who assume the name of god made their next move. If Siltran successfully got the hammer vassal weapon holder on their side, the situation between the nations would shift in their favor and Piensa would be unable to talk back so openly. That would be the time to open negotiations with the Bow Hero and prepare to fight the ones who assume the name of god. That was the plan. Things were already going better for Siltran, but this would settle it.

"I'd like to try with the people I know first. If that doesn't work out, we'll have to summon someone. I'd rather not drag someone from an unrelated world into this, if possible," Mamoru said.

"Understood," Natalia replied. "That does sound like the best approach." Each of Mamoru's companions then proceeded to attempt to take the hammer vassal weapon. Cian and others from among the kids Mamoru looked after were there too. Cian failed to take the hammer, falling back onto her butt as she pulled. She made a pained expression for a moment, then wiped her face and returned to Mamoru as though nothing had happened.

"No good, huh?" Mamoru said to her.

"Nope, no good," she replied. She sounded so much like Atla in that moment it reminded me of when Atla had attempted to take the gauntlet seven star weapon. We were going to be fighting powerful monsters and the ones who assume the name of god in the future, so I wanted as few casualties as possible. With that in mind, I watched the proceedings, hoping that someone would get picked to bolster our forces, but in the end, none of those Mamoru brought along were able to take the hammer vassal weapon.

"What about you and your allies, future Shield Hero?" Natalia asked me.

"It could be a massive pain in the temporal ass if any of us got chosen," I cautioned. We may even have to leave that person here in this time.

"That depends on the hammer vassal weapon, surely," Natalia replied, showing more forbearance than I'd been expecting.

"Dafu!" said Dafu-chan.

"Raph!" added Raph-chan, both of them chirping about something. Dafu-chan could use hammers.

"Maybe we should let this little one try," I suggested, picking Dafu-chan up.

"Dafu!" said Dafu-chan. "Dafu, dafu, dafu!" She was going wild. It looked like she really didn't want to.

"It's rare to see a Raph species that doesn't want to be held by you, Mr. Naofumi," Raphtalia commented.

"I guess so," I replied. We knew Dafu-chan was the past Heavenly Emperor, so there had to be some reason for this. "Okay . . . maybe let Ruft have a go. Even if he gets picked, when we go home, we'll persuade the hammer to release him." Ruft had looked pretty good swinging that axe around, so giving him a hammer could be a big attack boost for us.

"If you want me to, Shield Hero," Ruft said.

"It is highly unlikely that a Heavenly Emperor would ever be selected without extreme extenuating circumstances," Natalia said.

"What do you mean?" I asked.

"We're here to watch over the heroes. What do you think would happen if one was selected to actually become a hero? Do you think the spirit implements—the vassal weapons—have not considered this?" Natalia asked. I could see her point. If the ones who were meant to stop abuse were given the power to cause the abuses they were meant to stop, that could definitely be a conflict of interest, and one easy to give into.

"What does that mean about me?" Raphtalia asked, a frown on her face. She was the holder of the katana vassal weapon.

"That's a vassal weapon from another world, so it's not the same thing. The hammer vassal weapon is from this world," Natalia replied. Raphtalia was the holder of a vassal weapon from another world, so this rule didn't apply to her.

"That means Ruft is off the table," I said.

"Really? That's a shame," Ruft said. He seemed to want to give it a go, but not if Natalia wasn't going to allow it. I wanted to avoid contravening any of the rules of Q'ten Lo at the moment.

"You want to ask anyone else before the summoning, Mamoru?" I asked.

"I do have some other ideas. People I'd like to ask. Can we wait on the summons a little longer?" Mamoru replied. It sounded like he might have someone else he could ask—and it seemed like he was saying we were finished here for today. As we started to withdraw—

"Seriously . . . I hope we find someone soon," Natalia said.

"Dafu!" said Dafu-chan intently. But it was too late. Natalia reached out and stroked the hammer vassal weapon. With a popping sound, the weapon freed itself from the Rosetta stone and stuck to Natalia's hand. Dafu-chan's fur was raised, and she was growling. She'd tried to warn Natalia before she touched it!

Natalia could only gasp. She was staring at the hammer in her hand while the Rosetta stone turned into light and vanished. Everyone who had been getting ready to leave turned to look at Natalia.

"Oh my. The hammer vassal weapon has made a strange choice. Does it have any idea what this means?" the Water Dragon said, sounding bemused. Natalia had told Ruft not to

try and then been picked herself! The hammer vassal weapon was sparkling in Natalia's hand. She was the holder now, no doubt about it. Natalia herself had a hand pressed against her forehead and was shaking her head.

"Choosing a pacifier as its holder! What is the spirit of the hammer vassal weapon thinking?!" Natalia started raging at the hammer, but of course, it didn't reply.

"For better or worse, you've been selected as a vassal weapon holder. Now you will need to set an even better example for all heroes. Natalia the Hammer Hero! Redouble your efforts to maintain an honest heart!" the Water Dragon said.

"Silence!" Natalia raged back. "I feel like cursing this world and my fate, cursing everything! We've found a potential way to end the waves! Is this kind of exception to the rules even required?" She'd just become a holder and I was already worried about her getting cursed. She was setting the perfect example of what a hero shouldn't do, which was highly conflicting, given that she was also a pacifier.

"I think you might be suited to the role from a combat perspective," Mamoru said, trying to calm her down. His approach was quite different from the one I would have taken.

"Ah . . . good luck," Raphtalia said.

"Wow, this is amazing!" Ruft added.

"Raph!" said Raph-chan. They all seemed pleased for Natalia.

"I'm not happy about this," Natalia said with a sigh. "How did this even happen?" Having both the power of a hero and a pacifier could be powerful. She could use a hero's power while also holding the power to seal it.

Natalia looked even more exasperated than before as she followed us with the hammer vassal weapon on her back. We left the clearing.

Then something caught my eye deep among the trees. Something was moving in the underbrush with what looked like a golden tail.

"Mr. Naofumi?" Raphtalia asked.

"No, it's nothing," I replied. Probably just a monster watching what was going on. I set off after the others.

Chapter Seven: Origin of the Past Heavenly Emperor

We returned to the Siltran castle and let Melty and the others know that Natalia had been selected as the hammer vassal weapon hero.

"A new Dark Brave has been born! Wield that black power with abandon, oh fallen pacifier!" Filolia crowed from the sidelines. Natalia raised her hammer and took a step forward but then stopped.

"Hey, Filolia! Don't overly excite her!" Mamoru stepped in to caution her.

"It seems to make sense . . . but it won't be easy," Ren said, looking at Natalia with sympathy.

"Why does power always choose those who don't wish for it?" Raphtalia pondered, also looking sympathetic.

"Oh! I like that phrase!" Filolia responded. I thought it was good too.

"Why am I being counted among these . . . unique individuals?" Natalia bemoaned. I wasn't pleased with her tone. She was clearly using "unique" as a derogatory term. And if heroes were all "unique," that would include me. I wasn't pleased with that at all.

"That's pretty rude to the spirits of the holy and vassal

weapons," I commented. I had my own questions about how the spirits chose their heroes, but I didn't feel the same as the pacifier. She probably hated the whole world at the moment. I'd give her some time to settle down. "In any case, this puts Siltran on top. The threat of a Piensa invasion has been totally squashed." Piensa was left with just the Bow Hero. It didn't look like they had the Carriage Hero.

"True," Mamoru said. "I didn't expect things to develop this quickly." I agreed with that sentiment. Now we'd be able to take our time and search for a way back to the future. "We should continue to collect the weapons and enhance them, don't you think?"

"Sounds good," I said. "Collecting them isn't enough—they need to be strong too."

"She looks pretty strong already," Mamoru mused. "We probably don't need to worry so much." As we chatted, Natalia suddenly snapped back to herself and looked up.

"Hold on a moment. Now that I've been chosen as the hammer vassal weapon holder, what about that hammer I was given the other day?" Natalia asked.

"Restrictions. You won't be able to use it," I said.

"That's how it goes," Mamoru agreed. After someone was chosen as a hero by a holy weapon or a vassal weapon, they could only use that weapon in battle. That meant Natalia could no longer use the hammer that Holn had given her. Holn nodded upon hearing this.

"Honestly speaking, I'd prefer you used it in combat, but that isn't an option now," Holn said.

"Ah, if she can't use it, maybe I can," Ruft suggested.

"You're joking! I'm not giving that hammer to anyone!" Natalia replied immediately. She really didn't want anyone to hear what it had to say.

"Even if she can't use it as a weapon, surely she could just keep it on her back. But that sounds like a bit of a waste," I admitted.

"The weapon will still obtain the information I need," Holn replied. "It should pick up on her techniques." If Holn said it, that sounded legit.

"I'm not letting anyone touch this hammer!" Natalia cried out, still raging. "And I'm going to kill that evil alchemist one day!" It sounded like she was trying to calm herself down by focusing all of her hate on Holn.

"I hope she doesn't let her anger overtake her, Mr. Naofumi," Raphtalia said. The implication there was Raphtalia wanted to add "like you." I was wondering about that myself. It depended on whether Natalia hated Holn as much as I hated Bitch. They seemed to help each other out, so their relationship couldn't be that bad.

"Dafu, dafu, dafu!" raged Dafu-chan, seemingly triggered by Natalia's anger. But her outburst only made her look cuter to me.

"You'll only hear all those morose comments at the start. Once it's finished, it should be an excellent hammer," Holn commented.

"I hope you're right," Natalia said pointedly. With that, we welcomed Natalia as the Hammer Hero. I got the impression she would have liked to disappear, but her new duty would not allow for that. Being a hero really was the worst. It felt like some of these spirits—just some of them—were going to incredible lengths to troll our entire lives.

The night after Natalia was selected as a hero, I was alone in my room, drawing up some accessory designs and compounding some medicine.

"Raph!" said Raph-chan, bursting in.

"Dafu!" said Dafu-chan, joining her. Raphtalia was off again helping Keel and the others with their trauma treatments. We hadn't slept in the same room for a while now.

"Hey. You two want to sleep in my room tonight?" I asked my two visitors. Raph-chan and Dafu-chan slept in all sorts of different places. They had been helping Raphtalia recently, so they often slept with her.

"Dafu," said Dafu-chan. She took a step forward, stood up on two legs, and then leapt up into the air. With a theatrical puff of smoke, she turned into the form of the past Heavenly Emperor.

"Huh? What's up?" I asked, puzzled by the change. It probably meant she had something she wanted to discuss with me. "You don't turn into this form very often. Any special reason today?"

"It takes a long time to charge up the energy for this transformation, eh," the past Heavenly Emperor explained. "I should have kept more for this purpose." That explained it. Technically speaking, she was stronger than Sadeena. I would have preferred her fighting on the front lines; the reason she didn't turn into her human form often was because of the power it consumed. That was quite inconvenient.

"Sounds like you must have something you want to say— and you don't have long to say it," I jibed.

"I do not," the past Heavenly Emperor agreed.

"Shall we have Holn make a few modifications? Increase your transformation time?" I continued.

"I know you like joking around," the past Heavenly Emperor said, a frown instantly forming on her face, "but stop it. I already look like some freakish teddy bear, eh. I don't want things to get any worse."

"Whatever you say," I placated her. I'd already been pretty sure of this, but it seemed the past Heavenly Emperor didn't care much for Holn.

"The charge time is improving, anyway—but that only means I'm becoming more accustomed to this body, eh," the past Heavenly Emperor bemoaned. It sounded like she might be able to transform more often in the future. "I'm going to keep this short even though I've got a lot to tell you."

"Go right ahead," I said. I wondered if she had purposefully picked a time when Raphtalia wasn't here and what that might mean.

"First, I need to explain exactly what I am," she started.

"Raphtalia's ancestor, right? And coming after Natalia, I'm guessing," I cut in. "But that hammer of yours looked a lot like the one Holn had." We still had no real idea who this past Heavenly Emperor actually was. There was Raphtalia, Natalia, and her. That was about all the information we had. "In the original timeline, did that turn up later, and did they use it for the experiment?" I asked.

"No. The way that hammer came into being, eh, and its manufacture are without a doubt the same," the past Heavenly Emperor said confidently.

"Which means . . . you're residual memories from Natalia?" I guessed.

"Close to that, eh, but not exactly," the past Heavenly Emperor replied. "The answer is I was formed from that hammer, but further into the future from now when the personality transcription has been completed." This meant that the past Heavenly Emperor, sometimes known as Raph-chan II, was not Natalia herself, but rather had been formed from a hammer containing a copy of Natalia's personality. "It might be due to this unexpected trip to the past, and maybe because I'm growing into this body, but my memories are starting to come back to me. It doesn't feel exactly like I'm remembering them. This is . . . something else," the past Heavenly Emperor explained.

"Okay," I said. I had been hoping for some clues on the immediate future of the age we were now in, but that didn't sound promising.

"I can remember a little of what happened to the hammer after this. It was always taken out of Q'ten Lo as the weapon of the pacifier. An oracle would use its power to let the hammer take over their body and then punish rampaging heroes or monsters," the past Heavenly Emperor explained. That sounded like the trick Shildina had pulled when we first met her. So the past Heavenly Emperor was the one who got sent out from Q'ten Lo to fix things. She was fated to do a whole bunch of fighting, then. "Once I ended my life as a sentient weapon, there was nothing until Shildina awoke me."

"So tell me. Do you think the waves have ended in the future?" I asked her. She looked away as she replied.

"I can tell you . . . I recall fighting many new enemies over the years of my life. There were always those like Makina mixed in amongst them, but I cannot be sure they were always the allies of our true enemy," she admitted.

"I see." I rubbed my chin in thought. This trip back to the

past was definitely an irregularity. More and more things were pointing to that now. We didn't have any concrete answers yet, but the main issue still stood—we had to get back to our time as quickly as possible. "You don't seem bothered about talking to the Water Dragon either. Why's that?"

"I've never liked him. He talks too much and telling him any of this isn't going to change things," the past Heavenly Emperor said. It sounded like she didn't get on with him. He didn't seem to know much that could help us anyway. "If I show them this form, I'm worried about affecting the Heavenly Emperor further from this time . . . the original me, eh," she continued. I could see that too. Natalia didn't do so well with being "affected." She still had a lot of growing to do, mentally. She wouldn't be able to withstand the shock of discovering what was basically a clone of herself among a bunch of people from the future.

"So putting this all together, you're a hammer with a copy of Natalia's personality who's from further into the future than me," I said.

"That personality was extracted from the hammer and stored in a different vessel, eh," she corrected.

"And why do you say 'eh' all the time?" I asked.

"I don't know, eh," she replied.

"You're a blend of Natalia's and Holn's personalities, perhaps," I ventured. Holn had that whole "little old" thing when she spoke.

"I hope that isn't the case, eh," the past Heavenly Emperor said. "It's more likely I'm just getting old. I recall my verbal patterns being strange prior to my final destruction, eh."

"Okay then. What else do you need to say?" I asked, moving her along. I now knew this was future Natalia, but the human version of the past Heavenly Emperor looked so much like a slightly older Raphtalia that I found it hard to deal with her. "Are you going to give some speech about preserving the timeline? You're the one who killed that foxy lady, so you're in no position to lecture on that topic. That had to be a pretty big blow to the space-time continuum," I said.

"Huh? That fox woman? No," the past Heavenly Emperor said noncommittally. I would have liked a little more commitment there. A disturbing golden tail flickered through my memory. "If any changes are happening, I'm the one who wants to observe them. I'm not going to come down on you too hard."

"Awesome. I'll go ahead and have Holn make the Raph species rather than the filolials—" I started.

"That is certainly not permitted," the past Heavenly Emperor said quickly. "Know your place." I'd hoped she wouldn't take that stance. "I simply can't stand how she styles herself as an evil alchemist, eh." She definitely hated Holn.

"Are you expending all this charged up power just to complain?" I asked.

"No, of course not. There's something that's still vague in my mind, eh, but it could be a useful lead," the past Heavenly Emperor said.

"What is it?" I asked intently.

"Do you remember that device we saw in the filolial sanctuary, prior to coming to this time?" the past Heavenly Emperor asked.

"You mean the things that Motoyasu activated?" I asked. It had looked like a big clock.

"I think that . . . was a facility for the control of time," the past Heavenly Emperor revealed.

"There's no filolials in this time though, so they can't have a sanctuary yet," I said. "Was that shrine there before they came along?" Mamoru had mentioned a "sanctuary," but I deduced that they had to be talking about those ruins—in our time—that we'd visited during the Church of the Three Heroes debacle. Melty might know where it was, and what kind of facilities they had, but it seemed unlikely there was anything there. This was before the fusing of the worlds. The terrain was pretty different. That made it hard to locate things. Like with Melromarc and Siltvelt, there was a place called the Desert of Confusion on the way to Faubrey—again, in our time—but no such place here.

"If that shrine originated with the sword or spear worlds, that's going to be a real pain for us," I murmured.

"The worrying thing is how likely that sounds, eh," the past Heavenly Emperor added.

"Not a laughing matter," I said, wondering how the hell we would get there if that was the case.

"But we aren't without some hope. There's potential to get there if we can obtain the carriage vassal weapon," the past Heavenly Emperor revealed.

"Why would a carriage offer any hope at all?" I asked.

"The carriage is a movement-based vassal weapon, eh. Like the ship from Kizuna's world. It can trace the response from the sword and cross between worlds even outside of a wave," the past Heavenly Emperor revealed. That was a thing, was it? Ethnobalt had used the Ship vassal weapon to send us back to this world via an anchor accessory. The same kind of thing could be possible using different weapons.

Still, even if that gave us some hope, I was pretty pissed off to learn that our hope of getting home wasn't even in this world!

"Even the katana vassal weapon couldn't transport us over to Kizuna's world. You sure the carriage would be able to do something like that?" I asked.

"Like I said, it's just a hope at the moment," the past Heavenly Emperor repeated.

"Okay then." The next issue was getting our hands on the carriage vassal weapon. Mamoru made it sound like a vassal weapon that was really picky about picking someone to use it, and we didn't even know where it was anyway. I was pretty sure that Fitoria was the holder of the carriage in the future; maybe we could take the past Fitoria along with us to look for it. "I get what you want to say, but how do we look for something we have no idea the location of?"

"In this time . . . I recall it being in a place the heroes call the 'sanctuary,'" the past Heavenly Emperor said.

"So you do know," I replied sardonically.

"I remembered, eh," she replied. This was one unreliable Heavenly Emperor. Natalia would probably feel dejected to know she turned into this in the future. I also wasn't so sure we'd find anything useful in this "sanctuary." Mamoru made it sound like there wasn't much there.

"Ah . . . I'm out of time, eh," the past Heavenly Emperor said, and then she popped back into Dafu-chan shape in another puff of smoke. "Dafu," said Dafu-chan with a deep sigh. I wondered whatever she could dislike about this vision of cuteness. Maybe this was what Raphtalia would look like if she turned into a Raph species. I now knew this was Natalia as a Raph species, so I reached out to stroke her. Even as I extended my hand, however, Dafu-chan leapt away—sensing danger, perhaps. She even gave a threatening growl. It seemed she knew all too well what I had been planning to do. Maybe another time.

"Thanks for all the info. I'll talk with Mamoru tomorrow and get him to take us to this sanctuary place," I said.

"Dafu!" said Dafu-chan. Thanks to the information from the past Heavenly Emperor, I therefore decided to head to the sanctuary.

Chapter Eight: 0 Territory

It was the next day.

"Hey, Naofumi! Wake up!" Melty exclaimed in a panic. She was hammering on the door to my room.

"What's all the noise?" I said.

"Big trouble! Wake up and listen to this!" Melty shouted.

"Okay, okay. What's going on? Another Piensa attack?" I asked.

"Indirectly, yes!" Melty exclaimed. I shook my head. They weren't going to give up easily. I'd thought proclaiming loud and clear that we had the Hammer Hero would have shut them up, but it didn't seem to have worked. It might be time to crush them once and for all. That sounded like a faster move than waiting for Mamoru to take care of things. We'd give them a taste of what it was like to be invaded.

"We sent emissaries in order to form our own alliance to other nations. They've been attacking all of those nations!" Melty said.

"Finally showing their true colors," I muttered. We had them on the ropes, but that also made them dangerous. But we should be careful or they might hand us the justice in this situation.

"I don't know what they want. But they aren't holding anything back. Shadow barely made it back," Melty said.

"That'z right," Shadow said, arriving moments later. He was a mess and was basically being held up by Raphtalia. He was badly injured. Bloody bandages were wrapped around his head. The Raph specimen that had been with him was badly injured too. He was basically clinging to Shadow's shoulder. Things were bad if they had discovered Shadow's covert infiltration and caused this much damage to him.

"Mr. Naofumi, the situation is grave," Raphtalia said.

"I see that, but we need to prioritize healing them first," I replied.

"That would be welcome," Shadow said, "but I'm not zure even you can heal these woundz, Zhield Hero." The Raph specimen squeaked too.

"I think I can handle it," I said. They didn't look completely hopeless, like Atla had. In fact, they looked like a little magic or medicine would heal them right up without any trouble. But no one had done that yet, which suggested something else was going on here. There was only one way to find out—I incanted some healing magic at the Shadow and his ninja-cosplay Raph specimen.

"My time to shine!" said the Demon Dragon in my head.

"All Liberation Heal," I said. My healing magic was instantly activated. For a moment I thought it was working, but in the next instant their wounds burst open again. "What's the problem?" I exclaimed.

"The Pienza forcez have introduced zome myzteriouz new weaponz that cause incurable injuriez. The zoldierz from the nationz we tried to form an alliance with were attacked in the zame way. The battle was completely one-zided," Shadow explained. This was a new pain in the ass that I didn't need. It looked like some kind of curse. Perhaps it was similar to when I was badly wounded by Blood Sacrifice. I combined the power of my shield and the Demon Dragon to analyze Shadow's wounds. I hoped that some ritual magic or holy water could cure them. If not, they were eventually going to die. The continued bleeding was weakening them, I could tell.

"Raphtalia, we need to get them to the treatment center in the village," I said.

"Of course," Raphtalia replied.

"Naofumi. They'll be okay, won't they?" Melty asked.

"We'll heal them, don't worry," I assured her. "Can you get Rat and Holn, please?"

"Sure," Melty replied. We took Shadow and the Raph specimen to the village treatment center and began their treatment. Rat and Holn arrived quickly and joined me in analyzing the wounds of Shadow.

"I'm not seeing many signs of a little old curse," Holn admitted.

"Indeed," Rat agreed. "It's more like the wounds have been fixed in an open position. I think their condition would be even worse if it wasn't for the properties of Duke's healing magic." Rat and Holn's analysis revealed that incorrect treatment would have the opposite effect, and so should be avoided. The reason that my magic hadn't made things worse was because I couldn't attack. The effects of incoming magic were being reversed, which should turn healing into attack. Seeing as I was unable to attack, however, the healing magic just cut out instead. I wasn't sure whether to be happy or abjectly depressed at this new twist in my physiology. At least it had prevented Shadow and the Raph specimen from getting any worse.

"This whole setup is pretty nasty," Holn muttered. "I don't think Piensa has access to technology like this."

"There's a curse that prevents healing in the future . . . but nothing quite like this," Rat admitted.

"Diagnosis is one thing. But is there any way to fix it?" I asked.

"Maybe in a limited capacity," Holn said. "They might heal if the wounds were cut out completely."

"Cazes like that were zeen in the intel I gathered . . . The woundz zimply got deeper," Shadow reported. He had been collecting information on our enemies, and it sounded like that had included information on other victims. I cursed. Every treatment I had been thinking of would probably have the opposite effect.

"We could try using healing cultivation fluid," Rat suggested. "Let's see what that does." She took out a test tube of it and placed some on one of Shadow's wounds. Smoke rose with a sizzling sound, blood sprayed out, and the wound only got deeper. "That's having the opposite effect," she said, quickly stopping.

"I refuse to believe that anything is impossible to heal. That sounds like complete fiction," Holn said firmly. It certainly sounded like fiction to me too—like a weapon from some ancient myth from Earth that caused wounds that would never heal. "We might be able to overwrite it with a cell transplant. This is pretty thorough though, so I wouldn't be surprised if it blocks that too," she went on. I cursed again. This was black, twisted technology. It was just evil. It was almost as if S'yne's sister and her organization were here working in Piensa. We were in the past, so they actually might be . . .

"Do you have any other ideas?" I asked. If the wounds themselves couldn't be healed, maybe we could treat the area around them. But even placing a skin transplant over the top probably wasn't going to work here.

Then I recalled how Kizuna had saved the modified Tsugumi and ended the power of one of the resurrected.

"Raphtalia," I said. Ren and S'yne were here too, looking on with concern, but I thought it was fastest to ask Raphtalia.

"Yes?" she asked.

"Try cutting their wounds with Katana 0," I told her.

"Are you sure?" she asked after a pause.

"The 0 weapons don't have any attack power. They're also the only thing I can think of that might work against a bundle of pure evil like this," I said. This seemed as unfair, unjust, or irregular as anything we had seen so far. The 0 weapons seemed to exist to combat that brand of unfairness.

"I'll give it a try," Raphtalia said. She drew her katana, changed it to Katana 0, and slid the blade over Shadow's wounds. He moaned, trying to withstand the pain. Something seemed to be working. Maybe that was all we needed to do.

"First Heal," I said, applying some healing magic to the areas Raphtalia had tended to. But there didn't seem to be any major changes, and blood started to seep out again.

"I can't believe it," Raphtalia said.

"Even 0 can't help us," I muttered. Maybe this wasn't such an irregularity after all.

"This is extreme," Rat agreed.

"I must admit even my impressive brain can't seem to come up with a treatment," Holn said. "Maybe I could create some homunculi and transfer their souls over?"

"And you can do that in time?" I asked.

"I ztill have . . . a little time. I'm not . . . dying yet," Shadow said weakly. Probably not in the next few minutes, but with all the bleeding, I'd be surprised if he had two days. Maybe we should use that time to raid Piensa and find the one responsible for this.

"Will your idea work in time, Holn?" I asked again.

"A tall order. Even if I cultivate the cells at a breakneck pace . . . we can't be sure they haven't planned for this eventuality," she admitted. She was normally so confident, so the hesitancy in her answers shook me as much as anything else. That told me how hopeless this was. The only one who could remove this was the one who had caused it, but who knew what they would ask in order to do so?

"Naofumi. . ." Melty looked at me. Both of her hands were pressed together as though in prayer. If we allowed Piensa to invade, we might be able to save Shadow and the Raph specimen. It would delay us finding a way back to the future—indeed, it might prevent it completely. But that wasn't reason enough to dismiss it out of hand.

"Zhield Hero. You muzt not accept the evil of Pienza . . . for my zake," Shadow said. The Raph specimen squeaked too, both of them shaking their heads. "There'z ztill time. I underztood how the queen felt now . . . painfully underztand. At leazt I have zome time before I pazz to zhare my final wordz with you."

"Raph," managed the Raph specimen.

But I made a decision after losing Atla, and being saved by everyone, and then talking to Atla again. Whatever happened,

I made a decision not to lose anyone else. Whatever the cost, I wanted to protect them all. I clenched my fists tightly, pushing down the urge to scream out. Then I heard a voice from somewhere.

"Are you sure?"

It wasn't a voice I had heard before, but it also felt vaguely familiar. It was a bit like my own voice, but also not quite the same. I had no idea who it was. It might be coming from the shield, and it might just be ringing in my head.

The question the voice asked was more important than who was speaking.

Of course, I was sure. We'd had less contact with Shadow since wrapping up the stuff with the Church of the Three Heroes, but he had still done so much for our cause. Here in the past, he had gathered information on Piensa and helped Melty with her workload. I was also sure he had done all sorts of things to aid our cause. I didn't want to lose someone who had done so much to help out.

"This could be a path of thorns. There might be no going back. Will you still regret nothing?"

I was unshaken. I had made my decision. There was no

going back on it. If I could save the life of my allies, I'd do whatever it took.

"Then I shall answer your resolve."

It felt like the voice got louder for a moment.

". . . forgotten by . . . to 0 territory."

Beginning of 0 has changed! It became 0 territory: upper layer!
Attack -1
Enhanced magic passage rate
Learned Reverse Dimensional Defensive Wall (weak)

All of that popped up in my status. At the same time, a way to heal these wounds . . . a magic formula also appeared in my mind.

"Translucent black, vomiting forth to create nothingness! Allow me to guide that power and ask for realization!" I incanted.

"Mr. Naofumi?" Raphtalia asked, startled.

"Has something happened?" Holn asked her.

"I'm not sure. I feel something from Mr. Naofumi," Raphtalia replied. I was cursing to myself. This incantation was incredibly hard. It wasn't the normal puzzle style, and the Demon Dragon wasn't reacting either. It was like scooping fish from a pond that had been added to the normal style of puzzle; the pieces were the fish, but I had nothing but a flimsy membrane to collect them with.

"I, the Shield Hero, order the heavens and the earth to correct all order and return the puss to nothingness . . ." I tried again, but that didn't work either. It didn't seem to matter how many times I failed, but each one was increasing the length of time until the magic would be triggered. The difficulty of this was just so high! But that wasn't going to stop me.

"I order the source of all power! Eradicate this cursed blight from these victims of irregularity! Fill First Heal Zero!" I finally got it. With a crackling, it felt like all the magic was draining from my fingers.

"Some kind of incantation? Zero, did you say?" Raphtalia murmured. Even as she did so, what looked like some distortion of space itself appeared from my hand and flew toward the wounds on Shadow and the Raph specimen. The magic I had unleashed passed through them, running over their wounds, and then vanished into the air a moment later. After finishing the incantation, I collapsed on the spot, perhaps even losing consciousness for a moment.

"Mr. Naofumi?!" Raphtalia exclaimed. She quickly moved in to support me, preventing me from hitting the ground. I moaned. "Are you okay?!"

"Yeah, I'm fine," I managed. "I just blanked out for a moment. Lack of magic."

"I've never seen that happen to you before, Mr. Naofumi," Raphtalia said with concern.

"Just what magic did you use there?" Holn asked.

"Your guess is as good as mine," I replied. "Some magic that just popped into my head, basically." I was more concerned with the strange new skill that had appeared: 0 territory: upper layer. There was a value next to it as well: 3%. "What about Shadow?" I asked.

"I'm not seeing any real changes," Rat reported. I chugged some magic water to try and get my magic back up. I was still far from being fully healed, but the lethargy was at least gone. I was really hoping that had been more than just a waste of magic! I tried some healing magic on Shadow again. This time his wounds just closed right up.

"Oh wow!" said Rat.

"What did you do?" Holn asked. "I still wasn't close to working out how to heal them."

"I don't know myself," I replied. "Holn, that leaf you gave me which I put in my shield provided a certain skill. Well, that skill just evolved to let me use that magic." I didn't understand why myself, but for now we could simply celebrate the treatment of these untreatable wounds. "I'll heal the rest of them."

"Zhield Hero . . . thank you," Shadow said. The Raph species thanked me too.

"I don't need any more thanks. Heal those wounds and recover your strength," I told them.

"Underztood," Shadow replied.

"I think we need to give you some training too. Help keep you in the fight," I told him. He was fairly strong, but we hadn't applied things like the whip power-up method especially attentively. I needed to make sure I was suitably rewarding those who helped me out. Our enemies were ruthless. They would use whatever means they had at their disposal to injure and kill us. I wanted to make sure he would be able to make it through the next situation like this.

"Pleaze don't take it too hard on me," Shadow said. "I can reward you by turning into Raphtalia and zaying thingz zhe normally wouldn't zay to you!"

"You just got saved from a certain death situation! Don't put yourself in another!" I said. I wondered where these jokes of his came from. Maybe he was just trying to lighten the mood. "This sounds like we've got some trouble to deal with, anyway." Internally, I was feeling upset about all of this. I applied healing magic to Shadow and the Raph species again and then decided what to do next. We would have a meeting with Mamoru and his allies. This was going to put off our trip to the sanctuary.

Mamoru and his allies had heard of the attack and came to discuss it. I was explaining everything in the village refectory.

Hearing about this new threat from their enemy Piensa had created a heavy atmosphere in the room.

"Weapon attacks that only Naofumi can heal," Mamoru muttered, crossing his arms.

"At least we do have a way of healing them," Melty offered.

"Not one I can use repeatedly. It takes too much magic," I said. We weren't going to get far if I collapsed every time I had to use it. And it also took a long time to activate too.

"I wonder how they're doing it . . . maybe an imbued effect or something special about the materials?" Ren started to analyze things from the perspective of a blacksmith. We hadn't seen anything like this in the future. It was an attack so powerful even Holn couldn't come up with a way to cure it right away.

"If we could obtain one of the weapons that caused it, or bring some of the victims here and run a few little old experiments, I might be able to work out how to deal with it," Holn said. "The only issue is that I can't guarantee the lives of those subjects." Medicine had been built on a foundation of countless experiments and sacrifices. Holn was letting us know that even she might not be able to deal with something this evil without some such sacrifices.

"Not being able to heal from it makes it seem like it's like some kind of mythical weapon," Mamoru mused. I'd been thinking the same thing. There were a lot of weapons like that in mythology.

"That's right. There are lots of weapons with legends like this in our world," I agreed with him. Some famous examples I recalled from Celtic mythology were the Fragarach and Gae Bolg. Then there was the Harpe in Greek mythology. This was a world with many game-like elements. It wasn't out of place to have weapons with mythical or legendary properties. Maybe the reason the 0 series hadn't managed to resolve the effects was because they actually weren't irregular to this world.

One thing that was easy to understand about this curse to prevent healing was that the only way to make it so evil was through careful manufacture. There was a way to resolve the damage, but it had been willfully removed.

"There's also a chance they found the weapon in some ruins or something," I said. Although we hadn't found them in our world, there were apparently powerful weapons in this world that could rival the holy or vassal weapons. That reminded me of the one Ren had found in the filolial sanctuary. I remembered it was called Ascalon. If there was a famous dragon-killing sword here, all bets were off. There could even be things that other heroes had created replicas of. "The timing does seem a little suspect, however." If they had this in their back pocket the entire time, it seemed strange that they would wait until now to unleash it. It was more than just using it because they were on the ropes.

"Melty, did Shadow say anything else?" I asked.

"No. Just that they suddenly deployed this kind of weapon," Melty reported.

"This sounds like there's someone behind all this feeding things to Piensa," I mused.

"That sounds likely. So what do we do? Go on the attack ourselves?" Melty asked. I looked over at Natalia, who had her role as pacifier to consider.

"I admit, this is strange. But it's too soon to attack Piensa. If they aren't using hero weapons, then I can't cooperate with deploying heroes to destroy them," Natalia said firmly. She was answering strictly as the pacifier. Her stance that the power of heroes should not be used to ignite conflict was unchanged. "If those other than the heroes want to fight, be they from Piensa or Siltran, then they are free to do so."

"And the exception would be if someone else was behind all this, and the Piensa Bow Hero was somehow involved," I confirmed. Natalia nodded in response. So if technology had advanced to the point they could attack without using the power of the heroes, Natalia couldn't get involved. That really pissed me off. "We killed one of those actually causing the waves," I said, gritting my teeth. "What are they thinking, attacking us like this? Don't they like world peace?"

"For Piensa, we're the ones getting in the way of that— their own vision of what 'world peace' looks like," Natalia said. They believed that Piensa was the center of the world and an environment in which everyone obeyed them was true peace. That had worked out for them up until now. They appeared to have justice on their side and then used their muscle to push that through. Our appearance and subsequent involvement had messed up their plans. But I still didn't understand why they would cast their "justice" aside and launch an all-out assault using this new type of weapon.

"Sounds about right. They have been attacking other nations, saying that Siltran are the cause of all these troubles by keeping the strength to defeat the waves to ourselves," Melty added. "They are staking everything on defeating us—after that they can spin things however they like." They really were like Melromarc in the future. Maybe it was just human nature to prioritize one's own authority over something like the waves. The time period didn't matter; there were always countries like that. I was happy that I knew Piensa got wiped out in the future—the natural order restored. But considering that the roots of that same nation would become Melromarc made me sad too. Melty's own ancestors might be in Piensa right now. "I'll say what everyone here is thinking," Melty continued, looking at Natalia and me. "The ones who assume the name of god are behind this. Right?"

"That seems very likely," Natalia agreed. "But we can do little without decisive proof."

"Indeed, and it would be difficult to scout out such proof," the Water Dragon lamented. The dragon looked at me and added, "You're brimming with violence. Control yourself." I wondered if I really was so pissed off. I didn't feel like I was exuding violence. I didn't even feel like I was in a bad mood.

Back to the problem at hand. We were dealing with just the kind of scum who would try the roundabout approach next. Having these deadly new weapons appear at just the perfect moment seemed like all the proof we needed. But if we accused them of it now, they would deny everything. Even if we took Piensa off the map, the ones behind it would just do the same thing with a different country. The important thing here . . . was to keep Piensa dancing to their tune while luring out the ones pulling the strings and ending them. Easy enough to say, but we had no ideas for a plan to make it happen. This was going to be a difficult issue to resolve.

"There are still ways to deal with Piensa," Melty said. "They might have some powerful new weapons, but they still need to hit us for them to work. We can send in our powerful non-hero fighters on a raid, obtain some of the weapons, and put together a treatment plan."

"That sounds like the best approach," I agreed. "Take their weapon and use it against them. We don't know what the ones behind them will do next, but you can bet they will show their hand somewhere," I said. This was all such a pain in the ass to deal with. I was starting to feel the same levels of aggravation as I did with Bitch. "Can we go into Piensa, just for some recon? We aren't going to fight a war there, so that's fine, right?" I asked Natalia. She didn't say yes or no, just closed her eyes. It looked like she had given the green light. She just didn't want to be too open about it.

"What about the justification Piensa originally gave about occupying the sanctuary? We won't be able to make any moves while we scout things out," Mamoru said, asking his sheep therianthrope aide and Melty.

"They are standing by that," Melty said. "Domestically, they are saying that if they can occupy the sanctuary, the heroes will have to obey them, and then they can overcome the waves." The sheep added his own "baah" of affirmation. It was interesting that Piensa remained so fixated on this sanctuary place. I wondered what special reason they might have for that—a reason that made it more important for them to obtain the sanctuary than even their neighbor Siltran.

"Information obtained by Shadow suggests they've sent a small elite force toward the sanctuary," Melty reported.

"Okay. And how long will it take for Piensa to reach Siltran?" I asked.

"We still have some time as they try to get the other nations on board. I don't think they will attack right away," Melty guessed.

"The battlefield will be dangerous, but perhaps those other than the heroes should take part," I pondered.

"Fighting is one thing, Naofumi, but what about people getting injured?" Melty asked. I was the only one who could heal those wounds. I froze at the thought of anyone from the village getting injured or dying in battle. If we took the lead, it would also pass the hand of justice back to them.

"If I'm totally honest about it, I'd like to just crush them and move on. We don't need a big, protracted war," I said. Then Mamoru put up his hand.

"I'd like to talk to the Bow Hero from Piensa," Mamoru said. "Ask him if he's really going along with this immoral plan of theirs and whether or not they should really be using methods like these, even in wartime."

"If this was just a war of technology, we probably wouldn't have a leg to stand on, but timing-wise, this is just too suspicious," I said. "If all the heroes abandon Piensa, that would change the way the wind is blowing." Sending heroes into war was not allowed. They were, from one perspective, weapons of mass destruction. Conflict in this time period was about making use of these trump cards without actually playing them outright. But what if your enemy didn't have any hero cards in their deck, just some powerful new weapons? Without righteousness on their side, Piensa would descend to the level of a conquest-hungry enemy that needed to be defeated.

That strategy relied on being able to bring the Bow Hero to our side. It wasn't going to work if he was like Itsuki used to be.

But during the previous invasion, he had abstained from the fighting. There was a good chance we could get through to him.

"We need an attacking force to go into Piensa and a defending force to protect the sanctuary," I surmised.

"That sounds right," Melty confirmed.

"Leave the infiltration to me," Mamoru said. "But if you have anyone who could help out, we could definitely make use of them." Someone good at infiltration? Shadow had already been taken out.

"Mr. Naofumi," Raphtalia said to me. "I think I would be suited to infiltration." She was from a race skilled at illusion and concealment magic. From an abilities perspective, Raphtalia was best suited to the task.

"I'm not sure . . ." I said. I didn't really want to send her into enemy territory when those enemies had such deadly weapons.

"I'm not going alone. I'll have the Raph species helping me out," Raphtalia assured me.

"That's not all," Rat said. "Even if we can't heal the wounds, we can think up ways to escape those attacks. I might be able to make some single-use bio-armor, based on the body of Mikey Holn modified."

"That sounds promising," Holn agreed. "I'll have it look like a robe or something. When it's attacked it can swell up and prevent the attack from landing."

"Sounds convenient," I said. "That thing has multiple bodies?"

"It has slime characteristics, meaning it replicates by corrosive fusion," Holn explained. I wondered if I was meant to understand that. I imagined a powerful slime for a moment, absorbing prey into itself, consuming it, and increasing in mass as a result. Part of that slime could then be turned into a robe. It probably would survive an attack.

"Mikey can use illusions and concealment, too, due to his Raph species heritage," Rat continued. "He should be pretty well suited to infiltration."

"I'll go along too," Natalia said, raising her hand as though to cut off Raphtalia. Natalia was both a pacifier and a hero and could do pretty much the same things as Raphtalia, so she should be fine. "I need to check for myself whether the Bow Hero has stepped off the path. His priority has to be protecting this world from the waves, so I need to ensure he isn't involved in this foolish Piensa war."

"Dafu!" said Dafu-chan. It sounded like the past Heavenly Emperor (the future Natalia) was praising her. This was a moment for tension in the air, but Dafu-chan seemed to be ignoring that completely.

"Curse-inflicting injuries that can't be healed?" Filolia said with a chuckle. "What an exciting development! I'm going to send all who use such twisted means to the depths of hell!" She was off in her own head again. "Mamoru! A true hero can't back down from this! Heroes must lead by example!"

"Filolia . . . you're right. Let's start by making contact with the Bow Hero," Mamoru replied. This seemed like the moment to share the information the past Heavenly Emperor had given me last night and propose a full recon of the sanctuary.

"Okay. We'll let Mamoru take charge of infiltrating Piensa, and everyone else will go take this 'sanctuary' they are so keen on and turn righteousness in our favor," I said. Piensa's supposition was that the heroes would gather to the side who held the sanctuary. If Siltran took the sanctuary, then Piensa would probably say it didn't count because Siltran was an "evil" country.

"That's not really the kind of place to be used in these games," Mamoru said. "But I guess it would be worth you taking a look, Naofumi."

"Okay, Mamoru! Leave Piensa to Filolia and her band of Dark Braves! And you take Naofumi and his allies to meet the folks at the sanctuary!" Filolia said loudly. Natalia had an instant frown on her face; maybe it would be better not to include her in the "Dark Braves."

"The folks at the sanctuary?" I asked.

"That's right. The ancestors of those who acted as allies to the original heroes still live in the vicinity of the sanctuary to protect the place. Lizard men, uhnte jimna, and races like that," Mamoru explained.

"Ren." Eclair chose this moment to address the Sword Hero.

"What?" he replied.

"I'm becoming interested in the sanctuary myself. Could I join you?" she asked.

"Naofumi, what do you think?" Ren asked me.

"You didn't need to ask him. Just ask me," I said. Such a waste of time. I guessed that from Eclair's perspective Ren was the more approachable of the two of us. "Something on your mind?" I asked.

"Something personal, maybe. Like with Queen Melty or the former queen," Eclair said. I waited a moment. "The warrior who was my father's right hand . . . I was told he was the last direct descendant of the lizard men who allied with the Shield Hero. Unfortunately, he fell alongside my father, protecting the people du̇ing the first of the waves."

"He was important to you?" I asked.

"Someone I respected as a warrior and teacher, yes. He often looked after me when my father was busy and is the reason I have such compassion for demi-humans. My father helped him build his own family. I can only presume . . . they were lost too . . ." Eclair trailed off. There was a moment of silence. That was a sad story, for sure. I could see why she might want to meet others of his race. I had been filled with malice toward Ruft when he sent his minions to attack Lurolona, but after I learned he was just a decoration—basically a prisoner—I had started to want to save him.

"There's a portal located close to the sanctuary," Holn said.

"No time to waste, then. Good. Eclair, Ren, with me," I said.

"Thank you," Eclair said.

"I'll head over with you to check out the sanctuary, Nao-fumi . . ." Ren started.

"Leave defense of this nation to me!" Fohl said, raising his fist. This was the land that would eventually become Siltvelt, so I could understand Fohl wanting to protect it.

"No big risks, okay? Everyone else from the village, that goes for you too! If you see any suspicious weapons that could be this new type, don't get hit by them! Understand?" I shouted. Shouts of general agreement came back.

"You bet, Bubba!" Keel replied happily. I still wasn't sure she had conquered her trauma, but Keel and the others would form an important part of pushing back Piensa's attack. We didn't have enough justification for the heroes to fight. That was a pain, but we'd only be able to act if they played the hero card first.

Melty stood up and spoke too. "I'm interested in the sanc-tuary as well. Ruft, what about you?" she asked.

"I'm going along. I want to be ready to fight, no matter where the fighting breaks out," he said.

"Okay. Naofumi, let's get going," Melty said.

"Off we go," I agreed with her. We finished our meeting and set out on our separate ways to prepare for the conflict ahead.

Chapter Nine: Heroic Presence

Holn's transport skill easily sent us over to the vicinity of the sanctuary. I looked around to see a river running by, swaying grass, and rolling hills.

"I've seen this place before," Melty confirmed. "The sanctuary is that way," she said with a point.

"That's right," Holn replied with a nod.

"My mother took me around the sites of the four holy legends when I was a kid," Melty said. It sounded like she had been involved in researching the legends, like it or not. Eclair's father had probably been here too.

"Let's go say hello," I suggested.

"Okay," Mamoru replied. He led us off in the direction of the sanctuary. It was a lot like the filolial sanctuary in the future, a place that no one really was able to get inside. The whole place was just rubble. But in this time more structures remained and people could still go inside. It was the remnants of a country created by the first Shield Hero and Bow Hero as they took on the beginning of the waves. The world was a cycle of growth and decline, so they said, but it made me sad to see it. After we returned to our time, and restored peace to the world . . . Well, Piensa would ultimately fall anyway, even if it happened in the distant future and Mamoru's own nation of Siltran would end up being changed to Siltvelt. I wondered when Faubrey would come into being.

I was getting distracted. While Piensa was still occupied with creating the foundations for their assault, we needed to put together some way to resist them.

As I thought about these things, we arrived in what looked like a village.

"This is V'sheel, the village that manages the sanctuary," Mamoru explained as we stood at the entrance. I looked at the village and the people living there. There were some lizard men dressed in farmer-like outfits. They looked like bodybuilders. These bulked-up crocodile-looking therianthropes were tilling the ground with hoes. There were demi-humans with lizard tails . . . I guessed they were humans who could go therianthrope. There were also weasel-like people. They looked lean and quick. The women were doing chores, holding baskets and tubs, and children were running happily around the village.

"Ah, Master Mamoru." It was one of the villagers, addressing Mamoru at the entryway. The villager dashed over to me, tilted his head in puzzlement, and then moved over to Mamoru. Mamoru's allies also moved forward and started to greet the villagers. "What brings you here like this?" the villager asked.

"Some worrying news. It sounds like Piensa is going to make a move on the sanctuary again, so we came to check things out," Mamoru said.

"I see. They're shameless about spreading their muck on our legends, aren't they?! You should talk with the village elder," the villager said.

"Can you summon him?" Mamoru asked.

"Of course!"

The villager and Mamoru's other allies went off into the village. A short while later an elderly lizard man appeared. He was walking using a cane. It looked like his eyes weren't the best anymore. I didn't know why, but he was looking at me.

"Well, bless me. If it isn't Master Shield Hero Mamoru. Our village of V'sheel will never forget what you've done for us," the old lizard said.

"Elder, sorry. That's not Master Mamoru," said someone who looked like an aide to the elder.

"What? Really? I was directing my comments toward where I felt the presence of the Shield Hero," the crusty lizard said. "Presence," was it? I had picked up the ability to sense such things—including murderous intent—but it seemed this old codger had a pretty vague remembrance of Mamoru.

"Over here, elder. It is nice to see you again," Mamoru said. The elder lizard man looked over at Mamoru in surprise.

"Oh my? So who is this other individual so wreathed in the presence of the Shield Hero?" the elder asked. I wasn't aware I gave off any such presence. This guy had the strangest senses.

"There are reasons for that. My name is Naofumi Iwatani.

I'm also the Shield Hero. But the one you know is over there," I explained.

"I see. It sounds like we do have some things to discuss," the elder agreed. We were shown into the village and led to a large house. That said, it wasn't large enough for everyone, so just the heroes went inside.

"So this is what his homeland was like . . ." Eclair murmured to herself as she looked around the village.

"Is this definitely the place?" Ren asked.

"Yeah, these lizard men are the same race as him, no doubt about it. They're bigger than regular lizard men. That's what gives it away. I've seen them around Mamoru in Siltran, so it's been on my mind for a while," Eclair admitted.

"I see," Ren said. Eclair looked so happy, but Ren looked sad. Eclair didn't notice at all, her eyes sparkling like they had when she met the Hengen Muso Style old lady for the first time.

"My father said it was very difficult to get his right hand away from here. He had planned to live and die here as the last of his line," Eclair explained. Being able to visit a time when the ancestors of someone she so looked up to were alive was probably quite exciting. It looked like Ren and the others could stay outside and chat. We needed to head inside to discuss more important matters.

"How to go about explaining this?" Mamoru asked.

"Take things one step at a time, from the start," Holn suggested.

"Okay. Let's not say these things too loudly," Mamoru replied. He and Holn proceeded to explain everything that had happened since we met, without hiding anything about Filolia's rebirth or other potential crimes. Everyone in this village seemed to trust Mamoru implicitly.

"I see. From the future, you say," the elder lizard man said, looking over at me. "I am Seidohl. I'm the elder of the tribe that received these lands from the original Shield Hero and Bow Hero, the tribe that has protected them ever since. It's very nice to meet you."

"I'm Naofumi Iwatani—like I said before. This is a pacifier from the future, Raphtalia," I said. Melty, Ruft, Rat, and S'yne then introduced themselves as well.

"I'm so happy you told us your name right away," Raphtalia said, as sensitive about names as always. "If you don't let Mr. Naofumi know what to call you, he'll end up giving you a funny nickname."

"I see. And what were you calling me, might I ask? It would make me happy to know," the elder said.

"Elder lizard man," I replied promptly.

"A little obvious," Mamoru jibed.

"Shut it. Can we get to the point?" I said.

"So you already have a technique that can defeat those who are causing the waves. That makes me very happy," the elder said.

"That's a good thing, for sure. But now that things have turned against Piensa, they're coming to take this place. A small elite force is expected to mount an attack, so we came to check everything out," I explained.

"The sanctuary is an important place for us and the ruins of a once great city. It's easy to imagine what this hostile nation desires from it, but I'm not sure it will turn the tide for them," Seidohl said, his hand on his chin as he pondered the situation. "Very well. Accompanied by one with such a powerful Shield Hero presence, I can permit your entry into the sanctuary."

"Thank you so much," Mamoru said. In the future, Fitoria would be managing these ruins. The Lost Woods grown up around them. It had all sorts of ways to stop people from getting inside; I wondered if that was the same in this time period.

"Allow me to show you the way," the elder said.

"Thank you," I said. We finished our brief discussion and headed toward the outskirts of the sanctuary proper.

As we headed toward the sanctuary, I took the opportunity to look myself over carefully.

"What's the matter, Mr. Naofumi?" Raphtalia asked.

"Is my 'presence' really so obvious?" I asked. Atla had always seemed to be able to sense something, and now it extended to Cian, these lizard men, and even the weasel demi-humans. I had almost been completely mistaken for Mamoru. In fact, they had treated him like he was a cut-rate version of me!

"Well . . . yes, it kind of is," Raphtalia admitted. "There's a strange feeling about you. In the beginning, I was frightened of it, but with the passage of time, I've come to find it almost . . . appealing."

"I see," I replied. It sounded like Raphtalia could feel something as well.

"Fohl has talked about it," Raphtalia continued. "How he felt something strange about you when he first met you. I think Atla was also pretty aware of it too." It sounded like the blessing of the shield made a good impression on demi-humans and therianthropes.

"I have to admit, faced with all this, I do feel like you've got one over on me, Naofumi," Mamoru said. I wondered—not for the first time—why we two Shield Heroes were so different. Mamoru could attack things! He was the better option in many ways!

"How do you feel to have me, with my jokes and making light of the role of a hero, come off more like a hero than you?" I asked sardonically.

"More jokes," Mamoru said, shaking his head. "I don't always like the things you say, but this is surely because you've got more experience than me—and you have met all sorts of other heroes."

"We do have two more holy weapons than you," I said.

I'd struggled with resolving all the issues relating to those, including involving Ren. Counting all of those experiences . . . maybe that would make my presence more pronounced than Mamoru's. It might also have something to do with me holding the mirror vassal weapon. I was one and a half times a normal hero, which did make me feel a little superior.

Now I was starting to sound like Takt. The less of that the better. Being "superior" also seemed to get me into a lot more trouble.

"You think that's what all this is about?" Mamoru questioned me. "I see you as keen on tackling every problem and working hard for the sake of those who believe in you."

"You're starting to sound like Ren," I chided him. "You've got a pretty big following yourself. That's what I consider a hero."

"Did you call?" Ren asked. He had been talking to Eclair—no surprise there.

"No, nothing to worry about. I was just saying that flattery will get you nowhere with me," I said.

"It wasn't intended as flattery," Mamoru protested.

"Anyone who mocks you must pay the price, regardless of the cost. Nothing makes you feel better than landing that finishing blow, trust me!" I said.

"Mr. Naofumi, please control your face!" Raphtalia cut in from the side. That was easier said than done. We had faced more than our fair share of annoying punks in the future. At least they seemed to be keeping a low profile here in the past.

"Things might be better here than in the future," I admitted. They didn't have to deal with records from the past being completely wiped out for one thing. The people still seemed pretty smart and capable.

"I'm not sure I like where this is going. You make it sound like our hard work is meaningless," Mamoru said, furrowing his brow.

"It's not meaningless. You'll lay the foundations for things that still exist in our time. But also, like Holn said, nothing lasts forever," I replied. It was best not to let him sink into total despair. We needed him to stay on task after we were gone.

"Wise words," Holn said. "Everything will fade with the passage of time."

"Sure, but I still can't agree with enjoying destroying my enemies," Mamoru said.

"That's the better way to be," Raphtalia said sympathetically. "We have so much trouble with Mr. Naofumi in that area." I didn't care if they understood me or not.

"Even a little kid knows not to do to other people something they wouldn't like to be done to themselves. I like to take people who haven't learned this lesson and put them through the wringer and then laugh when they complain about it. If they aren't prepared to potentially suffer something, then they

shouldn't do it in the first place," I said. It was their fault for doing things they weren't prepared to suffer for themselves. Most
of them were unable to accept it, of course, and howled like
whipped dogs.

"Ren. You loved it when Bitch died that time, right?" I
asked, looking for some support.

"Yeah." Ren nodded. "I guess I understand that much."
Talking about Bitch made Ren's eyes cloud over. He hadn't
completely overcome all that yet.

"I wish she'd done us all a favor and died for good," I
added. She needed to pay for everything she'd done. Seeing as
we knew she would come back . . . even though we didn't know
where the respawn point would be, I'd love to be able to camp
it. Just kill her the moment she came back—as slowly as possible, of course. Her other victims, like Lyno, would be satisfied
with that too.

"Enough talk like that, Mr. Naofumi," Raphtalia said.

"You think?" I asked. I found it lots of fun to daydream
about.

"I do. Your heroic presence will become more and more
clouded if you continue down this path," Raphtalia warned.

"I don't feel that happening," I snarked back. I had every
intention of fulfilling my duties as a hero, but I wasn't buying
into this "presence" thing. I wondered if life force could be
used to contain it. Life force might even be what was causing it!
I concentrated and tried to contain it.

"Mr. Naofumi, what're you doing now?" Raphtalia asked.

"Trying to contain my life force," I explained.

"I don't think that's going to change anything. It's not related to that," Raphtalia said. That left me wondering what I could possibly do.

"What do you think a 'hero' even is?" Ren asked, his eyes distant.

"Don't ask me," Mamoru said, in sync with Ren for a moment, his eyes looking the same and staring off at the same spot.

"What's this?" I said hotly. "You think I'm dumb, do you? Motoyasu is the dumb one!"

"I'm not denying your characterization of Motoyasu, but just feeling how unfair the world can be . . . you are reliable, Naofumi, no doubt about that . . . but that's something strange about you that I still can't quite accept," Ren said.

"You're really starting to piss me off!" I raged. "We're going to come back to this!"

"Mr. Naofumi, if you don't stop playing the bad guy, people are going to start looking at you like, well . . . you're actually a bad guy," Raphtalia cautioned me with a look similar to the one the others were giving me. I wasn't "playing" at anything! I cursed. I hadn't done anything to make them look at me like this.

"Your attempts to play the bad guy have been self-destructing a lot recently," Melty chipped in, turning back from the head of our column to glance at me. That was the last straw. I needed them to shut up!

"I think our Shield Hero does a great job of lightening the mood," Ruft said, offering a counterpoint to Melty. "It makes him more approachable."

"That might be true, but sometimes there's a serious mood for a serious reason. He's even been breaking out into slap stick recently, so I hear," Melty commented. I had no recollection of that! It was starting to feel like everyone was ganging up on me. I decided to just keep my mouth shut. I continued to follow the others with my lips firmly sealed. We did encounter some monsters along the way, but nothing the current party couldn't handle. I almost thought we would run into the predicted Piensa elite unit, but we didn't see anything of the sort. Maybe we had beaten them here.

We reached the sanctuary without any real trouble.

It was definitely in ruins. There were rows of worn-down stone houses and a crumbling old castle beyond them. The Demon Dragon's castle had nothing on this place. In our time this had all been swallowed by a sprawling forest, but in this time the plants hadn't gained much of a foothold yet.

I wondered where the spot we camped out was. The terrain was so different we'd probably never find it.

"What is here, anyway?" I asked. Piensa seemed to want this place, but I had no idea why. I couldn't see much point to these ruins. It seemed like nothing more than a site of indigenous faith treasured by the people who lived here for pretty standard reasons. Melty and Mamoru made it sound like some kind of unknown power was still slumbering here, but I wasn't seeing that yet.

"Piensa claims that weapons, magic, and power left by the heroes from the past still sleep here, but we've only ever found one thing," Mamoru said. "We were also told not to really talk about it."

"There might be something else, somewhere else here, that we haven't found, but it's just the one thing at the moment," Holn said.

"The carriage vassal weapon," I stated. It was an assumption based on what the past Heavenly Emperor had told me. Mamoru nodded, not hiding anything.

"If you know that much, no need to beat around the bush. Come on," Mamoru said. He led us through the ruins, between the abandoned houses and through the bare remains of the castle—little more than walls marked out on the ground. We eventually arrived at what looked like nothing more than a pile of rubble. In one corner, though, the floor had a familiar-looking relief. It was like the one we had seen in the Ancient Labyrinth Library in Kizuna's world. Mamoru pointed his shield at the relief, and the crystal in the center extended a beam of light. It seemed to be resonating with the gemstone in the shield. Then the floor rumbled open and stairs leading downward appeared.

"That's quite the setup," Melty breathed, impressed. It reminded me of the underwater temple at the Cal Mira islands.

We continued down the stairs that had appeared. They went pretty deep down into the earth. Raphtalia made some magical light that allowed us all to see.

"Why did this country end up like this?" Melty asked. "In our time it's been completely forgotten, so perhaps you can shed some light on it for us." She was very curious about the lost history of this world.

"They say it was wiped out in a single night by Suzaku. The creature appeared without any warning and attacked," Mamoru said. I recalled that the Spirit Tortoise and other beasts in our time had appeared once and been sealed away. That meant they had caused damage at some point in the past. This country was one of those that had suffered. "The stories say the rulers here had become pretty corrupt. It's even used as a cautionary folktale—purifying fire, that kind of stuff."

"No matter the gold of the golden age, all things eventually fall . . ." Melty said. Siltvelt had done pretty well, considering what we knew from the future. The name of the nation had changed, but their descendants were still doing well back in our time. Mamoru had made a lasting difference.

"I think . . . we're almost there," Holn said. Then the end of the stairs came into view. Beyond that was what we were here for. It was a weapon buried in the same kind of stone plinth that we'd seen around the rest of the seven star weapons. The vassal weapon itself was shaped like a simple-looking chariot.

"This is the legendary carriage vassal weapon," Mamoru said. His party, the lizard men and weasel demi-humans, all bowed their heads.

"I thought as much," Melty murmured, taking in the carriage.

"You know who the holder of this vassal weapon is in the future, don't you, Naofumi?" Mamoru asked.

"Yes. She's stubborn about pretty much everything, so she didn't tell us herself. So I wasn't completely sure," I replied.

"I see," Mamoru said.

"It's someone who's also here in this time," I continued. Mamoru and Holn both looked at me, clearly having finally worked it out themselves from that comment.

"It's little old Fitoria, isn't it?" Holn said. I nodded. "If you know that much, future Shield Hero, there's something else we ought to tell you."

"What?" I asked with some trepidation.

"There's another reason why the filolials love to pull carriages," Holn said. She had previously explained that they were monsters who had been created to help promote the flow of goods around Siltran. "Mamoru, can I go ahead?"

"Yes, why not? Naofumi and his friends can handle it. There's no reason to keep it a secret," Mamoru said. Holn turned back to me and continued.

"I've also told you that the carriage vassal weapon is a stubborn one, haven't I?" Holn said.

"I do recall that," I replied.

"Do you know which of the holy weapons—the shield or the bow—the carriage is affiliated with?" Holn asked. I hadn't given it much thought. The reason for our insufficient power-up methods since arriving in this time was the differences between holy weapons and vassal weapons. The power-up methods that Ren's sword could perform came from the sword, spear, projectile, staff, and gauntlets. Meanwhile, the power-up methods that Mamoru and my own shield could perform came from the shield, bow, claws, hammer, and whip. The remaining two were the axe and the carriage. The carriage was in front of us now. That meant the one affiliated with the sword or spear was the axe, which probably wasn't even on this world at the moment.

"The shield holy weapon has the claws and hammer as its vassals. This is simply a little old fact, one that the pacifier should know too," Holn said. I recalled that the demi-human nation of Siltvelt had been responsible for the claws, and the other demi-human nation of Shieldfreeden had held the hammer. They might have moved around depending on the time period, but this overall trend had to remain the same.

"Which means, by process of elimination, the bow's vassal weapons are the whip and carriage," I stated.

"That's right. The holy and vassal weapons have formed up their own separate factions and cliques," Holn said. The Shield Hero is with the claw and hammer heroes. Mamoru stood in the front, while Filolia raised the claws and Natalia her hammer. "I think the shield holy weapon selected these two as its vassals due to the synergy between them," Holn explained. That made sense to me. Mamoru might have been Filolia's superior, but he had to bow his head to Natalia. I wondered if the hammer was the vassal weapon that had poor compatibility with me. A shield was effective against cutting attacks from swords or claws but weak against opponents who used impact weapons— like a hammer. The damage might not be limited to the hand holding the shield either; I could see it being imparted inside the armor too.

"And what about the two types the bow holy weapon selected as vassals?" Holn asked. She sounded like a school-teacher. The answer was the carriage—or, in this case, more like a battle chariot—and the whip. A whip was used for striking. I mainly had a negative image of it being used to hit animals like when a lion tamer used a whip to control the king of the beasts. The best thing about the whip was personal enhancement, which allowed the owner to not only enhance themselves but also those around them.

As for the carriage . . . it looked like a Roman chariot. It was a vehicle that allowed for fast transportation around the battlefield. I considered what it might mean to add the Bow Hero to that equation—the Whip Hero controlling the animal pulling the carriage while the Bow Hero fired arrows from the back. That would provide excellent mobility and overcome the issue of the Bow Hero having powerful attacks but preferring to stay out of close combat.

"That's a pretty good combination," I said.

"Indeed, it is," Holn agreed. The carriage was all about defense and movement. If needed, it could even be used to protect those riding it. "Which brings me to my point. This stubborn carriage vassal weapon placed an order with the whip vassal weapon."

"An order for what?" I asked.

"A monster that was born to pull a carriage. And I presume you know what I created as my response to that order?" Holn said. The answer was the filolials—monsters created from Mamoru's girlfriend. The filolials had stood out, even in the time period I was originally summoned to. There were no other monsters that took such pleasure from the simple act of pulling a carriage. There were other monsters that could do it, like dragons or caterpillands, but I hadn't encountered any other monsters with that desire so embedded in their basic makeup.

The role of the whip vassal weapon was to control monsters

and the carriage was pulled by something. That had led to the desire for a monster that could handle a carriage and love it.

"In the past, the carriage vassal weapon always selected monsters as its hero: a dragon, a griffon, or a pegasus . . . but do you think any of these could handle a carriage?" Holn asked.

"No, of course not," I replied. "They would be better off dropping the carriage altogether and fighting on their own. But couldn't you say the same thing about filolials?" I'd never seen Filo use a wagon or carriage to attack, that was for sure. She loved her own special wagon and wouldn't dream of taking it into battle. Then I recalled that she had run down Motoyasu that one time.

"Let me change the question. Who do you think could make the best use of the carriage, its skills, its magic? Who could effectively use it to defend the hero?" Holn asked.

"No idea about that. I've never even seen a carriage skill . . . Oh no, wait, I have," I corrected myself. Now that I thought about it, Fitoria had used something like that on the Spirit Tortoise during its rampage. Her carriage had increased in size to match Fitoria, turned all spiky, and slammed into the Spirit Tortoise. That had to be a skill. She had even shouted "Crash Charge."

"I remember seeing her use at least one weapon. A battle wagon covered in spikes for ramming into the enemy," Melty said, describing the same thing I'd seen. It was a ramming weapon with spikes arranged out in front and was pulled by multiple filolials into battle. The power of them charging together could cause a lot of damage. It had been used to break down doors during sieges.

"That's the role it plays," Holn said. "Even without the blessing of a hero, filolials have incredible strength when it comes to pulling things around. They might not handle precision so well, but they can be powerful even without having to be a filolial queen." I'd seen Filo pulling a wagon loaded down with heavy cargo like it was as light as a feather. I'd been surprised that a single filolial could handle such a load, but she clearly had a bonus there based on her race. "To love all forms of carriage and sometimes use them as weapons is the kind of monster that the carriage vassal weapon desired from the whip vassal weapon."

"This one sounds like a real narcissist," I said, looking at the carriage again.

"I'm not denying that," Holn replied. I kinda wished she had, but if it had asked for the creation of a monster that would love it, I guess she couldn't. "Now, I want you all to think for a moment about what would have happened if the future Shield Hero and friends didn't show up here," Holn continued.

"Can we skip the thought experiment?" I asked.

"You have so little finesse, future Shield Hero. But okay. If Mamoru's attempts to revive Filolia had been less than successful, what do you think he would have done next?" Holn asked. It still sounded like her quiz was continuing.

"Why don't you ask Mamoru?" I said, a little testily. Holn took that graciously and looked over at Mamoru. His face clouded over and his eyes went distant.

"If I'd never met Naofumi, and had faced too much difficulty reviving Filolia, I think I might have wanted some consolation . . . a child with her," Mamoru admitted. "Through further research of her blended soul."

"I remember what the future Shield Hero and Melty said when they first saw Fitoria," Holn said.

"Hold on!" I exclaimed, seeing where this was going.

"I think the difference between the future Fitoria and the Fitoria in this time is the volume of soul inside her. The future one includes material from both Mamoru's and Filolia's souls and is sent out into the world as their daughter," Holn explained.

"So what's Fitoria at the moment?" I asked.

"The most stable of receptacles . . . a soulless puppet. An artificial life-form that responds to only the most basic of questions," Holn replied.

"The Fitoria at the moment is a familiar, right?" I confirmed.

"She doesn't yet contain what you would consider self-awareness or a soul. But she's in a state where she could in the future," Holn explained.

"What about Raph-chan?" I wondered immediately. She seemed to be aware of herself and she answered any questions put to her.

"Your familiar comes from a different world from this one, doesn't she?" Holn said.

"I can't believe it . . . That's the truth about Fitoria . . ." Melty breathed. Everyone present from my side was stunned by this new piece of information.

"I'm presuming his desire was to have her live as a hero and live the life that her departed mother couldn't," Holn guessed. She had been created to use the carriage vassal weapon and in Mamoru's grief she'd taken on the role of his daughter. If that was Fitoria . . . then what a tragic fate she had. The future Fitoria had possessed the desire to fight for the world. I wondered if that had been implanted inside her too. Her feelings on the subject had been very intense. She had been willing to oppose the four holy heroes themselves for the sake of this world. "I think the reason filolials are in principle so happy and easygoing is because of the desire Mamoru had for his daughter to be that way."

"But now . . ." Mamoru started, but then his eyes unfocused.

"What's up?" I asked.

"Fitoria is asking to be summoned here," he replied.

"Does she know what's going on around you? Like Raph-chan does for me?" I asked.

"Maybe. C'mon Fimonoa!" he said, shouting a skill like C'mon Raph. With that skill, he summoned the prototype Fitoria who suddenly appeared in front of us. She didn't say anything. She just stared at Mamoru.

"Now that you've got Filolia back, Mamoru, you might not need to take things this far," Holn said. Fitoria looked at her and then at Mamoru and then spoke.

"I'm becoming this because I want to. Because we were created by someone special," she murmured. Then she spoke more loudly. "We haven't been born yet." With that, Fitoria touched the carriage vassal weapon . . . and nothing happened. It just sat there, unchanged, with no sign of accepting her as its holder.

"A large-scale change is required for the carriage vassal weapon to accept me. My proposal . . . Master, make me into your daughter . . ." Fitoria requested. Everyone fell silent at that. She had said "we haven't been born yet." When I messed around with Raph-chan's stats, I had changed her a lot. That had resulted in Raph-chan changing the monsters in the village into the Raph species, which was still producing consequences today.

"I think . . . I might have come too far with this to go back," Mamoru said, giving a deep sigh as he took in Fitoria's request. "But I'd like to decide by discussing it with Filolia first. Would that be okay?"

"Answer accepted," Fitoria replied, moving over close to Mamoru and then stopping.

"I've shown you the sanctuary," Mamoru said, moving on. "In regard to what we need to do next . . ."

"Capture the unit from Piensa coming to infiltrate this place and obtain the carriage vassal weapon to make them give up completely. It also sounds like we might be able to use the carriage vassal weapon to cross over to the world of the sword and spear and get something there to help us get back to the future," I stated.

"First I'm hearing about this!" Melty said.

"Do you know that shrine that's a nest of filolials in the future? It's likely that device Motoyasu activated there has something to do with all this," I replied.

"Yes, that does sound like a possibility," Ren agreed. "If it isn't here in this world, it must be over in the other one." It was a possibility worth investigating, that was for sure. The possibility of crossing to another world seemed unlikely, but we might be able to connect back to the future from the sword and spear world.

"First things first. We need to drag the ones behind Piensa into the open and take them out," I said.

"That's right," Raphtalia agreed. "I think Mamoru is going to need some time as well. Let's head back." Everyone nodded at Raphtalia's proposal and we left the carriage vassal weapon in its underground lair before returning to our village.

Chapter Ten: Exclusive Equipment

We decided how best to proceed and worked out a plan for patrols of the sanctuary. That night I was back in the sanctuary with Raphtalia and the others. We were taking a look around at the place but also expecting an infiltration attempt to come at any time. Mamoru had told us of a sightseeing spot—hot springs—that were located nearby. After taking a patrol around, we were going to go and take a bath. After agreeing to make contact by shouting or using magic if anything happened, we all split up to look around. That left me alone with Raphtalia.

"I'm surprised to be here again, even though we are in a different time period," Raphtalia said.

"Me too," I replied. I recalled when we had been caught up in the machinations of the Church of the Three Heroes and Fitoria led us here. In the future there was nothing left of the sanctuary but the barest of ruins. In this time, there was a lot more of it remaining. It was mossy and crumbling but still intact. We were standing in a slightly open area, talking, as I considered again that there was no escaping the weathering of time.

"Our village might end up like this one day," I said.

"I think Q'ten Lo is the exception, not the rule, when it comes to remaining since ancient times," Raphtalia stated.

"That could be thanks to the protection of the Water Dragon, or the chain of Heavenly Emperors, or maybe something else," I said. Melty had told me that Siltvelt didn't emerge from Siltran overnight. The nation created by the first heroes had eventually crumbled. There was no guarantee that our own village would make it into the future. It made me sad to think of that. Maybe the ones who assume the name of god had obtained an eternity that escaped from such degradation, but it felt like their hearts had become corrupted in exchange.

"The God Hunters." We'd heard a lot about them but had no idea who they really were. They at least seemed to be leaving things around that helped us out.

Then there was 0 territory. I wondered what that was. Something was warning me not to use it too much—like it was something dangerous. Seemed like I'd go to a place I wouldn't be able to come back from. It had allowed me to save Shadow and his Raph specimen, so that was good . . . but I still needed to be careful with it. It had already reduced my attack by 1, something I couldn't especially afford. If continuing to use it continued to lower my attack, I could fall to 0.

"It's important to wish it lasts forever, I guess. But probably a mistake to actually desire eternity," I said. I thought about Fitoria in the future. She wasn't immortal, but she didn't age. The Demon Dragon had told Ethnobalt that he would eventually understand the foolishness of humans. Monsters and humans had a very different mental makeup, but maybe that's the kind of thing monsters turned into if they lived too long. They were either like Fitoria, unable to hate humans but still kept their distance from them, or the Demon Dragon, who hated humanity and plotted to wipe them out. These two different reactions might be rooted in the same emotion: true eternal life and having the ones who assume the name of god grant that wish.

It reminded me of the famous magical lamp from *Arabian Nights*. There were other stories with similar devices—things that granted wishes. Thinking about them now, I remembered a few characters who appeared in such stories and chose eternal life. But even if they did, they often ended up regretting that choice; but if such a thing were actually possible . . . maybe the one who chose it would end up seeking entertainment by toying with other worlds. It might be tough to live forever. I'd even heard that death could be a release for such people. Water would stagnate if it didn't flow . . . just like souls.

They weren't immortal, but the revived—those under the thumb of the ones who assume the name of god—might be in a similar situation. I wondered if the revived themselves had ever considered the nature of their revival. Some of them probably thought of it as a second life but kept the memories of their first one. If they were going to use those memories and try to live better lives, so be it. But all the revived we had met were not making any such attempts at that. They seized authority and power, living however they pleased, causing hassle for other people and the entire world, and killing anyone who got in their way. They also gathered attractive members of the opposite sex and treated them like personal belongings. Maybe being reborn with your memories intact led to such corruption of the soul.

When I was in Japan, I'd seen plenty of content with being "reborn" as a way to reach other worlds. At the time, I'd thought it might be quite cool . . . but having actually been summoned to another world, I'd gotten caught up in so much crap and been through hell. The idea that a different world would be a friendly place for me was long gone by now. This whole conflict had been kicked off by those who possessed eternal life, which made me think that Holn and her disdain of the concept was the right idea.

I also couldn't accept that the ones who had caused all this were going to live forever. So many innocent lives had been lost due to the eternal ones who assume the name of god. I could only hope this fight would come to an end back in our time. We had the techniques to hunt these "gods" now, but we still didn't have a way to resolve the situation. The only thing I could really think of as a vague idea was to get to the world of the ones doing this and stop them from ever being able to do it again. Take the fight to them and wipe them out.

I recalled how Glass came here with similar intentions, seeking to kill the holy weapon heroes that supported this world in order to defend her own. Just killing one of them had the potential to end the world. That might be a better approach than having to wipe out everyone. S'yne's sister had warned us that the holy and vassal weapons might not always be our allies; this might be one of the reasons. Even that eternal world probably had its own holy weapons, so maybe we could use them to wipe it out. The holy weapons existed to protect the world while also having the role of potentially ending it. Of course, this only applied if the world of the ones who assume the name of god also had holy weapons. I'd not heard anything about them in the Japan I came from, at least. Of course, they might be hidden, or not talked about, just tucked away somewhere . . .

"Mr. Naofumi?" Raphtalia asked.

"Huh? Yeah, I'm here," I said, coming back to myself. I was here talking to Raphtalia, but I'd wandered off into conjecture without any answers. I need to get my head back in the game. "Even if it isn't for as long as Q'ten Lo, I want our village to last for as long as possible."

"Yes, Mr. Naofumi," Raphtalia agreed. For some reason, that made me think about what she called me.

"Hey, Raphtalia," I said.

"What is it?" she asked.

"Aren't we a little past the whole 'Mr.' thing by now?" I asked her. It had never really felt especially "fantasy" to me.

The fact that other women were constantly coming onto me was probably because Raphtalia and I never seemed to be making any progress. Things actually weren't proceeding at all, of course. I also didn't need the heat we'd face if we went recklessly into a sexual relationship. If it was finally proven that I was unable to cause pain, I really had no idea what might happen.

But enough about that.

"I'm not sure," Raphtalia replied.

"To start with, we used it to make it clear I was in a position above you, correct? But our relationship has moved beyond that now," I said. This really had been a long time coming. I'd been hoping that Raphtalia would one day stop using "Mr." on her own accord, but it felt like we'd reached the point I needed to point it out before anything changed. She always gave smart answers when I was playing dumb, like we were in some kind of comedy duo, and if I made a mistake, she was there to put me right. That was why she had my complete trust. And yet she continued to use "Mr." in front of my name. That was my thinking behind asking her to stop . . . but Raphtalia's face was starting to blush. Maybe it was embarrassing. It involved calling me by something new, after all.

She was clearly trying, her lips moving slightly . . . "Mr. Naofumi," she eventually said, unable to overcome the mental block. She tilted her head. "Mr.—" she tried again and made the same mistake. It almost sounded like she thought "Mr." was a fixed part of my name. "This is harder than I thought," Raphtalia admitted. She concentrated harder, her face turning redder. I was amazed that embarrassment stopped her from doing this, after all this time. "I've been calling you Mr. Naofumi for so long I'm not sure I can stop." Raphtalia was still embarrassed about it, and it was even starting to rub off on me. I was also aware my thinking was going in a strange direction.

"If we got married . . . would that make you 'Raphtalia Iwatani'?" I asked.

"I hadn't really thought about it," Raphtalia stammered.

"Maybe 'Raphtalia Heavenly Emperor Iwatani'?" I said.

"Please, don't make fun of me!" Raphtalia replied. This felt more like our spot.

"I hope you can drop the 'Mr.' one day," I told her.

"Yes. I'll do my best . . . Mr. Naofumi, if that's what you want," Raphtalia said.

"It's not about what I want. I want you to want to," I said. My jokes helped her forget her embarrassment, and she started smiling. "Do you have Japanese surnames here in this world?" I asked her.

"I've heard some of them before. They can be used by those with the bloodline of the heroes," Raphtalia replied. It sounded like there might be a "Suzuki" or a "Sato" running around out there.

"If I needed a name more suited to this world, maybe I

could use the 'Rock Valley' that I went by in Zeltoble?" I said. That would keep Raphtalia's name from standing out even if we got married. For some reason I recalled that S'yne's surname was "Lokk," which sounded a bit like "rock." Maybe that was just a coincidence . . . "Ah, that reminds me." I took Raphtalia's hand and then placed an accessory onto her arm.

Shield Hero's Charm (Raphtalia Exclusive)
Defense up (high), emergency healing, protect effect up, proof of trust, Heavenly Emperor power boost, enhanced illusion magic
Spirit seal, all status up (medium)
Quality: excellent

It was shaped like a rosary of beads that wrapped around her arm. I had used the balloon remnants to make a string and symbolize everything we'd been through together. I'd made the beads from hardened medicine, miraka ore from the Cal Mira islands, materials from the Spirit Tortoise and Phoenix, sakura stone of destiny, and even the leaves Holn had provided. For all of that, it looked like a simple rosary.

I'd also carved a flag into one of the beads. Raphtalia had loved those little flags that always came with the kid's meal. Flags had a special meaning for Raphtalia, including the flag she saw when we started reviving Lurolona.

That was how I completed this accessory for Raphtalia; the name had come out a little more embarrassing than I might have liked.

"Oh my," Raphtalia said.

"You wanted something practical," I said. When I'd asked her what kind of accessory she wanted, she had asked for something practical. That was certainly what this was—even if it was a little embarrassing.

"That's true, but I'm happy to get a present from you," Raphtalia replied.

"I'm not sure a rosary is the best gift," I said.

"Do you think so?" Raphtalia asked.

"Yeah," I replied. A rosary probably wasn't the best accessory to give a girl you liked. If anyone else got a rosary at a time like this—a moment they might be expecting something more romantic, like a ring—they'd probably get angry. "Do you like it?" I asked.

"Yes. I'll treasure it forever," she replied. She carefully wrapped the rosary around her arm and then gave a nod. She looked so happy looking at the rosary it made me happy too. There were even tears in her eyes. All the effort it took was worth it.

"Just don't treasure it so much that you don't even take it into battle," I told her. Too many gamers hoarded the good stuff and ended up never using it. They'd have a chest packed

with full heal items long after defeating the final boss. "Even if it breaks it, I don't care as long as it saves you. I'll repair it as many times as it takes. Keep it close to you at all times."

"I understand. I'll treasure it all the same," she told me.

"Next time I'll make something a little more fashionable," I said. She wore her miko robes most of the time, so something like a Japanese hair comb would make sense. "A hairpin styled like a leaf might suit you," I murmured.

"I'm sorry, but . . . after Raph-chan had that leaf on her head, I'd rather avoid the same look," Raphtalia admitted.

"Oh, that was so cute," I said, unable to help myself. "Ruft was copying her too."

"I'm not going to wear anything based on what you just said," Raphtalia replied, standing her ground.

"I know, I know," I assured her.

"You're ruining the mood," she replied. I wondered why these moments never seemed to last between us—it was me, of course.

In that moment the clouds parted and moonlight shone down onto us. Illuminated with a pale glow, Raphtalia looked even more beautiful than usual. She had started out as a little kid, but now she was a beautiful woman. Her actual age was close to that of Keel and the others, so she was impressive.

"Come then, Mr. Naofumi. Let's finish our patrol and then head over to these hot springs that Mamoru told us about. I'm sure everyone else had gone on ahead," Raphtalia said.

"Okay," I agreed. When we finally arrived close to the hot springs, Raph-chan was there waiting for us, looking up at the moon.

"Raph!" said Raph-chan.

"Hey, Raph-chan," I said. "How was your patrol?"

"Raph," replied Raph-chan. It sounded like there wasn't much to report. Then Raph-chan noticed the rosary on Raphtalia and put her little paws to her mouth theatrically with another "Raph."

"You don't do that often," I commented. "Are you trying to fool around like Keel?"

"Raph," said Raph-chan, as though she had no idea what I was talking about. She patted her tummy a few times and looked back up at the moon. The setting really suited her: tanuki in moonlight. It was like a painting.

"The moon looks so beautiful it makes me want to throw a harvest festival," I said. If we got all the Raph species to play their tummy drums together, it would be like something from a Japanese fairy tale. Once the world was at peace, we could call Glass and the others over to our world and have a big moon party.

"Is that something from your world?" Raphtalia asked.

"Yeah," I replied.

"Raph!" said Raph-chan. She incanted some magic and started to glow like a firefly, illuminating the area around us.

The effect created a really nice atmosphere. We started to walk again toward the hot springs, which the others were probably already enjoying.

"Looks like these springs have a nice view," I commented. They were outdoor baths with a stepped layout. There were separate changing rooms for men and women, but that was about it.

"Hey, it's bubba and Raphtalia!" Keel shouted as she spotted us.

"We were worried something happened," Fohl said. Ren had already finished bathing and was cooling off, sitting on a rock nearby, while Eclair was bathing next to Melty. Keel and the others were racing around, playing tag or something. Mamoru had said he would probably come by with his party later. Everyone had their weapons close at hand, in case anything kicked off. The whole thing would probably have been a lot more relaxed if it wasn't for our current situation.

"Come on, Mr. Naofumi. Let's take a nice bath too," Raphtalia said.

"Yeah, okay," I replied. I liked our bath at home, but this was nice as well. There was going to be fighting here one day, but I could pray it wouldn't start while we were bathing.

Luckily, it didn't. We enjoyed some relaxing time all together and ended the day well rested.

Chapter Eleven: Dinosaur Hunting

It was a few days later.

"Thiz iz no way to treat zomeone recovering from a zerious injury," Shadow complained with a moan.

"Raph," said his ninja Raph specimen. We had been moving between the sanctuary and the village, working to protect them both. We'd also received a request from the village close to the sanctuary to deal with some dangerous monsters lurking nearby. Mamoru and his party were busy with preparations for the infiltration of Piensa, and so we hadn't seen much of them. As a side note, Eclair had quickly become friendly with the lizard men and was often seen training and sparring with them. Maybe because Mamoru was lending them some strength—applying the Whip power-up method—but the lizard men were putting up a good fight even against Eclair.

"You've recovered enough for this. Shut up and get moving," I said. I'd decided to take Shadow and his ninja Raph specimen along in order to level them up a little.

"You do look like you've made a full recovery!" Keel yipped.

"I'm a zeriously injured individual!" Shadow complained. I also had Raphtalia, Ruft, the noisy Keel, and—for the first time in a while—S'yne too. I hadn't even talked to S'yne much recently, what with all her magic training. I didn't like her just watching me from a distance all the time, so I decided to bring her along. Raph-chan and Dafu-chan had gone with Natalia to help Mamoru. I could summon them via a skill if they were needed, so that wasn't a problem. Raphtalia and the others could also stop Shadow from trying to escape if he decided this was all too much hassle. It was a good all-round party.

"I'm not sure about working Shadow quite this hard," Raphtalia cautioned me.

"The very fact he suffered such a wound is why we need to bring him," I replied. Shadow might have learned a lot of technical things from our village and Q'ten Lo, but in a matter of pure stats, he had performed a limit break but was still behind Keel and the others. This was maybe the only time we were going to have to do something about that. He certainly was tough. He had been up and walking around soon after his wounds healed. If he had been bedridden and unable to move, I wouldn't have been pushing him this far.

"My role iz only to collect information, infiltrate targetz, and protect Queen Melty," Shadow said sullenly. He had been all for joining Mamoru in the Piensa infiltration, providing information on routes through the nation and acting as a guide, but I had put a stop to that and practically dragged him along with us.

"You must have upset Bubba something fierce for him

to be taking you out like this so soon after a big injury," Keel pondered. "When I got hurt badly, I was left in the village for everything." She was right. During the fight with the Spirit Tortoise, we'd been forced to leave her behind due to her wounds.

"If you want to help with the infiltrations so much, you need to be strong enough to escape from any possible enemy attack," I said pointedly.

"I have no responze to that," Shadow admitted. "But you are a demon, Zhield Hero. I need zympathy, not combat."

"What do you mean, zympathy?! I couldn't be more zympathetic if I tried!" I shot back. He had just healed up and wanted to head straight back into a warzone! I needed to prepare him as best as I could first. What was that, if not "sympathy?!"

"If you raise my level here, Zhield Hero . . . will you end up making me your lover?" Shadow asked.

"Huh? Is that how this works?" Keel asked naively.

"Keel, shut up," I snapped before addressing the main crazy person. "You think I'm raising my allies' levels in order to make them my lovers?" I asked. The only ones thinking like that were the old Motoyasu and the resurrected. Before we even got to that point, I couldn't ever understand why I would want my lovers to be strong.

"Mozt of thoze you go out to raize levelz with are your loverz," Shadow said.

"I don't think you really understand the situation," Raphtalia said. "Keel, that isn't what's happening here, so don't worry."

"What about Fohl? And Ruft?" Keel asked persistently.

"Me? Lover of the Shield Hero?" Ruft asked. "Ah, love me, love me just like this!" Ruft struck an affected pose. He really did love his Raph therianthrope form. I thought it was cute too, but it was having the opposite effect at the moment.

"Keel, Ruft, you're only going to make things worse for Mr. Naofumi by getting involved in this. Please stay quiet," Raphtalia chided them.

"Huh?" Ruft said.

"I'm not sure what you mean, but whatever," Keel replied. I turned my attention back to Shadow.

"I'm not your lover," Shadow confirmed with me.

"It might have been better if you did die, at least once," I said. I had no idea what he thought I was. Yes, I had lost it that one time and grabbed onto Fohl, but there was no reason to keep basing their entire assessment of me on that one mistake!

"Holn haz told me that you fall for the heart, not the body, Zhield Hero. Race and gender mean nothing to you," Shadow said. So that was the reason for this! Turning the Shield Hero into some kind of idolized pansexual! The idea that love could overcome all boundaries should be reserved to the thinking of dragons and Motoyasu!

"You've been zpending a lot of time with Keel recently. Are you trying to make her yourz too?" Shadow asked. I presumed he was talking about the incident that had triggered Keel's trauma.

"So that's what's going on!" Keel said.

"Keel, have you forgotten already? That was punishment for you saying the wrong thing. Do you want to be punished again?" I asked. I'd given her a thorough stroking when we were in the trading wagon as punishment for her telling me I should get with Raphtalia and other mockery.

"Ah! Your punishment feels good, but it scares me too, so no! Raphtalia! Forgive me!" Keel yipped, both hands together, bowing her head as she asked for forgiveness.

"The details of that incident don't concern me, but please don't overstimulate Mr. Naofumi," Raphtalia said.

"I took Keel along on that trip as a punishment in the first place, but I spent most of the trip talking about accessory making with Imiya," I said. Keel and Imiya played the role of loveable mascots for the village, perhaps, but that wasn't the kind of "love" being intimated here. Imiya was cute, in the same kind of way Raphtalia was, and she seemed to be into me. But I'd think about that once the world was at peace. Otherwise, there would be some real wild beasts awaiting me back in the future—wild beasts named "Sadeena" and "Shildina."

I wondered where this rumor that I raised party members' levels to make them my lovers started from. If I could pinpoint the exact individual, they would need to be punished. It sounded like something that Keel might have kicked off. It might be time to activate her slave seal!

"Why are you glaring at me, Bubba? What have I done now?" Keel asked.

"He suspects you of spreading those rumors about leveling people up in order to make them his lovers," Raphtalia said.

"No! You've got that wrong!" Keel instantly protested. I wasn't sure about that. Rumors could spread, whether the originator intended them to or not.

"Okay. Where does Cian fit into the crazy scenario?" I asked.

"Zhe'z zomeone already intimate with a different hero, making her an exception. I don't have any hero I'm ezpecially cloze to, so I'm a likely target," Shadow explained.

"Well, you can relax. This is all in your head. I don't even know if you are male or female, to be honest," I replied. I had always presumed "he" was male. "I've never even seen your face. How could I fall for you? The only way to tell you apart from all those other shadows is the way you talk." I'd seen him turn into the queen once. I actually had no idea of "his" gender. He seemed able to pretend to be Melty too. When I was on the run during Melty's kidnapping, he had turned into a villager. He really could be a man or a woman, so I had no idea.

"Are you zeriouz?" Shadow said, shocked. "You really don't care about me, do you?! I'm juzt another namelezz, formlezz blob to you, aren't I, Zheild Hero?! Raphtalia, pleaze tell me! Why doez thiz feel zo much like defeat?"

"I think you would be better to just ignore him completely," Raphtalia advised.

"That juzt makez the zting of defeat even worze!" Shadow complained.

"Shadow . . . I don't even know if you're a bubba or not, but do you really want Bubba Shield Hero to look at you in that way?" Keel asked.

"I don't think he (or she) wants it either way," I said.

"I know Bubba can be foulmouthed, but that only shows how much he cares," Keel explained, just making stuff up like normal.

"The easiest way to tell the difference between a man or woman is to ask Motoyasu," I said. He saw all women other than Filo as pigs. His eyes were very accurate. He could probably tell if Shadow was a man or woman with just a glance. "But maybe you're happy being a genderless shadow?" This whole debate was starting to feel pretty pointless. Be nice to women and hard on men, was that it? Ridiculous. If that was my outlook, I wouldn't be so eager to send Bitch to hell.

"I underztand exactly how Melty feelz," Shadow exclaimed with a shout, shaking his fist. I wondered what that meant.

"Where does Melty come into this?" Keel asked. "Raphtalia, do you know?"

"I think it's to do with being called by title rather than name. Mr. Naofumi called her 'second princess' for quite a long time," Raphtalia explained.

"Oh, okay," Keel said.

"Whatever the reason, stop believing this crap about leveling people up to make them my lovers. You're meant to gather intelligence for us! I'm starting to doubt your skills," I said.

"I'm ztill at the ztage of determining if thiz iz crap or not! I'm running an experiment! Uzing Keel!" Shadow declared.

"Me?! Am I fated to become Bubba's lover as well?" Keel yipped.

"Keel, there's no need to worry about this," Raphtalia assured her again.

"Enough, all of you!" I shouted. "Just shut up and follow me! If you want me to remember your name, tell me what it is!"

"No! No way!" Shadow protested. He was just messing with my head now. He didn't even want to say his name. If he was a ninja, maybe he didn't have a name at all. I had no points of contact with any other shadows, so it was fine to just leave him as "Shadow," but I was getting a bit exhausted in terms of reaching that point.

"Just quit it. I've had enough of talking about this. If you want to go back into Piensa, then you need to raise your level and get stronger first. Unless you want them to find you again!" I said.

"I didn't expect to get caught like that either," Shadow said. His account of events was that he had been hiding on the battlefield when he was discovered and attacked before he had a chance to escape. I was impressed that he managed to get away from such a situation while injured. Maybe he had used a smoke bomb or something—or pretended to be dead. His survival skills had brought him back to us, anyway. That was a fact.

"Raphtalia, how do you rate Shadow's infiltration and disguise abilities?" I asked. Raphtalia sounded puzzled for a moment.

"Well . . . he's good enough that even someone with a high level of exposure magic would still take a while to find him. If he disguises himself as well, that would make it even harder to spot him," Raphtalia said.

"I can't even sniff him out," Keel said, also offering her praise of Shadow's infiltration techniques—but I hardly rated Keel's detection abilities very high.

"Look what I can do," Shadow said. It looked like he was taking off his clothes, but then he had suddenly changed into Sadeena.

"Wow! Amazing! Sadeena!" said Keel excitedly.

"What do you think, zweet Naofumi?" Shadow said. I had no reply. I knew he was good at disguising himself, but he had picked the wrong disguise with this one. "Thiz will give me the advantage over the Zhield Hero!" Shadow crowed.

"Fine. You'll make a great shield yourself for fighting these monsters. Sadeena can handle anything," I said.

"'I'm only joking!" Shadow quickly fired back. "I'm not

fully recovered!" He quickly changed back to normal. We hadn't had many chances to talk like this in the past, and now we were getting one . . . I actually preferred it that way. He was like a comedian trying to push through a bit that wasn't working. I never thought he had this kind of personality. I needed to have words with Melty to put him right.

"Enough talk. Time to level up," I stated firmly. "We might encounter Piensa infiltrators too, so keep your wits about you—especially you, Shadow, with your skill set."

"I would rather thiz goez off without any zuch excitement," Shadow said. Our goals were to level up while patrolling places a Piensa unit might try to come in from. I'd formed the party from those with skills in detecting others. I would have normally left Ruft with Ren or Fohl, but he needed some work on his level just like Shadow did. He was in a key position, after all—just like Melty and Shadow. Melty herself was off with Eclair and Ren.

Before we left the village, they had been using the names "Raph Species Squad" and "Filolial Squad" to differentiate the two groups, but I was choosing to ignore that.

After a lot of unnecessary noise, we were finally underway. This party of excitable individuals and I were going to defeat the monsters in the vicinity of the sanctuary and gain an understanding of the routes the enemy might use to attack. We could have just waited for them in the sanctuary itself, but we needed to keep the village safe too. It was also an excellent chance to obtain some materials from unknown monsters.

We proceeded along the route we had been asked to clear out.

"There sure are a lot of them," I commented. "Is there a larger monster population back here?" We continued along the beast track and reached an area with exposed rock . . . it looked like something from the land time had forgotten. There were monsters called the kaiser rex, which looked like an earlier form of the Tyrant Dragon Rex, and then emperor triceratops, king stegosaurus, and lord pteranodon, all dinosaur-type enemies with a royal connection. They were strutting around like they really did rule the place. I guessed we could clear them out too . . . and I was really getting time-travel vibes from this scenery too. Those "other worlds" were such a crazy mashup of concepts. I was willing to bet there would be dinosaur-type therianthropes as well. The lizard men already kinda looked like crocodiles.

I was also a little puzzled to find these dinosaurs so close to human habitation. I knew ecosystems changed over time, but there seemed to be far too many monsters here.

"Hey, Shadow," I said.

"What?" he replied.

"Are there monsters like this in our time too?" I asked.

"I don't know, but I've seen bonez in the Faubrey muzeum," Shadow revealed. If we took Rat along, I was sure she'd go crazy for that. This was a world full of dragons and griffons, so why not dinosaurs too?

When we first encountered the first rex, we thought it had been unlikely that we'd defeat it head-on, but I was sure we'd have no problem this time.

"Let's start the fighting," I said.

"Yes, okay," Raphtalia replied.

"I'm ready too!" Ruft added.

"It reminds me of that monster we met when you saved me, Bubba! I won't be left behind again!" Keel barked.

"I've got this," S'yne said. Each of them took out their respective weapons and prepared for combat. Ruft was using an axe. He seemed to have taken a shine to heavy weapons.

"What can we hope to offer in thiz battle?" Shadow wondered.

"Raph," said his ninja Raph specimen. Both of them sounded uncertain.

"Don't worry. Much worse things than this come out on the ocean tours with Sadeena," I told him. The oceans were a treasure trove of crazy. The experience down there was delicious, but we wouldn't be able to hack some underwater grinding without the killer whale sisters. On dry land and against these kinds of monsters, I wasn't expecting any trouble.

"Just stick close to me until you level up a bit. You've got some combat experience, so you shouldn't get too cocky even once your level increases a little," I said.

"That'z true," Shadow replied, but he didn't sound especially confident.

"Let's go!" Raphtalia drew her katana and rushed toward the dinosaurs. They had noticed us and were already moving in with predatory intentions. Ruft was right behind her, and then S'yne was close behind. A kaiser rex opened with a roar, leaping toward Raphtalia and breathing fire. Then it tried to bite her. It was a wild but carefully targeted fire-bite attack. The jaws of the kaiser rex closed fast and hard over the spot where Raphtalia was standing.

The image of Raphtalia vanished completely. Then she popped up at the side of the kaiser rex and slashed into its ribs with her katana. The attack made a satisfying noise, blood sprayed out, and the monster groaned. Raphtalia passed beneath the beast and not a single drop of blood landed on her. She cut as she went along to induce further cries of pain.

"It's got tougher skin than I expected. It feels like the flesh is clinging to my blade," Raphtalia reported.

"I'll give it the axe!" Ruft quipped, seemingly popping into existence in the middle of the air. The kaiser rex was still focused on Raphtalia and didn't even notice the axe coming for its head until it was too late. "Just to make sure!" Ruft transitioned into a kick on the spot he had just hit and then unleashed some magic. "Zweite Illusion!" Ruft said and dropped back. The kaiser rex rushed off roaring at a ninety-degree angle from us. It started biting and swinging its tail at thin air. Ruft had applied some illusion magic.

The kaiser rex was a monster but still showed signs of intelligence by sniffing around to try and locate its real target. Its jaws snapped down again but came back empty once more. The illusion magic Raphtalia used could confuse even a monster's sense of smell. Rat and Holn had been impressed by this facet of their magic. Fox-type demi-humans and monsters could use their sense of smell to defeat illusions, but Raphtalia and the others could overcome even that obstacle. The tanuki always seemed to outfox the fox in Japanese folklore, so maybe that was part of it. The past Heavenly Emperor had displayed the ability to confuse the sense of smell of Takt's fox woman. Their powers were legit, but it might be dangerous to literally assess our combat abilities based on folklore from my home world. Raph-chan seemed to have better illusion skills than even Raphtalia at the moment, making Raph-chan our most proficient user of illusions.

"Raphtalia and the others have made an opening!" Keel barked. Then she gave a mighty howl and swung her sword down from above. It was just a normal longsword, but she looked like some kind of berserker with it in her diminutive paws.

"S'yne!" Raphtalia called.

"I'm here!" Cutting in a little late to the party, S'yne split her scissors into two blades and slashed into the kaiser rex. The monster was completely defenseless, and S'yne's attacks quickly found its throat, slashing it.

"I'm ending this!" Raphtalia returned to deliver the final blow. "Instant Blade! Mist!" The kaiser rex was writhing in pain. Then Raphtalia relieved it of its head. The dinosaur collapsed into the dirt, going extinct without pretty much any opportunity to meaningfully fight back.

"It was faster and tougher than I was expecting," Raphtalia commented.

"But it seemed very weak to illusions," Ruft replied.

"That's true. We're a good match for it," Raphtalia agreed.

"What about me?" S'yne asked.

"You stopped it from moving around too much. That was a big help," Ruft told her.

"I didn't lag behind too much, right?" Keel asked, also seeking affirmation.

"You're fast on your feet, Keel, which really helped confuse it," Raphtalia told her.

"You really think so? I want to be faster though, like you, Raphtalia. Maybe I can ask Bubba Sword Hero for a better sword," Keel wondered.

"That's a good point . . . Why do you even use a sword, Keel?" I asked. She chopped off the kaiser rex's tail and then turned to me. She was small but nimble, I'd give her that.

"Huh? You gave it to me, so I'm using it," Keel replied.

"I bet you could use the same kind of attacks monsters do, like biting and stuff," I said. She had decent fangs when in therianthrope form. I almost thought just biting the monsters would do more damage. I'd seen her with something clamped in her jaws once, shaking it from side to side like a dog did.

"Bubba, do you think of me like a monster?" Keel asked.

"Have you ever looked in the mirror? I bet Raph-chan could use a sword better than you. Everyone needs to use the right weapon for the job," I said.

"You could fight in your demi-human form, Keel," Raphtalia suggested.

"I can move around more easily like this," Keel said after a moment's thought. "I'll stick with it." She always seemed to choose her dog form for battle. It made her even smaller than normal; I was impressed she could fight at all.

"Your therianthrope form is great. Very cute too," Ruft said, choosing this moment to get involved.

"It's not cute! It's cool!" Keel yipped back.

"Come on, Keel. Your cuteness is your biggest selling point," Ruft replied.

"I know, but I want to be cool!" Keel retorted. The sight of Keel and Ruft bickering as they defeated monsters was pretty surreal, like cute village mascots causing hardcore violence.

"Let's keep moving," Raphtalia said smartly. The party

turned smoothly to face the incoming emperor triceratops.

"They're making zhort work of thiz," Shadow said. "Bazed on the incoming experience I'm receiving, I would have expected theze battlez to take a little more time."

"That's just how strong we've become," I replied. "Ruft has decent specs and just blends into fighting alongside the others without any trouble. Keel is still a little slow off the blocks." Ruft was Raphtalia's cousin, which explained a lot. The bonuses from his therianthrope form were not to be sniffed at either. When compared to the rest of the party, Keel was definitely a step behind.

"Bubba! I'm going to prove myself! That's what all my training has been for!" she yipped at me. Sure, whatever, I thought to myself. "Special attack time!" Keel yelled. She gave a howl, light glowing around her, and then she charged as a shining dog back into battle. "Zweite Wild Fang!" she shouted. It looked like an attack incorporating magic. Keel could use beast magic, which included howling to boost her own stats. For this attack, she had wreathed herself in magic to increase her attack power and then performed a charging magical strike.

"I don't feel like I can make a contribution to thiz," Shadow admitted.

"Raph!" said the ninja Raph specimen.

"Don't worry. When they fight something that's too slow to hit them, I don't make much of a contribution either," I admitted. My role was just to keep attack support on them and maintain buffs. I also needed to make sure Shadow and the Raph specimen stayed safe, so I couldn't move around a lot. It didn't seem to matter for this one, anyway.

"Air Strike Shield, Second Shield!" I shouted as an incoming lord pteranodon dropped down fast to launch a hit-and-run attack on Raphtalia. My shields appeared in the perfect spot to block it. It screeched more like a chicken than a powerful dinosaur, surprised at whacking into my sudden defenses. Then S'yne turned her scissors into a ball of twine, wrapped up the lord pteranodon, and Raphtalia finished it off with her katana. S'yne proceeded to deploy a spider web of threads in the event of any other attacks from the air.

"Over here! Ah! Keel!" Ruft called, even as he avoided an attack.

"I've got you!" Keel replied. Ruft had confused a king stegosaurus with some illusion magic, and he was proceeding to take it apart with his axe while Keel helped out. With all the illusions in play, the dinos were attacking thin air half the time. There wasn't much for me to do. These looked like powerful monsters, but they didn't have any illusion resistance.

We continued to clear out the excess of monsters, with Shadow and the ninja Raph specimen increasing in level and abilities along the way. The incoming experience was pretty good. It was almost a match for hunting with the sisters. I wondered why experience was so good in this time period. Mamoru and his gang were pretty strong, but in terms of level, they weren't setting any records. I wondered what they did about class-ups. They didn't have a Dragon Emperor, no filolials, and no Raph species either. So how did they perform limit breaks to class up? Maybe in this time they could limit break just by having a hero around.

"Let me get into the action!" Shadow said, feeling more confident with his boosted abilities and joining the battle with Raphtalia and the others. "Hide Behind!" Shadow launched some magic at the kaiser rex. The monster jerked and looked behind himself. That seemed like a pretty funky effect.

"That's dark magic, isn't it?" Raphtalia said. She could create both light and dark illusions. She had a pretty deep understanding of dark magic.

"Correct," Shadow replied. "I've focuzed my learning in magic that controlz and directz the attention of my targetz." That made sense. He was skilled at a kind of infiltration that took a different approach from Raphtalia and the Raph species, such as making enemies turn away so he could sneak past them or hiding his presence. Kizuna had a pseudo-ninja among her allies too. Maybe these two operated in a similar fashion.

Raphtalia and the others quickly took the distracted kaiser rex apart.

"If I have thiz Raph Zhadow with me, there'z no target we cannot infiltrate!" Shadow said.

"That's the name you've given to your Raph species?" I asked.

"It iz a zhadow from the Raph zpeciez! Zimply a dezcriptive term, not a name!" Shadow replied.

"You are such a pain in the ass!" I replied. I wasn't sure if he/she/they was just messing with my head now, but I'd had enough of all this ninja stuff! Believe it!

"Raph Shadow . . . can't we do better than that for a name?" Raphtalia asked. She seemed to want to fight Shadow on this point too. Names weren't an area I had any right to speak about, but I could see why she might want to complain.

"Hey, have the Raph Shadow equip this," I suggested, taking out a wrapped package I had brought along. The Raph Shadow climbed down from Shadow's shoulder and took the item from me.

"I thought that waz your lunch!" Shadow said as though he thought I carried food with me everywhere I went. If we needed to eat something, we could just portal back.

"It isn't?" Raphtalia asked. "I thought the same thing."

"Me too!" Ruft chimed in.

"And me! I was looking forward to a nice meal!" Keel yipped.

"Me too," S'yne added. I felt a sinking feeling that everyone had drawn the same conclusion. I wondered if the idea that some kind of packet I had with me meant I was packing food came from my cooking skills.

"This is not food-related. It's something experimental. I put it together to try with Raph-chan," I explained.

"That sounds like something I'm going to object to most strongly," Raphtalia said immediately.

"If this prototype goes well, we'll make one for you too, Ruft," I said.

"What? What is it? I can't wait!" Ruft said, excited by the prospect of anything Raph species-related. The Raph Shadow opened up the package and confirmed the contents. It was armor based on the teakettle design I had come up with.

Prototype Raph Species Teakettle: Raph Species Exclusive
Defense up, slash resistance (medium), thrust resistance (medium), fire resistance (high), wind resistance (high), water resistance (high), earth resistance (high), magic defense processing, enhanced illusion magic (medium), magic/heat conversion, exhaust floatation, enhanced mobility, Spirit Tortoise power, tortoise shell

"Okay, what is that?" Raphtalia asked.

"I guess you don't know Mt. Kachikachi. It's based on the tanuki that appears in that fairy tale. I made it for the Raph species," I told her.

"I remember when you had the idea," Raphtalia said. "What

I mean is, when did you get the time to make it?"

"I ordered Ren to do it. What do you think?" I replied. "Paws up, Raph Shadow! We need to get this on you."

"Raph?" said Raph Shadow cautiously with a worried expression about putting it on. It did look a little heavy for a Raph species that normally went around dressed as a ninja.

"Don't worry. The metal originates with Spirit Tortoise materials. You won't lose any mobility, but one of those nasty new weapons won't hurt you either," I explained. I pushed the teakettle down over the head of Raph Shadow. The ninja gear Raph Shadow was already wearing was the same as the clothing Filo wore. It was made from magic turned into thread. It might be fun to have Raph-chan dress up in something like this. The miko priestess outfit I'd made once might be a good place to start. Raphtalia had got angry and confiscated it.

The head, arms, and legs of Raph Shadow all popped out of the teakettle, making it almost look like a tortoise's shell.

"Raph!" said Raph Shadow, frowning at this change in appearance.

"Wow. Were you going for the turtle look?" Keel asked, sounding unimpressed. I couldn't see the problem myself.

"Oh wow! That's amazing!" Ruft's eyes were sparkling. He almost looked jealous!

"No, it isn't, Mr. Naofumi," Raphtalia said, taking a very different tone.

"I made an accessory for you too, Raphtalia. Let me have my fun," I said.

"If I'd known it would become a bargaining chip, I might not have accepted it," Raphtalia replied.

"If this works out, I'm going to consider giving them to all the Raph-chans. It could be a boost for both defense and magic," I continued. I made sure everything was in place, then pushed Raph Shadow to walk. I'd been worried that walking might be difficult, but Raph Shadow jumped easily back onto Shadow's shoulder. "You can vent magic and float for a short period too," I explained.

"Raph?" said Raph Shadow, leaping off Shadow's shoulder again. Heat started to be expelled from the skirt section of the teakettle, allowing Raph Shadow to float for a limited time in the air.

"All the basic principles look sound," I commented. Rat and Holn had also been involved in putting it together. Holn had been particularly interested after she saw my designs.

"Raph!" Raph Shadow pulled a shortsword out from inside the teakettle, once again displaying the ease of movement even with this new armor equipped. Floating in the air was a big boost to mobility too.

"It doezn't impede movement at all!" Shadow exclaimed. "How did you make thiz work?"

"This is the power of exclusive equipment," I replied.

"I don't think the name 'ninja' can be applied to thiz though," Shadow continued.

"Either change the moniker from 'ninja' to 'fairy-tale creature' or use magic to hide the armor," I replied.

"An interesting conceit," Raphtalia said, quick on the uptake. "How about I make my miko outfit look like my old armor?"

"That's not allowed," I said quickly. I needed Raphtalia's miko getup to stick around—it was just so easy on the eyes.

"I don't understand your basis for these decisions," Raphtalia replied.

"It's so cool," Ruft said. "I might use magic to make my armor more like that."

"Please don't waste your magic on anything of the sort," Raphtalia told him. She had just talked about making her own miko outfit look like armor but now cautioned Ruft against the same thing. That sounded like a double standard to me.

"Shall I make an exclusive miko outfit?" S'yne asked. She was the Sewing Kit Hero. She would be perfectly suited to such a task.

"Can you do it?" I asked.

"Leave it to me," S'yne replied confidently.

"Why don't you ask about the outfits your ancestors wore and make something for yourself too?" I asked.

"That would look a lot like what I already wear," S'yne

revealed. Fair enough. R'yne did wear something similar, but Filolia wore a very different one-piece.

"I want some exclusive gear too! It'll make me stronger, right?" Keel cut in.

"Keel! A trading outfit?" I asked.

"You made me wear that to interact with customers!" Keel barked back, getting worked up. "I don't want to get stronger wearing that!" I thought it was perfectly suited to her.

"A loincloth, then?" I asked.

"You want me to fight in my underwear?" she shot back. "I don't care if it makes me stronger!"

"Keel, you couldn't go out in public dressed like that," Raphtalia chided her.

"I do it in the village all the time," Keel retorted. She did still walk around in a loincloth sometimes when she wasn't off trading. It suited her, so no one called her out on it, but it could become an issue.

"Enough chatter! Back into combat!" Shadow said. He pulled out a shortsword and quickly dashed at the kaiser rex, slashing into it. Then he took some of the blood from the blade onto his hand and incanted some magic. "Blood Drain!" He lifted his weapon into the air. Blood was sucked from the wounds, forming a red ball in the air that gradually turned black. "Into . . . Blood Rain!" Red rain started to splatter down, falling on the kaiser rex that Shadow had already attacked and the other dinosaurs too. Smoke started to rise from them. "Now!" shouted Shadow.

"Raph!" Raph Shadow said. She was throwing out iron skewers as she still floated in the air. They jabbed into the hide of the dinosaurs, making the creatures stagger in pain.

Raphtalia, Ruft, and S'yne didn't miss a trick, launching a fresh assault. Their attacks seemed more effective than before.

"That seems to have lowered their defense," I said.

"Wow! This is great!" Keel yapped.

"Correct. Thiz iz dark magic that lowerz defenze while alzo attacking," Shadow explained. Making it rain blood was a pretty evil-looking attack, but I couldn't deny how useful the effects were. Shadow had become stronger already and continued to try and keep up with the speed of Raphtalia and the others. He had mentioned wanting to be faster, so he was probably focusing on that.

"That's a sharp weapon you've got there," I commented.

"It's a Zpirit Tortoize dagger made by the weapon maker you favor zo much, Zhield Hero," Shadow explained. That would explain how strong it was.

"That's enough for today," I eventually said at the point Shadow and Raph Shadow could move faster than Ruft. "We've definitely reduced the surplus monster population." I was comparing Shadow and Raph Shadow to Ruft because he was already fast enough. I'd asked Ruft to work on his attack power over his speed or magic. He was swinging the axe around pretty smoothly. I was pleased with his progress. The main remaining issue was that he was just using a regular old steel axe.

"I'll have Ren make an axe for you, Ruft," I said.

"I'm only using this at the moment because I love swinging it around," Ruft replied. "Anything would be fine."

"Ruft, are you sure you aren't focusing too much on strength and techniques?" Raphtalia asked.

"I'm keeping an eye on my balance, don't worry," Ruft replied. "I only learned a little swordplay from Shildina and some life force techniques from the old lady before we came to this time." We still needed to work on his technical aspects though.

The sword that Ren had made from Filo materials Melty now carried for her own protection. She was sharing it with Eclair as needed.

"Maybe I should be thinking about narrowing down my weapon choices too?" Keel pondered, looking at her sword.

"What do you want to use?" I asked her. She thought for a moment.

"Before we came here, I saw that guy . . . L'Arc, was it? He had a scythe. That was so cool!" Keel replied, swinging both arms around as though she were reaping some souls. "Filolia's claws look like fun to use too. I'm not sure I could pick between them," Keel said.

"You seem to get on well with Filolia," I commented.

"Huh? Yeah, she's funny! She wants to be cool too!" Keel exclaimed. As we chatted and prepared to head back, Shadow and Raph Shadow both suddenly looked over toward some bushes a little distance away. Raphtalia and the others looked over there too, noticing the same thing.

"I don't think we're finished here just yet," Raphtalia commented.

"I'm guessing we've been infiltrated after all," I said.

"I know you're hiding there! Come out!" Shadow shouted, throwing a knife for good measure. Some figures promptly appeared from the underbrush.

"Bah! How did they spot us?" one of them said. There was a fox demi-human with two tails, a puma therianthrope, and an eagle-looking therianthrope with a scythe-like weapon. I presumed these bird types were also categorized as therianthropes in this world. Then two more appeared, one holding a staff and another holding a dagger.

Chapter Twelve: Unexpected Visitors from Piensa

"Oh wow, look at that! Yes, there was a funny smell in the air!" Keel said, sniffing around. The one with the staff and dagger was behind the three others, making it hard to see them.

"It doesn't matter! We were going to fight them either way!" the fox demi-human said and then smashed something down onto the ground. Iron fences erupted from the ground a short distance away, sealing us inside a cage. I recalled this item. It was a magical tool used to cut off means of escape. Motoyasu and his crew had used it during the Church of the Three Heroes incident. This one looked pretty similar to that, but with lightning and fire swirling close to the cage. So they had it in this time too. It looked pretty powerful.

In the same moment, a dragon appeared in the air and unleased some magic with a roar. I felt the tension in the air as the dragon Sanctuary expanded outward. They really didn't want us running away.

"I recognize them," Shadow murmured to me.

"Hold on. Isn't that the one we cut down with these new weapons? That's odd. He isn't meant to be able to survive that," the puma therianthrope said to the fox demi-human as he pointed at Shadow.

"I don't know. Maybe it's someone else dressed the same," came the reply.

"That must be it," the puma responded. "No way anyone could survive what we did to that guy." I heard Shadow take a few deep breaths to control his anger and then he murmured to me again.

"We zhould keep it quiet that you managed to heal me, Zhield Hero. It would be a great dizadvantage to let them know we can do that," Shadow said. He was right. No need to make their lives easier.

"How strong are they?" I asked him. "Are they allies of the Bow Hero?"

"They are in the upper rankz in Pienza but not affiliated directly with the Bow Hero. They are ztrong though. Fighting them will not be eazy," Shadow cautioned. They weren't quite on hero level then . . . more like Keel, perhaps.

"Let's chat a little," the fox said. "You must have heard talk about these new weapons of ours by now." It sounded like they wanted to negotiate first. It wasn't a bad idea to play along. There were some selfish people in this time, but they also seemed less inclined to have already made up their minds before we even started talking.

"Yeah, we've heard some stuff," I replied. "So what do you want? I thought you were here to capture the sanctuary?" They didn't seem to have the numbers for that, unless they simply wanted to get their hands on the carriage vassal weapon. From how it was protected, they would need the Bow Hero for that though.

"That's part of our orders," the fox replied, "but our primary target is you, the heroes." It sounded like Piensa had become interested in us after we took out one of those running the waves. But they couldn't believe these heavy-handed tactics were going to work. Melty and the others had messed them up once already.

"Bubba?" Keel asked.

"Keel, quiet!" Raphtalia shushed her as Keel looked around. "Don't cause any trouble for Mr. Naofumi at the moment. Stay silent."

"What are you saying?" I asked.

"Leave Siltran behind and come join Piensa. Siltran could never have withstood Piensa without your help, even with the Shield and Whip Heroes on their side," the fox said. It sounded like word of Filolia hadn't got around yet. It wasn't especially easy to explain away her coming back to life.

"What about the newly appeared Hammer Hero?" I asked. Word that Natalia the pacifier had been selected by the Hammer and was working with Siltran to quell the turmoil had rapidly spread around the world.

"We know about the pacifier, of course, but she'll understand. A unified world is vital to overcome the fighting ahead and end the waves," the fox replied. That almost sounded logical, but also very arrogant. Natalia certainly wouldn't "understand" either. "Piensa would welcome you. The king has promised it. That has to be appealing!"

"Unfortunately for you guys, no, not really," I shot back. The two-tailed fox frowned at my quick rejection.

"We're offering the full support and cooperation of a powerful nation in order to help protect the world from the waves. Isn't that exactly the kind of environment you want to complete your duties as a hero? We've all the people—and the women—you could need. We can definitely offer more than tiny little Siltran," the fox said, pulling out all the stops to get us on the hook. Back in our time, I was already a Duke in Melromarc, the nation that basically ruled the world. There were no merits for me in joining with this relatively soon-to-be-doomed nation. They had already deployed weapons that caused incurable wounds. Who knew what they would do to us if we joined them?

"Sorry, but I don't care for you whoring out your women, and I don't need a fancy bed to sleep in either," I retorted. "The waves are here. They're happening. It would hardly be heroic to bow to a dictatorship trying to seize control of the world."

"Or maybe you could consider the Shield and Whip Heroes to be the ones causing the unnecessary conflict," the fox countered. "All this fighting is only happening because they aren't willing to obey Piensa's orders."

"And yet you use the word 'orders.' I feel sorry for the Bow Hero being stuck with you," I said. Just this short conversation had already revealed they had no intention to cooperate. They were too accustomed to giving orders from a place of absolute authority. Mamoru and Holn were completely in the right here. I recalled the former queen and her calls for nations to set aside their differences and overcome the waves together. She had been a good ruler. Trash had taken up the same tune since his return to form. Having intelligent people on the throne definitely made a difference in our time. Faubrey could be overbearing and had tried to lure the heroes to them, but they hadn't demanded a monopoly and hadn't sent them into warfare either. Those aspects seemed worse in this time. "What are you planning to do about your relationship with our world?" I asked, bluffing them a little.

"Piensa has some thoughts on heroes from outside coming in and causing trouble, of course," the fox replied. "But such transgressions can be forgiven."

"Forgiveness, huh. That isn't something we need from you. I can already see that you try to use force to settle everything. It's easy to imagine what you will try if you ever do unify this world," I shot back. The desire for domination was without bounds and the waves were known to fuse worlds together.

"I don't think it's a bad proposition to join with mighty Piensa in ruling any number of worlds," the fox said.

"A selfish proposition, sure," I shot back. Even the guys from Kizuna's world weren't this arrogant. At least they put the threat of the waves first . . . The resurrected were another story, of course.

"Your reaction suggests these negotiations aren't getting us anywhere," the fox said. "We would prefer that you accepted our terms."

"I'm sure you would. What are you going to do next?" I asked. They all looked so hostile I couldn't see them just backing down and going home.

"The fact that you were able to kill those causing the waves is a thorn in the side of Piensa," the fox admitted. "If we can't turn you into our allies, then we just have to remove you from the board." The others behind the fox took this as the signal to ready their weapons. It seemed like a good point to call in Raph-chan. I focused on the skill C'mon Raph. With a sound like something tearing, Raph-chan appeared. It seemed she was even capable of breaking barriers now.

"Raph! Raph, raph!" said Raph-chan intently. It seemed like our other allies were in trouble too. At the same time, she was pointing up at the dragon in the sky above us. She wanted to say something to do with that.

"Raph Shadow, can you use your magic inside the Sanctuary?" I asked.

"Raph . . ." came the forlorn reply and a shake of the head.

This was heading toward tit for tat with sanctuaries, then, but I couldn't account for interference from the cage. It was probably better to wait and have Raph-chan incant her own Sanctuary magic later.

"Couldn't we do this after we've stopped the ones causing the waves?" I suggested.

"Such a proposition does not suit everyone on our side. If we can defeat you, then we can obtain your technology for ourselves anyway," the fox replied.

"You seem to think we're going to be a pushover. I've got bad news for you in that regard," I sniped back.

"Do you think we would show ourselves without some kind of trump card?" the fox countered. Then both the fox demi-human and puma therianthrope threw their weapons toward us.

"Watch out!" Shadow shouted.

"Go! Fragarach Custom!" one of the enemies shouted. With a noise that sounded dangerous, the swords that the fox demi-human and puma therianthrope threw flew up to us and started chopping.

"Shooting Star Shield!" I shouted in reply, putting up a barrier and sending out float shields to block the attacking blades. For a moment it looked like the disembodied weapons were giving up, dropping down to the ground, but then they attacked again, hard and low. They seemed to have some kind of auto tracking.

"Oh! Is this it? They move around so quickly!" Keel said, eyes wide as she watched the blades in the air.

"They will purzue a target until they land a blow. I'm zurprized at you being able to block them, Zhield Hero," Shadow said.

"They do seem pretty powerful," I replied. A heavy attack clashed with a float shield in that same moment, pushing it backward but luckily not breaking it.

"Impressive! I didn't expect them to deal with that!" the puma said.

"Let's try this next!" the fox replied. The entire Piensa squad rushed toward us. The fox and puma took out fresh weapons. Shooting Star Shield still seemed enough to handle the problem. Then the one with the dagger changed his weapon into an auger and threw it at us.

"Shield Breaker V!" a male voice shouted, and with a shattering noise, my Shooting Star Shield broke apart instantly.

"What?!" I exclaimed. The voice sounded as though it had enhanced the skill . . . which told me exactly who we were facing! I needed to boost everyone's abilities or we wouldn't stand a chance! I focused on magic and incanted. "All Liberation Aura!" I placed support magic on all my allies and then caught the swords of the incoming fox and puma on my shields. As power swelled up inside them, Raphtalia, Shadow, Keel, Raph Shadow, and Ruft all gave shouts and launched their own attacks into the opening created by me blocking the incoming attacks.

"Bind Wire!" S'yne shouted, matching the others' attacks with wires to bind up our attackers. They seemed maybe on equal footing with Keel, but they weren't ready to fight Raphtalia. Even Shadow could probably hold his own now with the new levels he'd received.

"I, the Staff Hero, command the spirits and command the world. Dragon Vein. Combine your power with my magic and bravery! As the source of your power, the Staff Hero implores you! Let the true way be revealed once more and provide them with everything!" The magician with the staff finished her magic. "All Remove Everything X!" The next instant, the three in the lead sped up! They slashed easily through the threads S'yne created and came right for us. With an assortment of clashes, Raphtalia combated the fox demi-human. Keel, the Shadow, and Raph Shadow attacked the puma therianthrope. Ruft and S'yne fought the eagle therianthrope. The eagle was surrounded with wind and floating skillfully in the air.

"Oh wow! This is amazing. Talk about a rush of power!" the eagle said.

"It can't be . . . can it?" Raphtalia said, eyeing the two at the back while her katana was locked with the fox in front of her. I was dealing with the flying swords, but who knew how long that would last? They were going to land a hit eventually.

"Thiz iz . . . problematic," Shadow said.

"Raph!" agreed Raph Shadow.

"They suddenly got a lot faster," Ruft added.

"Bubba, are we going to be okay?" Keel asked.

"You back there! What are you?" I asked directly, glaring at the two holders of what had to be the staff and projectile vassal weapons.

"The guy with the shield seems to be their leader! Oh, great staff wielder, take him out!" the fox cried out.

"Take them all out, one after the other!" the puma said. The staff holder didn't look like she wanted to talk. Then she pointed her staff at me and shouted.

"Air Strike Blast V! Second Blast V!" Two beams of light were emitted from the staff toward me. I put my shield up and took them head-on. I was able to stop them, but they were powerful! With a grunt, I deflected the attacks, shifting them away to the side. But then a flurry of axes flew toward me as though waiting for that very moment.

"Air Strike Throw, Second Throw, Torrid Throw! Tornado Throw X!" the male voice shouted.

"Shield Prison!" I read the incoming arcs of the hand axes and other weapons and then used a life-force-enhanced cage of shields to block the rotating tornado. The shield cracked and shattered around me, but the use of life force kept me safe. For now.

There was no mistaking it after all that.

"Where did the Staff and Projectile Heroes come from?! I don't understand this!" I raged. I checked their faces. It wasn't Trash and Rishia. Of course not. The one with the staff was wearing a robe. Her face couldn't be seen, but from the body, I was guessing it was a woman. The one with the projectile was a guy in his twenties with short hair and robber-style clothing. These two had to be the Staff and Projectile Heroes from this time period.

"You're the ones who popped up out of nowhere!" the fox demi-human said, weapon still locked with Raphtalia.

"You're innocent in this. We watched your fight. We wanted to support you . . . but that's why we have to fight now," the Staff Hero said.

"The only way to protect our own holy weapon hero is for you to die!" the Projectile Hero said.

"Hold on! Both of you! Let's discuss this!" I shouted.

"We can't betray what we believe in. Fight us! Fight us or die!" the Staff Hero screamed in desperation and then un-leashed more magic toward me. "All Release Flare X!" Blazing flames gathered around me and then exploded. I gritted my teeth and poured life force into my accessory, enhancing the magic-reflect function. If I used it too many times, it would break, but anything was better than being hit by the incoming attack. I felt the accessory crack, but a barrier that reflected magic was also thrown up around me and the explosive magic was automatically reflected away.

"What? Reflection?!" The Staff Hero gave a shout of surprise as the concentrated ball of fire descended on her.

"Watch out!" The Projectile Hero leapt at the Staff Hero and got turned into a fireball instead of her. I had protected Raphtalia and the others while also protecting the opponents they were immediately engaged with. The Projectile Hero was not so lucky. He screamed in pain as his back was burned to a crisp.

"Hold on! I'll heal you!" the Staff Hero said. "All Release Heal X!"

"Phew . . . thanks," the Projectile Hero said, recovering. "That Shield Hero can reflect release-class magic? Now I can see why they're so strong. We could learn something from this."

"They did defeat one who assumes the name of god. Impressive," the Staff Hero agreed. It sounded like they were praising us, but their hostility toward us only grew.

"It sounds like we could work this out if we only discuss it," I said.

"We aren't allowed. That's all we can say. We have to fight you at full strength!" the Staff Hero replied.

"If we don't take your heads . . . you don't know what'll happen to our world!" the Projectile Hero added. Even though they "weren't allowed" to say too much, they almost didn't seem to want to stop talking about it. I was getting some idea of what was going on. As soon as the mysterious new weapons that inflicted wounds that couldn't be healed appeared in Piensa, it was easy to imagine who might be behind all this.

"Those scum have taken the holy weapon hero and the people of your world hostage and told you to kill us, correct?" I extrapolated. Their silence told me the rest of what I needed to know. Any resistance, any betrayal, would not be forgiven. They had said too much already. I'd worked the whole thing out.

We were talking about the kind of scum who operated a bizarre game of death from a position of complete safety. They were going to come as hard as possible at anything that could possibly threaten them. At the same time, they also didn't want to risk their own lives, which led to the use of tactics like this. Working in the shadows, they provided Piensa with these powerful new weapons and sent heroes from other worlds to kill us. They would clearly just keep coming until we were wiped out. Maybe they were calling our bluff. If the God Hunters were here, they wouldn't be trying something like this. It reeked of desperation. Piensa should be ashamed for having any involvement in it all. I glared at the fox demi-human, who seemed to be the leader and had done most of the talking so far.

"What? Our illustrious heroes have some kind of issue?" the fox asked, seemingly clueless.

"You don't know?" I replied.

"We're elite soldiers, but we don't get that information," the fox explained. The fox seemed like a commander but was still taking orders. The entire nation was structured for warfare. "I admit that I'm impressed by your handling of our trump card." The fox offered an honest opinion on my blocking of every attack from the two swords. "One little scratch and we'd get the upper hand at once."

"These are the famous weapons that inflict incurable wounds," I confirmed.

"That's right." The fox nodded. "Aren't you scared?"

"Of this? Please," I said.

"Impressive! Time to get serious!" the fox barked.

"You asked for it!" I replied. Then I performed weapon fusion with the Spirit Tortoise Carapace Shield and another shield—the Iron Shield Pistol! Then I activated Magic Bullet! I incanted magic again and activated it. This was the only way to respond to the X-class support magic that our opponents were using.

"First . . . All Liberation Aura!" A ball of support magic was released from the gemstone section of the Spirit Tortoise Carapace Shield. "Raphtalia, you're up! Everyone else! Just repel their attacks a little longer!" I shouted.

"Okay! Ruft, help me!" Raphtalia replied.

"I'm here!" Ruft said.

"Raph!" said Raph-chan, also taking part. The three of them synced up and deployed a magical circle.

"Five Practices Destiny Field Expansion," Raphtalia intoned. "Sakura Stone of Destiny! In the name of the pacifier, I ask for strength!" Raphtalia changed her weapon to the sakura stone of destiny katana, and Ruft's axe sparkled with a cherry-pink light as well.

"My strength is draining away!" the puma complained.

"I guessed these were also pacifiers . . . but this timing is too much!" the fox complained. Now the fighting changed in the favor of our side with Raphtalia and the others pushing their opponents back and then moving to smash the flying swords out of the air.

"You've been keeping these crazy swords under control all this time?" Ruft said in surprise.

"Uwah! There's no healing a single cut from these! Stay away from me!" Keel said.

"Take this chance to stop them!" Raphtalia shouted.

"I've got thiz!" Shadow replied.

"Shadow! Don't go too far forward!" Raphtalia called, but it was too late; one of the swords slashed into Shadow as he broke ranks. But Shadow faded and turned into darkness. The sword remained where he had been. Then the actual Shadow and Raph Shadow knocked the sword away.

"Another application of Hide Behind," Shadow explained.

"Behind . . . Wire," S'yne said, binding up the swords of death in a bundle of threads. The sword quickly cut through the threads on the blade but was having trouble with the threads on the handle.

"Change Shield!" I shouted, giving up on intercepting their swords with float shields. Instead, I changed the float shields into mirror shields using Change Shield and then used them to reflect the ball of magic fired from the Spirit Tortoise Carapace Shield. This was like the combination attack I had pulled off with the Demon Dragon when using the mirror vassal weapon. Now I could do it alone. The reflective float shields moved away from my awareness and auto launched a different skill that I had activated when I was using the staff vassal weapon. The name popped up, so I shouted it and activated the skill.

"Magic Prison!" I had no idea how many reflections imbuing life force would make it possible, and no idea how much the enhancement multiplier would increase with each reflection, but this should allow us to compete with the support magic the enemy was using. At my shout, the reflected All Liberation Aura ball shattered apart and was applied to everyone I had designated as allies. It instantly felt like my body had become lighter. I used my float shields to pin down the flying swords again, which assisted Raphtalia and the others in switching back to offense.

"Get ready! Eight Trigrams, Destiny Thrust!" Raphtalia said.

"From me too! Eight Trigrams, Destiny Smash!" Ruft added. Raph-chan was keeping the barrier going while Raphtalia and Ruft unleashed a synced-up special attack directly at the now-weakened Piensa therianthropes and their flying swords.

"You won't take us out that easily!" the fox shouted. All of our attackers broke off and leapt backward to safety. The attack from Raphtalia and Ruft headed for the swiftly slashing swords. The weapons continued to flail around, but they were smashed left and right by the attack.

"There's no escape. Deploying Optical Wings," S'yne said. Rushing after the enemies as they dropped back, she split her scissors into two swords and then deployed the wings of light on her back.

They were indeed wings. They were delicate butterfly-like wings sprouting from her back. They looked a little different from the ones I'd seen R'yne use, but they were visible to the naked eye and moved beautifully. S'yne zipped up to where the eagle therianthrope was flying.

"You dare pollute the skies, outsider Sewing Kit Hero?" the eagle squawked.

"It was a mistake to think you're the only one who can fly!" S'yne retorted. She flapped her wings and butterfly dust drifted toward the eagle therianthrope, causing small explosions on impact. Then S'yne flowed into a familiar double-sword combination attack. She slashed vertically with the scissor half in her right hand, performed a spinning attack with her wings, then slashed horizontally with her left hand, while her two familiars performed an attack from behind.

"Too many attacks!" the eagle blustered. "Feather Shot!" Trying to escape from being mobbed, the eagle unleashed some attack magic against S'yne's sister, but she simply dodged back for a moment to avoid it and then closed in again. The eagle swung his scythe wildly, but S'yne confidently intercepted by grabbing its shaft.

"See how you like it!" S'yne shouted, redirecting the weapon and chopping into the eagle with it.

"I know—" S'yne said.

"I know someone much more skilled with a scythe than you. You need to train harder," her familiar spoke for her. That was the first time I'd seen that in a while.

"They're too fast for us! Illustrious heroes!" the fox shouted.

"We have to do everything," the Staff Hero complained and then started to incant some magic again. "I, the Staff Hero, command the spirits and command the world. Dragon Vein. Combine your power with my magic and bravery! As the source of your power, the Staff Hero implores you! Let the true way be revealed once more and strip from them everything! All Release Debuff X!" The Demon Dragon lurking in my mind analyzed the magic and informed me that it was like the All Liberation Down X that Itsuki used. I'd expected a move like this and we were pretty buffed up, so I could just let it through.

But why should I?

"Did you think debuff magic would work so easily? Pathetic!" I shouted, more at the Piensa guys than the Staff Hero herself. I revved up the old Hengen Muso Style Lost Technique: Magic Eradication, which gathered together the magic the Staff Hero unleashed and then wiped it out. Even if I couldn't block the casting, I could nullify some debuff support magic like this, no problem.

"He repelled the debuff magic? Impossible!" the fox exclaimed.

"You've got some moves, I can tell, but we've just been through a whole lot more shit than you have," I said flatly. We wouldn't be here otherwise.

"These guys are tricky and tough!" the puma said.

"I think you'd have more luck trying to convince Piensa to give up world domination than you would trying to kill us," I told them. "You must have some idea what's really going on behind the scenes over there."

"Maybe. But that's for the top brass to know. We don't have the right to question them," the fox said. It sounded like a military through and through. I would have appreciated it if the knights in our time had retained this ability to keep emotions out of things, at least. But then again, I reasoned that anything passed down from these demi-humans or therianthropes would go to Siltvelt or Shieldfreeden. I looked over at Raphtalia and the others and gave the signal with my eyes. Raphtalia returned her katana to her sheath for a moment and then started to charge her life force.

"My universal collaborators! Respond to my call and materialize your magic power!" Raphtalia called, drawing on the power from the distant Raph species in order to unleash a big attack.

"Raaaaph!" said Raph-chan. Light from the vicinity flowed into her. She became a jacket of light again and Raphtalia put her on. Ruft crouched and fluffed up his tail, preparing for a big attack. S'yne had her wings out and her scissor blades crossed in front of her. Keel's normal cheerfulness had changed to anger. She was growling. Her pupils were open wide and she was ready to leap into action at any moment like some feral predator—or at least an angry, husky puppy. Shadow and Raph Shadow both had daggers in their hands, hiding in the darkness, waiting for a moment to strike. It was an unconventional party, but not a bad setup.

"No point in keeping our trump cards in the deck!" the fox shouted. The Piensa side started to throw out all the swords they had, not just the first two.

"Shooting Star Shield!" I shouted. The cooldown finished and stopped the four incoming deadly swords. It was important to have Raphtalia and the others attack, but if they got hit by these, then healing them here would be hard. They moved quickly and could leave us totally on the defensive.

"Weapon Prism X!" the Staff Hero shouted, firing what looked like a rainbow-colored gemstone up into the air above us. I wasn't sure what was going on.

"Zhield Hero!" Shadow shouted. "That'z like the zkill Trash usez!"

Chapter Thirteen: Beast Transformation of Rage

That shout did jog something in my memory.

"Fragarach Custom X!" the Projectile Hero shouted, launching a skill with the same name as the deadly weapons.

"Air Strike Shield! Second Shield! Dritte Shield! Change Shield!" I shouted, rattling off my own skills. "Everyone, stay back!" I deployed plenty of shields alongside my floating ones and then turned them all into my sakura stone of destiny shield and readied another skill. A moment later the thrown sword hit the gemstone and multiplied into countless weapons before raining down on us. My shields started to absorb the impacts, cracking and breaking as they did so. These shields should have had incredible effects against a hero's weapon. Our enemies clearly knew something of pacifier techniques. Their holy weapon hero was being held captive. They weren't going to listen to anything our pacifiers had to say anyway—or they had already been conditioned not to.

With a grunt, I stepped forward to take as many of the flying swords on my own body as I could. I wanted to keep the damage from Raphtalia and the others as much as possible. My defenses were quickly shredded and I started to take cuts into my body. It really hurt, and it was only a matter of time before I got torn to pieces. They were crafty, coming up with an attack like this. I recalled how Trash had used a skill called Magic Prism as part of a skill combination, allowing him to reflect magic exactly as he desired and use it to attack. It looked like their target might have been me all along, because the flying swords were still focusing entirely on me. I wasn't going to let them get away with it!

I used the life force Gather the best I could, activating Hate Reaction and increasing its accuracy.

"Mr. Naofumi!" Raphtalia exclaimed.

"Shield Hero!" said Ruft.

"Bubba!" shouted Keel.

"Don't worry about me! Go!" I shouted back.

"I can't!" Raphtalia cried out.

"Don't worry! You guys focus on attacking! While they hit me, you hit them!" I replied through gritted teeth. I didn't know how long this weapon-reflecting skill was going to last, but I wasn't going to last much longer myself if we didn't take our attackers out!

"—got this!" S'yne was the first, flying right for the Piensa forces and the Staff and Projectile Heroes.

"Optical Wings! Give me more . . . more power!" S'yne shouted. Her wings glowed even brighter and she hit the lead Projectile Hero with an incredible impact. It was easy to imagine how the Projectile Hero would fight based on what we'd seen Rishia do. It wasn't a weapon especially suited to close combat.

"Raphtalia, keep up! This is no time to hesitate!" S'yne called back.

"But Mr. Naofumi! Those swords!" Raphtalia shouted.

"Don't worry! Just end this fight as quickly as you can!" Ruft told her.

"That'z right! If we don't defeat theze enemiez, the Zhield Hero will fall! Attack with everything you've got, right now!" Shadow shouted.

"Raph!" Raph Shadow shouted. All three of them were telling Raphtalia to get her head back in the game. But she continued to watch me, stunned into inactivity.

"Bubba . . . I'm going to do it . . . I've decided! I'm going to become stronger to help you all out!" Keel snapped back to herself with a roar and started flipping in the air. The icon to confirm beast transformation support popped up in my field of vision. Directions for Change Shield also appeared along with it. I'd seen this pattern before, but it still took me a moment to realize . . . this was for Keel! It seemed other magic could increase the variations of available transformations. I took a moment to consider who else could collaborate on this. Raphtalia and the Raphs could offer light and dark, which might be interesting, but I couldn't be sure that would make it any stronger. They could use illusions already, so we didn't need that. The same went for Shadow. S'yne . . . I wasn't sure about.

As for my healing and support magic . . . I wasn't sure they would help. I just didn't want Keel to push herself too hard. If things took a wrong turn, I would just end it.

"Change Shield!" I activated beast transformation support along with Change Shield at the same time. The two float shields changed into the black and white Shield of Compassion and Shield of Wrath. Keel's body thumped, jerked, and her fur turned red and black. She gave a louder roar as she morphed into a four-legged form that was wreathed in black fire. Then she rushed forward. At that speed, she could actually match S'yne and Raphtalia.

"What now?!" the puma exclaimed.

"A beast transformation!" the fox shouted.

"No more hurting Bubba!" Keel growled. As she dashed forward, she left afterimages behind. She turned into the form of a cerberus amid the black fire and threw herself boldly at the Piensa soldiers.

"I can't let Keel do all the work!" Raphtalia said. "This power is a marker for illusions! True magic that lays waste to all, illusions that confound our foes! The Heavenly Emperor orders you! Sink my enemies into an ocean of illusion! Demon Emperor: Illusory Layers!" Raphtalia promptly launched her own magic, sinking all our foes into deep and complex illusions.

"More trouble!" the fox exclaimed. "This is powerful illusion magic . . . I know these are illusions and I can't get rid of them! What kind of monster is she?!"

"Even the staff vassal weapon can't analyze this spell," the Staff Hero reported. "This is how strong you need to be to defeat our true enemy?"

"We can't just give up!" the Projectile Hero replied. "If we can't tell where they are, we should attack in all directions at once!"

"Okay!" the Staff Hero agreed. The two of them raised their weapons and started firing off skills.

"Skill Prism V . . . Shooting Star Cannon!" the Staff Hero shouted. A reflecting gemstone rose up into the air and started to fire in all directions, targeting everything other than the Staff Hero's own allies. They were playing it safe after learning I could reflect magic.

"Shooting Star Shot X!" the Projectile Hero shouted. He tossed out what looked like countless grenades across the vicinity and then stars scattered out from those in every direction. I was taking heavy damage. My field of view slowly was turning red, but I could still tell what these were—the shooting star skills from the Staff and Projectile weapons.

"I'm not backing off!" S'yne yelled, taking damage but sticking to the Projectile Hero.

"She's willing to give her life for this!" the Projectile Hero exclaimed. "Of course she is! I have to fight back at full strength!" He was still under the influence of the illusions, but the Projectile Hero at least managed to respond to S'yne's attacks. He was taking a lot of hits, but there was no sign of defeating him yet.

Then the fox demi-human used some kind of spray across the general area.

"Thanks! That's a useful item that removes illusions!" the Projectile Hero said. "Sorry, but I'm not losing to you," he shouted at S'yne.

"And I'm not losing to you either!" S'yne shouted back.

With a growl, Keel clamped onto one of the tails of the fox demi-human and started to shake it in her jaws.

"That burns!" the fox cried with a scream. "Get off me!" Keel took the incoming blows from the fox, but her teeth remained locked in place. The fox was being burned by her fiery bite.

"Don't forget about me!" the eagle therianthrope said, dropping down in front of S'yne to protect the Projectile Hero without a moment's hesitation. These two might not be the best of friends, but they still had to fight together.

With a shout, Raphtalia rushed in, smashing everything down with her katana while Ruft and the two Shadows came up the rear.

"I can't hold anything back!" Raphtalia shouted. "Please, let us defeat you!" She swung her katana down at the Staff Hero, but the puma therianthrope circled in between them, catching the blade on what looked like a piece of cloth. Raphtalia's sword slid off to the side and I heard a weird sound.

"This feels like—" Raphtalia started. Then her own blade appeared from the air behind her and stabbed her in the back. Some kind of twisting of space was going on there! Exactly like the special defensive walls we had seen the ones who assume the name of god use and the force that S'yne's sister belonged to.

"Wow! This is the real thing," the puma exclaimed. "I didn't actually expect to catch such a powerful attack with something so flimsy. It doesn't matter how strong their attacks are! We can still win!"

"No, you can't! Not like that!" Raphtalia replied. She grabbed her katana for another attack but changed it to Katana 0 first. The cloth was cut to shreds with a single strike. The puma grunted.

"The illusions have ended! You can fall back!" the Staff Hero shouted, stepping bravely in front of the puma alongside the Projectile Hero. "This is our chance! While the Shield Hero can't move!"

"Time to drop the hammer! Mjolnir X!" the Projectile Hero exclaimed.

"Jormungandr X!" the Staff Hero added. A massive hammer flickering with lightning was joined by the staff that was glowing with purple light. Then both were readied to throw at Raphtalia and S'yne.

I'd heard the name of the projectile skill before—the famous weapon of the god of thunder. I could see how that would become a skill. For the staff skill, Jormungandr was an interesting counterpoint to Fenrir Force, which I had used with the staff myself. Jormungandr was the name of one of the older siblings of the god-eating wolf Fenrir. Those were the kinds of skills found in the staff.

Raphtalia imbued life force into the katana in her hands, instantly expanded a magic circle on the ground, and then sliced downward.

"You will not hurt Mr. Naofumi any more than this!" Raphtalia shouted. "Divine Clash of the Five Practices!" I could tell she was pushing herself hard, because blood erupted from her shoulder. It stained her jacket red, finally giving her the "red jacket" I had also been contemplating for her.

"The magic is binding me . . . I can't move!" the Staff Hero complained.

"I'll help, Raphtalia!" S'yne shouted. She caught up the incoming lightning hammer with a bundle of threads as she turned her scissors back into one weapon and slashed at the Projectile Hero. Out of the two of them . . . the Staff Hero was a bigger threat than the Projectile Hero in this situation.

"Divine Clash of the Five Practices, and then . . ." Raphtalia said, cancelling out the incoming attack with big techniques of her own. Then she drew the second katana at her hip, going into her accelerated state and unleashing another skill.

"Bubba! Things might get hot, but just hang in there!" Keel exclaimed. She tossed the fox demi-human away, still using just her mouth, and then it opened wide and expelled a torrent of black fire. It did look really hot, but I didn't feel any heat at all. Maybe because the source of her current power was a link to my own rage. The fire Keel was blowing all around me wiped away the countless flying swords. I knew they would be back quickly, but I needed to use this moment to help Raphtalia.

"Attack . . . Support," I managed to get out, launching some spikes at the Staff Hero. They weaved between the countless deadly weapons and struck the Staff Hero full-on. I saw Raphtalia glance my way, just for a moment. There were tears in her eyes. I'd probably get in trouble again later.

"Spirit Blade! Soul Slice!" Raphtalia said, using the opening I had created.

"What?" the Staff Hero exclaimed. Then he screamed as Raphtalia's katana landed. All of the Staff Hero's SP drained away as she toppled over and fainted.

"Are you okay? Hey!" the Projectile Hero roared, dashing over to the collapsed Staff Hero and lifting her up. But she wasn't moving at all. In the next moment, the countless swords flying around me vanished into a mist, leaving just the original four circling and attacking.

"Shooting Star Shield," I said, creating another barrier to

hold them off. I'd been chopped up so badly it was hard to locate all the individual injuries.

"For the Shield Hero!" Ruft shouted, smashing down with his axe.

"I'm here too!" Shadow added, joined by Raph Shadow, who unleashed a quick series of slashing attacks, pushing back the fox demi-human and puma therianthrope.

"Me too!" Keel shook her head, as though dispelling a dizzy spell. Then she sucked in a deep breath before unleashing a torrent of fire toward the enemies. The fox barely managed to take what looked like three claws from inside her clothing and catch Ruft's axe with them. She was still sent flying away. The puma therianthrope was cut into by the two Shadows while also getting burned by the black fire.

"Keep the prezzure on! Blood Drain!" Shadow commanded.

"Raph!" said Raph Shadow.

"My blood . . . is being sucked out? What now?!" the puma exclaimed, roaring.

"Let'z zee how you enjoy experiencing the pain of woundz that cannot be healed," Shadow said. He worked with Raph Shadow to draw the blood from the cuts on the puma therianthrope and then turned to attack the eagle that S'yne was still tussling with. "Blood Rain!"

"Huh? Is this . . . blood?" the eagle said, then started screaming himself.

"That's my opening!" S'yne didn't miss her chance, chopping into the eagle.

"I won't lose to you!" the bird replied. "Any wounds caused by this will never heal! You'd better not—" But S'yne just carried on, taking the thrust of his scythe into her body. "Such . . . noble determination . . ." the eagle managed and then plummeted down to the ground with a crunch. S'yne landed with the scythe still jabbed into her. She turned off her wings and came over toward me. At the same time, Raphtalia had her katana at the throat of the Projectile Hero. If he moved a muscle, he was dead.

"This fire has an effect to delay healing!" Keel crowed, doing a pretty good impression of me. "How does it feel to get a taste of your own sick medicine?"

"This is . . . going badly," the fox said. The four swords the fox and puma threw returned to them for a moment. They then deployed two of them again, but against Raphtalia. As she dealt with the two swords, the Projectile Hero took that opening to drag the Staff Hero away. "We have to fall back. Their Shield Hero will surely die from those wounds anyway."

"Yeah," the puma agreed. "A shame, almost, seeing as how strong he was."

"These are orders from our nation . . . from Piensa royalty. All's fair in love and war. Your own strength was what led to you being targeted," the eagle said.

"I won't apologize for anything," the Projectile Hero said. "We did this to save our own world." The Staff Hero was still knocked out, but I guessed she would have had something to say too. Each of the enemies nodded at the fox's command, but they left us with a nice parting message. The two swords around Raphtalia also returned to their owners' hands. The fox took out what looked like a piece of cloth and placed it over all of them. By the time it reached the ground, they had vanished. There was no sign of the cloth either.

"Have they hidden themselvez?" Shadow asked.

"No. It doesn't feel like that," Ruft replied.

"They aren't here," Raphtalia confirmed. "They must have run far away." It was some kind of way to travel between dimensions, maybe. They had selected retreat. They knew how their weapons worked, after all. Considering the beating they had given me, they probably didn't expect me to last very long. They could have tried to hold on a little longer, but they knew when it was best to give up. I felt the inescapable dragon Sanctuary end too. They had really covered their tracks.

"Mr. Naofumi!" Raphtalia exclaimed, rushing over to me as I breathed hard.

"Bubba!" Keel shouted and then grunted as I ended the Shield of Wrath Change Shield. The beast transformation ended and Keel collapsed on the spot. The power of the Shield of Wrath had helped to somewhat reduce the damage caused by their deadly weapons, but I was reaching my limit too.

"I can't believe . . . using your power is this rough, Bubba," Keel managed.

"You saved us, Keel," Raphtalia told her.

"But . . . I couldn't do half as much as I'd have liked. I need to get . . . much stronger than this," Keel said, managing to drag herself into a sitting position.

"Zhield Hero! Are you okay?" Shadow asked.

"Do I look okay?" I replied. I had bloody cuts all over my body! I was lightheaded from the blood loss. But if I collapsed here, I was going to die, no doubt about it. Pure force of will was keeping me standing.

"Raphtalia, make sure they don't double back. S'yne—" I started.

"Forget about—" S'yne cut me off.

"Ms. S'yne says that you should worry about yourself first," her familiar translated.

"Okay. Give me some support," I said. I took some magic water out from my shield and then started to incant some magic. It wasn't easy to use such difficult magic when I was so low on blood. This definitely wasn't something I could ever use in battle.

"First Heal Zero," I said listlessly, starting by removing the incurable wounds that had been caused to my own body.

0 territory: 5%

That text passed through my mind and then my magic dropped to zero and I almost passed out.

"Mr. Naofumi!" Raphtalia's shout dragged me back to consciousness and I chugged the magic water. After that, it was up to the Demon Dragon.

"My time to shine!" said that voice. "Liberation Heal!" My wounds closed up without further ado, but I had lost so much blood that physically I wasn't completely recovered yet. My head was still spinning . . . but S'yne needed healing too.

"S'yne, you next," I said.

"I can hold on," she replied.

"No, you can't. Ruft, hold her," I said. I wondered what she was talking about, saying she could "hold on" with a weapon sticking out of her. She tried to back away but Ruft held her—gently but firmly—in place, and I cast the magic. My consciousness blurred again.

0 territory: 7%

"Now to heal you," I stammered.

"Mr. Naofumi . . ." Raphtalia sympathized, joined by the others. Healing my wounds hadn't replaced all that lost blood. I'd concocted some medicine later that would promote blood production. It was a dangerous medicine to use, even in this world.

"Everyone, be ready for more fighting," I told them. "If they came here for us, it's safe to assume they've gone for Ren and the others too." I checked the red wound on Raphtalia's miko outfit. It was pretty deep. It was a very strange situation to literally stab yourself in the back. "All Liberation Heal," I incanted. I cast healing magic on everyone there, and then I needed another magic water . . . but that was too much hassle. I took out a rucolu fruit, which I kept for emergencies, and stuffed my cheeks with it. It recovered my magic and SP at the same time . . . but did nothing for how lethargic I felt. I wondered if there was nothing I could do about how much magic this new technique used. The magic composition itself was overly difficult. Liberation was a walk in the park in comparison. There was no way I'd ever be using this healing magic in battle.

Raphtalia had been hurt the deepest. I breathed a sigh of relief after healing her wounds. My armor had been slashed up and was covered in blood too . . . That was going to take some repair work. More crap to deal with.

"We'd better get back to Ren and Fohl," I said. "Smash this cage."

"Okay!" Raphtalia said.

"I've got this!" S'yne added with a nod.

"Why not juzt releaze it?" Shadow asked.

"If you can do that, be my guest," I told him.

"I have learned zome zuch techniquez," he replied. He walked around the cage, observing it carefully. "But in thiz caze, I'm not zure how to proceed. Zmazhing it will be fazter," he concluded.

"You heard Shadow," I told the girls.

"Okay! It might have a counterattack function, so stay back a little!" Raphtalia imbued life force and magic into her katana and then unleased a skill. "Instant Blade! Mist!" she shouted. Sparks erupted from the cage. Lightning and fire flickered out as the counterattack she had predicted, but she slashed them away too. She had managed to cut it, but not all the way.

"Those counterattacks will be a pain if we let anyone else try," I pondered. "It's too small a target to really hit Attack Support . . . not impossible." Keel hadn't recovered from her beast transformation yet. It had really taken it out of her. The Demon Dragon had pulled it off with no trouble, so I'd thought Keel could take it . . . but she wasn't quite at the same level. She'd been a big help, but we'd better not rely on her doing that too often.

The Attack Support thorns thudded into the cage, and Raphtalia cut it again to shatter the prison around us. If it recovered from that, then we'd have to think of another way to handle it, but that seemed to have done the trick. There was a gap big enough for people to pass through safely.

"I'll put a Shooting Star Shield up just in case . . . Now let's get out of here," I suggested. The remaining cage sections were still sparking with electricity and I protected everyone with Shooting Star Shield as we passed through the gap.

"Great! Let's get to Ren." I turned to Keel. "You can—" But she cut me off with a moan.

"Bubba, why am I so pathetic? I can't even keep up with Ruft," Keel said. She had both hands covering her face, trying to hide her bitter tears from me.

"You bet you can keep up! You saved us all. If you still think that's not enough, then just get stronger. That's all you need to do," I told her.

"I do want to be stronger," she replied. "That way I can help you all out, Bubba." She sniffled, still trying to keep her tears in. "Raphtalia, can you send me somewhere safe? I'm only going to hold you back like this."

"Oh, Keel," Raphtalia said sympathetically.

"Please . . . I can hardly move. I don't want to hold you back," she said.

"Okay. Scroll of Return," Raphtalia said, using a skill that would send Keel back to the dragon hourglass in Siltran. I silently thanked Keel for everything she had done. I joked around with her a lot, but I wasn't going to let her powerful determination go to waste.

After treating ourselves on the spot, we headed in the direction where Ren and his party were also fighting monsters.

Chapter Fourteen: Known Vassal Weapon Heroes

We reached the path that Ren and his party were using to patrol the sanctuary. They had probably faced the same kind of attack that we had: trapped in a cage to prevent escape with a dragon Sanctuary over the top. I could only pray that they were safe. We hurried in the direction Raph-chan indicated. It didn't take long to see the same kind of cage that had held us.

"Raphtalia!" I shouted.

"Okay!" she replied. I launched Attack Support at the cage and Raphtalia cut into it with a skill. We rushed through the hole and into the cage itself. We found Ren, Eclair, and Chick all breathing hard, badly wounded, and standing in formation to protect Wyndia and Melty from further enemy attacks. The sword Melty was holding was creating a wall of wind, offering further protection. I guessed Raph-chan had managed to reach us thanks to that Filo-based sword. But even these defenses weren't enough to protect completely against an incoming hail of spear attacks. All of them were bleeding from multiple locations.

"Naofumi!" Melty said, her expression brightening as she noticed our arrival. "Naofumi and the others are here!"

"That's good," Ren managed. "Nice to get some reinforcements." There were countless spears circling around him, waiting for an opening. They had used swords with me, but now these were spears. Maybe they were worried about Ren, the Sword Hero, copying one of their deadly weapons.

"Reinforcements?" exclaimed one of their enemies. They looked to have a similar composition to the group we had fought against: one with the axe, another with the gauntlets, a wolf demi-human, a tiger therianthrope, and another that looked like a human. Piensa was apparently a mixed nation of humans and demi-humans. It looked like the human was in charge of this group.

"The Shield Hero?! I thought the first squad took care of them!" the human said.

"Would you believe us if I told you we drove our friends off?" I asked. That shut their leader up for a moment. I could see the cogs turning.

"They're here, so we have to deal with them!" said the one with the gauntlets. "I'll handle it!"

"Hold on!" said the leader, but it was too late. The Gauntlets Hero—who was dressed in clothing a lot like Fohl—closed in and unleashed a series of skills at me.

"Air Strike Rush V! Second Rush V! Torrid Rush V! Moonlight Kick V! Boldest Boulder-Busting Body Blow V!" he shouted in a sequence I had definitely seen before. Fohl had used the same combination when I was sparring with him. I blocked the spears flying toward me with my shields while taking the impact from each Gauntlet strike on my main shield, dampening, deflecting, or dismissing each attack.

"Impossible! He's reading my every move!" the Gauntlets Hero exclaimed.

"You know we have one of you guys too?" I said.

"Yes, but that's no reason to give up!" the enemy Gauntlets Hero replied, glancing over at the one with the axe—a short, stocky girl—and signaling her with his eyes. A hockey mask appeared. I'd seen this trick before as well.

"Jason Murder X!" the Gauntlets Hero shouted. Yep, I'd definitely seen this! This version looked more powerful than the one Armor had used. Slashes from what looked like a red chainsaw were attacking everyone around us.

"Get down!" I shouted. This attack had something of a fixed trajectory. I ducked down to avoid it and then grabbed the arm of the Gauntlets Hero.

"Are you sure you want to do that?" he asked. "Turtle Crush X!" He used his other arm to unleash a skill on me. I felt the impact coming and knew what kind of skill it was. I used life force to redirect it back into my opponent, but I was lacking enhancements in this time. It still caused me some damage.

"A counter?" the Gauntlets Hero said with a grunt, blood exploding from his mouth. He gritted his teeth and punched at me so hard again it looked like he wanted to shatter his own arm.

"Let go! Crescent Break X!" This came from the Axe Hero, who jumped toward me to protect the Gauntlets Hero while swinging her axe in a wide arc. It was a powerful attack that left a crescent moon shape in the air as it came down.

"I won't back down!" Raphtalia shouted.

"Don't forget about us!" Ruft added. S'yne and Shadow shouted too, all of them using their own weapons to stop the axe and knock it away.

"Keep the pressure on!" Melty shouted, raising her sword. Wyndia, Raph-chan, and Chick all shouted their agreement and transitioned into some cooperation magic.

"Filo! Lend me your strength across time! Mother Earth, pure flow of the Dragon Vein, lead those who wish to live, and bring us power! Dragon Vein! Hear our petition and grant it! As the source of your power, we implore you! Let the true way be revealed once more! Give us the power to overcome the obstacles before us! Intense Cooperation Magic: Thunder God!" Melty incanted. Their combined magic appeared in the air above them, raining lightning similar to Judgment down on the Piensa forces!

"Lightning magic? Take this!" the leader shouted, working out the effect of the incoming attack and then spreading out some of that cloth that bent space. The falling lightning hit the cloth and then stopped, vanishing in the air. What a pain in the ass.

"We expected that!" Melty shouted, slashing her sword to the side. Chick squawked as well, flapping her wings. Blades of wind slashed out that were mixed with droplets of poison.

"Nice try!" the tiger said, spinning his spear skillfully to catch all the incoming droplets. It might have poisoned him if they had landed . . . but then the tiger put a hand to his mouth. His face was pale. "Is this . . . blood?" Raph-chan and Chick had knowing smiles on their faces. A purplish mist appeared around the Piensa forces. It looked like Chick had been quietly dispersing her poison as Raph-chan had been concealing it. We had a ninja sucking up enemy blood and using it like a weapon and Ren throwing out attacks left and right. Raph-chan and Chick were showing them how a real ninja rolled.

"I'm zenzing an unzettling prezence!" Shadow said. "Where'z it coming from? Zomeone iz making fun of me!"

"If you can tell that much about it, you don't need to look any further than Mr. Naofumi," Raphtalia quipped. He seemed to have an impressive sixth sense, but this wasn't the time to deal with it.

"They're using poison mist!" one of the enemies shouted.

"We have some healing spray!" another replied. "Deploy it at once!" They seemed ready for anything. The wolf demi-human got out a canister and stamped down on it, spreading a mist around the Piensa forces.

"Go! Gae Bolg Custom!" shouted someone from the

Piensa forces, throwing out a horde of spears. They were targeting . . . Melty and Wyndia!

"Melty!" I cried out. Eclair and the others were also shouting her name. Eclair had been fighting alongside Ren, but she broke off and dashed toward Melty. Shadow repelled one of the Axe Hero's attacks and then did the same.

"Wyndia!" I shouted. I sent out Attack Support and then dashed over to protect Melty. Ren slashed into the spears with a roar in order to protect Wyndia.

"Shooting Star Sword X! Phoenix Gale Blade X!" he shouted. He scattered stars from his two swords to send the spears flying as he charged in, surrounded by fire.

"Shield Prison!" I protected the two girls with a cage of shields.

"Powder Snow!" Raphtalia shouted. She unleashed a skill that forcibly extracted the magic of an opponent on the Gauntlets Hero. He grunted as it took effect.

"You won't take us alive! Tornado Axe X!" the girl with the axe shouted. She spun around like a tornado as she closed in to protect the Gauntlets Hero from Raphtalia. "Bedrock Breaker X!" With a heavy thunk, the axe smashed out a crater and an earthquake rippled out. Raphtalia leapt backward to avoid the attack. Then the Axe Hero grabbed the Gauntlets Hero and fell back. She was working to save her ally.

Even as that happened, Ren was incanting magic.

"Liberation Magic Enchant!" he shouted, gathering the residue from Melty's cooperation magic into his sword. "Lightning Sword!" Then he unleashed it. Lightning crackled around his blade. Ren glared the enemy down. He looked like a brave and powerful hero. He was a flashy swordsman out of his own adolescent dreams. Looking at him in action, I could tell he wanted to graduate from that aspect of his personality. He had things he was good at and things I relied on him for.

"Lightning . . . Hundred Swords X!" Ren raised his sword and countless blades wreathed in lightning rained down around him. The Piensa forces were using those same cloths to deal with the rain of swords. The Axe Hero was just smashing them away. But she couldn't handle them all and was bleeding from numerous places.

"The Sword Hero . . . is so hard to fight!" the Axe Hero said through gritted teeth. She was glaring at Ren.

"Naofumi, about those two," Ren said.

"Yeah. Those are vassal weapons, aren't they?" I said.

"Looks like it," Ren said with a nod. "They've handled some of the attacks I launched as though they've seen them before."

"That goes both ways," the Axe Hero said. She was listening in on our conversation. "You have a Gauntlets Hero among your allies."

"And he's better than your guy," I said. I'd only taken a few blows from the guy, but it felt like he didn't have any life force training. I'd been able to damage him by using a reverse of the defense- ignoring or defense-rating attacks and sending it back to him. Fohl would have discharged that and let it flow away. He was definitely better in that regard. The weight of the weapons might be a factor too, but that could be down to a difference in support magic.

"I'm not going to let you write him off that easily," the Axe Hero said, "but I have to admit . . . you're strong."

"Has your holy weapon hero been taken hostage too?" I asked directly. Her reply was silence, just like the first two. When she eventually spoke, it was just the normal bluster again.

"For the sake of our world, and the sake of our hero, we can't lose here," she said. I decided to try something. It couldn't hurt.

"Can you tell us the power-up method for the axe?" I asked. It was a vassal weapon from a different world, but maybe we could use the seven star weapon axe power-up method to enhance Ren. That was something that the shield couldn't do.

"Naofumi, that was too blunt," Ren said.

"It's muscle enhancement," the girl replied. "The details are complicated. It would take time to explain." That was interesting. Any enemy we asked in the future would have shot that down at once. In that respect, I much preferred this time period with its serious heroes who fought with a sense of duty. "I'll tell you what I can—"

"Enough wasting time with chatter!" the Piensa leader cut in, earning a glare from me. She had just been about to spill the beans! "Retreat! I'm not happy with this result, but we've managed to cause some injuries. Now we just need to wait for them to weaken and then come back. The only way to heal those wounds is to come to Piensa. I hope you make the right decision." The countless spears returned to the leader's hands while the Axe Hero lifted the Gauntlet's Hero onto her back and rushed away as well. Then they used the same kind of cloth as the first squad to vanish completely.

A bunch of new heroes had shown up as reinforcements, after all. They had no idea what else might happen. A tactical retreat made sense for them, especially if (they thought) they'd caused incurable wounds.

"They backed off," I said. "That's pretty different from all the brain-dead resurrected and religious cults we've been fighting up until now." They were heroes and soldiers thinking about winning the war, not the battle. Their reactions were also totally different from when I dropped that monster train on them during our prior conflict. Fighting at this more personal level, they would be a force to be reckoned with. They had these strange weapons too. They probably hadn't used the swords because they were scared of Ren copying them. Even if they had been rigged to self-destruct if they fell into enemy hands, all Ren had to do was grab one during the fighting, copy it, and everything could turn in our favor.

"We survived, but they've deployed some annoying new faces," Melty bemoaned.

"Looks like the ones who assume the name of god are pretty worried about us," I commented. "They've taken the heroes from other worlds hostage to make their vassals fight us." I explained everything we had learned while I healed Ren and the others.

"An efficient way to fight an opponent who possesses the ability to kill them," Melty replied. "Really lowers the risk to their eternal stinking lives."

"They use the same dirty tactics in the future," I said. It felt like we were dealing with the same shit back there. After we killed one of them, maybe they had switched their approach to prevent any more deaths. It sounded plausible. They had also seemed to enjoy a big theatrical performance, so it did feel a bit different.

"It seems Piensa—and those behind them—want to cause incurable wounds to us and use that as leverage to take things in their desired direction," Melty said.

"Yeah. Either kill us outright or threaten us into working for them," I replied.

"For that to work, though, their incurable weapons have to actually be functioning," Melty pointed out.

"Right. I'm sure they have some backup plans if they discover the weapons aren't working," I said. I could heal the wounds, which was definitely something, but they would still prove deadly to almost anyone else inflicted with them.

"If we let the other nations know that Piensa has joined forces with the ones who assume the name of god, we might be able to form our own alliance, but that wouldn't be easy," Melty pondered. She made the same expression Trash did when thinking about a tricky operation.

"I'm sure some of them would sign up for it, but more of them would be too scared of the ones pulling the strings and choose to surrender rather than fight," Raphtalia concluded. It didn't sound like an effective solution. We also didn't want to have to answer questions about why my allies and I—the only ones who could actually kill this terrible evil Piensa had shacked up with—were avoiding direct conflict. Piensa might make a big thing about it or they might not. We needed to work with Mamoru to narrow down our strategy a little more.

One thing we had definitely learned was that we'd moved beyond the point where extracting the Bow Hero would solve this problem.

"A shame we didn't get the details of the power-up method from that axe girl," Ren said.

"Even if we did, we don't know it would have been the same as the axe in the future," I told him.

"That's an issue, sure," he admitted. Power-up methods didn't respond unless you were absolutely sure. We would need definitive proof that both the present and future axe had the same power-up method . . . "But the holy weapon hero they believe in is the Sword Hero, for sure."

"No doubt about that," I agreed. Serious fighting against actual heroes, not resurrected, would be such a pain in the ass. I didn't want to consider it. It would be great if we could find some common ground like we had with Glass and L'Arc, but that would be difficult if their holy weapon hero had been taken hostage. There were some gaps we could exploit—the fact they were doing this under duress and the fact we had the means to resist the ones doing the threatening. If we could rescue the hostage, they might well immediately side with us. "Defending isn't enough anymore; we need to go on the attack."

"Indeed. They seem to be prioritizing you over the sanctuary now," Melty said.

"What about everyone else?" I asked. "I bet they would come for Fohl too."

"I'm worried. Let's go!" Raphtalia said. We headed out to check on the other patrol groups and the village.

"Hey! Is everyone okay?" I shouted as we returned to the village. There were signs of fighting. A bloody Fohl was slumped at the entrance with Mikey behind him. Mamoru, Rat, and Holn were tending to everyone.

"Hey, Brother. We're okay. No loss of life. They attacked

with their strange weapons, as we expected. We held them off for a while and then a flare went up in the distance and they retreated," Fohl explained. I checked Fohl's wounds. He looked like he had some incurable ones.

"Their plan was to injure and weaken, surely," Holn said. "The future Shield Hero also drove off the ones attacking him, correct? They seemed to be in contact with their other allies."

"I'm not surprised," I said. "Were there any vassal weapon heroes among your attackers?"

"No. You saw some?" Holn asked in surprise. It sounded like we were only facing four of them. When we beat our group and then rushed over to help Ren, they must have made the decision for a full retreat.

"We'll get to that. I need to heal everyone first. Gather everyone with incurable wounds together. Best to handle this in one shot," I said. We decided to get into further discussion after the incurable wounds had been dealt with. "At least not many of you got hurt." Fohl and Holn had taken the bulk of the injuries. None of the others were especially badly hurt.

"Mikey was pretty good at protecting people who were about to get hurt," Rat explained. His clay-like body gave him excellent defensive properties. He did look a bit reduced in size though.

"Raph," said Mikey.

"The prototype Mikey vests also did a good job protecting

everyone wearing them," Rat added. She pointed at a pile of them that were discarded after the combat ended. It looked like a mountain of reddish lumps of flesh.

"They still broke through and focused their attacks to strip the armor away," Holn said. "I'm just happy it wasn't worse than this." I might have done better with some of that armor myself, but considering the volume of attacks I had suffered, it wouldn't have made much difference. Any protection I was wearing would just have been chopped up too. "With all of these injuries to examine, it will help my research."

"If you find a good counter, we need to get the information out there," I said.

"I'll do the best I can," Holn confirmed.

"What about you, Mamoru?" I asked him.

"Well . . . we were in the middle of infiltrating Piensa when the Raph species started to get worked up about something. We hurried back and took part in the battle," he explained. It sounded like they hadn't been attacked themselves. They had still been sneaking around—they probably hadn't been spotted at that point.

"The power of Filolia drove our enemies away!" Filolia exclaimed. She looked pretty happy with herself. I wondered what she had done. "It's a hard life having such a worthless sister."

"Please, don't get too carried away," R'yne said pretty halfheartedly. I pointed over at Filolia and Mamoru gave a wry smile.

"She shot out feathers from her wings, which confused the auto tracking on their weapons. That, combined with the Mikey protection, allowed us to put up a good fight. We only failed to keep Fohl safe because he was fighting on the very front line," Mamoru explained. Her feathers were treated as magic, making them a convenient form of attack that wasn't bound by rules regarding weapons.

Then Natalia and the Water Dragon came over.

"This is a critical situation. As both a pacifier and a vassal weapon hero, I can confirm that Piensa has crossed the line," Natalia declared.

"What about the Bow Hero?" I asked.

"He will still have a chance to explain himself, but I see little chance for him to talk his way out of this. Siding with Piensa makes him an enemy of the world. They have gone too far," Natalia said. Piensa had the advantage, but that was only because the ones who assume the name of god were involved in all this. My allies and I had been the secret weapon Siltran had been holding, and now Piensa had some vassal weapon heroes in pretty much the same position. The brief chat we had shared had revealed the complexity of the situation. We were in Siltran because we couldn't get back to our original time, and our holy weapon heroes hadn't been taken hostage.

"We need to be careful," the Water Dragon cautioned. "The fighting is only going to escalate from here."

"Indeed," Natalia agreed.

"I'm interested in why the Bow Hero didn't show up," I said.

"True," Natalia said. "It made things easier for us without him around, but it makes you think."

"There's a reason he didn't show up," I continued for her. From what Mamoru and Raphtalia had said about him, he didn't seem completely without promise. It was possible he had been imprisoned, or even killed, for speaking out against the direction Piensa was taking.

I really hoped Piensa weren't that stupid. They would need him to enhance their forces, if nothing else—even if those vassal weapons were the seven star weapons from the future, and they could perform some enhancement themselves. There were power-ups that Ren and I couldn't use. And the power-ups they were using were being reflected in Ren's power-ups. I thought for a moment about which power-up methods Ren was using on our allies. The staff was magic, the gauntlets were skills, and the projectile involved using money to increase the weapon upgrade limit. The axe was some kind of physical enhancement, we had learned. The effects were likely similar to the whip. If the ones who assume the name of god were involved in this, who knew how many worlds we would be facing enemies from? They probably wanted to confirm whether we were connected to the God Hunters or not. It didn't feel good being under the microscope like this.

"How are your investigations going, Mamoru?" I asked.

"Even inside Piensa, they are only claiming to have introduced some new technology that is giving them an edge. We need to dig a little deeper," Mamoru replied. They hadn't made much progress yet. This was something that was going to take time.

"At the same time, we need to work on obtaining the carriage vassal weapon and going to the world of the sword and spear," I confirmed. The heroes being held hostage were probably on their home world. Holy weapon heroes had difficulty traveling between worlds without special permission. The ones who assume the name of god might have dragged them here against their will, of course. We couldn't give up on recusing the hostages, wherever they were being held.

"We'd have a lot less trouble if you could cross to the sword world with a wave summons, Ren," I mused.

"I feel you. I've been thinking the same thing," he replied, his hand on his sword. These weapons could be such a pain in the ass. Sometimes I thought they were just messing with us on purpose. They really had something against doing what we wanted.

"If the weapons wanted to get in the way more than they have already, then what? They could prevent us from leaving this world?" I pondered. Mamoru was the hero in this time. If the shield still refused to let me leave, I'd order Atla to give the Shield Spirit a good kicking.

It felt like the gemstone on my shield flickered. Either the spirit was begging for me to call Atla off, or Atla was letting me know I only had to give the order.

"We might be able to sneak over in the chaos during a wave," I pondered. The ones causing the waves had placed a target on our backs, however, so it seemed unlikely they would let us get away with that. I wouldn't, if I was in their position. They might wait until they had a way to deal with us, then cause a wave to finish us off. I wasn't going to wait for that either.

"Mamoru, Filolia. Have you made a decision about Fitoria?" I asked. Filolia flushed red at my question and looked down at the ground.

"Suddenly getting a daughter . . . and then putting such a cruel burden on her. I don't want to accept it . . . but Fitoria wishes for this to happen, so I can try," Filolia said.

"Sounds like we're a go," Holn commented. She took out what looked like a Dragon Emperor Core and passed it to Mamoru. "I was planning on overseeing you making this, but we need all the time we can get, so I went ahead."

"Holn . . ." Mamoru said.

"I've packed in everything I could imagine you would have done, Mamoru, if you were making your child with Filolia," Holn explained.

"Is there anything you can't make?" I asked from the sidelines.

"I've adapted the Dragon Emperor's inheritance system and the tech I used for Natalia's hammer. It's not what you'd call a soul. It's more like something that will accelerate Fitoria's advancement into self-awareness," Holn explained. She wanted to bring down dragons as the most powerful monsters, but backing up that attitude had required a lot of study of those very monsters. That allowed her to apply all sorts of different techniques. "If you activate this crystal while performing a ritual in front of the carriage vassal weapon, it should be automatically adjusted to select her as the holder of the carriage vassal weapon."

"Okay. Let's get back to the sanctuary and pick up the carriage. There's no more time to waste," I said. In that moment, a wave of dizziness washed over me.

"Naofumi, are you okay?" Ren exclaimed.

"Yeah, I'm fine. I lost a lot of blood, and so I'm not back to full strength yet. I need a little longer, that's all," I replied. I'd fetched some rucolu fruit from the village stores and was wolfing them down. They were packed with nutrients that only I could unlock—for me, these were better than most medicine.

"I'm not sure I approve," Ren said.

"Mr. Naofumi, please stop pushing yourself so hard," Raphtalia added.

"I'll be careful," I told them. "We're just going to see a man about a carriage. Nothing to it."

"If you say so," Raphtalia replied.

"We should also pick up Keel from the Siltran dragon hourglass," I mentioned.

"Keel really proved her worth," Raphtalia said.

"She certainly did," I replied. We swung by to pick up Keel, finding her healed and happy. Her tail whipped from side to side as she leapt toward us.

"Bubba! Everyone! Did things go okay without me?" she asked. I picked her up for once—it couldn't hurt sometimes—and she started licking my face. She really was a dog!

"Yeah, nothing to report. What about you?" I asked.

"I'm still sore all over, but I can move around again," Keel yipped.

"If you aren't fully recovered, don't push yourself too hard," I cautioned her.

"I don't want to miss anything because of this," she replied.

"I heard what you did," Fohl said. "Good work."

"Bubba Fohl, beast transformation really hurt! How do you put up with it?" Keel asked.

"I don't do it all that often, but did it really hurt that badly?" Fohl asked. Holn stepped in at that point and started to question Keel.

"My estimates suggest it shouldn't place too much stress on you. What did you do?" Holn asked.

"Bubba lent me some strength," Keel replied.

"I had to use the cursed shield. It can be useful in a crisis," I said.

"Not surprised that caused some stress," Holn replied.

"I was filled with power too! But it felt kind of horrible . . . like I hated everyone. That's your trump card, huh, Bubba?" Keel said. It sounded like Keel had experienced some of the mental pollution from the Shield of Wrath. I was glad she hadn't been infected by the curse herself, but the blowback had still been harsh on her. "Now if I could maintain that strength for longer . . ." Keel said, looking at me with expectations on her face.

"I'd prefer it if you found a different way to get stronger," I said. Then I had a thought. "Are you okay with not getting turned into a cerberus?" I asked. She had been told she'd never be able to change back after transforming once, but she performed the beast transformation anyway.

"I'm fine. If I can obtain that strength and power, I'm fine," Keel said. I still didn't think it was the best approach.

"We should at least run some tests," Holn said. "We need to make sure the stress of this isn't causing any other issues."

"You finally see how dangerous your experiments are?" Rat said, homing in on Holn.

"Greater output than the individual can support is not a good idea," Holn admitted.

"You need to keep that in mind when you're around Duke," Rat said.

"You don't miss a chance to put the boot in," Holn said wryly.

"The same goes for you," Rat replied.

"There's a risk to Keel's life," I decided. "We won't use it again until Holn and Rat finish their tests."

"Okay," Keel finally said. "I'll toughen up." This had been a good learning opportunity for her. I wanted her to continue to grow and to learn the meaning of our fight.

"You need to take better care of yourself," Raphtalia said.

"That's rich, coming from you, Raphtalia! Everyone in the village is always thinking the same thing about you guys!" Keel shot back.

"She's got us there," I replied. We always did whatever it took to win, however crazy. Keel had taken notice.

We ended the discussion and moved things back to the sanctuary.

Chapter Fifteen: In the Sanctuary

"What's this?" Holn said. We had explained the situation to the lizard men in the village close to the sanctuary and were proceeding to complete the ritual to select the holder of the carriage. Holn's surprise was due to the gemstone on the whip vassal weapon starting to flash. "Something going on?" Holn held the whip in her hand and tilted her head. Maybe it was a warning about some kind of trouble.

In that same moment, a loud noise rumbled out, and smoke rose from the direction of the sanctuary. We all felt the nasty presence at the same time and started running toward the disturbance.

"What's happening?" I asked.

"That's a trap in the sanctuary," Holn explained.

"There are traps?" I said, surprised. We hadn't seen any of them.

"That's right. That one was set up to be triggered if anyone tries to force open the door to the carriage vassal weapon chamber without permission," Holn explained. They had some security in place.

"This means Piensa has other infiltration squads here?" I asked.

"It looks that way," Holn agreed. "But I don't think the Bow Hero would have triggered the trap on the carriage vassal weapon. I have a bad feeling about this." I'd be more interested if she had any other kind of feeling, given the situation. We quickly arrived at the source of the smoke.

"You're here already," said a voice. A wind whipped up, dispersing the smoke, and from it there emerged one of the ones who assume the name of god—one of the ones causing the waves. It was the one we had seen before, the one with the dog mask on. A barrier was crackling around him, and he somehow had the carriage vassal weapon floating at his side. It was trying to resist him but doing poorly. "I knew that nation was after something like this . . . but I'm surprised at the shoddy security," dog face said. He looked at us as we arrived, seemingly asking for our agreement. "This place is important too. The ancient heroes left all sorts of little traps to annoy us. No more problems from any of this now."

"You!" Ren had Sword 0 out purely on reflex, readying it to fight.

"Hold it," dog face barked. "I'm not here for that. But I can see the helping hand we offered your enemies was not enough to stop you. What crazy little ants you are." The one who assumes the name of god muttered to himself, using the carriage vassal weapon as a shield and dropping back away from us.

"What do you want? What are you doing with the carriage

vassal weapon?" I asked. Dog face looked at me with smoldering anger.

"I don't have to tell you anything," he growled. "You will pay for your grievous sin of killing a god."

"What do you mean by 'grievous sin'? We were simply punishing a crazy spree killer," I replied.

"And so you interfere with us, espousing justice," dog face said. Of course, he thought we had the God Hunters behind us. "Looking at the situation, you're not so different from us! Using heroes as your pawns and enjoying the confusion you cause us!" He seemed to have got the wrong idea—unless that was how the God Hunters operated. If I tried to correct him, I might give too much away, so I decided it was best to just let him rant. "You're stronger than before. Look at how angry you are. Such murderous intent! Are you trying to threaten me?" dog face accused, glaring at me. My murderous intent had gone unchecked since the moment we first met this guy, but I wasn't sure it had increased since then. I didn't know what he was talking about. We had uncovered the hammer vassal weapon's power-up method, so we were stronger than before, that was true. "The ones backing you will understand now! I'm taking this carriage to stop them from sending you to attack us! Now they'll see! This world is overflowing with those who seek nothing but domination! There's nothing here worth saving!"

"I can't argue with that last part," I replied. Every era

seemed the same in that regard. In our time, we had Melromarc, Faubrey, and Siltvelt all brimming with the desire for conquest, and the nations here in Mamoru's time seemed little different. The fact the heroes hadn't come together to stop the waves was proof enough of that. At least they were trying to avoid conflict between the heroes here—that was one improvement over our time. Back there, Motoyasu, Ren, and Itsuki had all considered the other heroes nothing more than rivals to defeat, at least in the beginning.

"Mr. Naofumi!" Raphtalia said.

"But we fight for those who that doesn't apply to," I continued. That was my answer, and I was sure it was the correct one. It was the answer I'd reached after coming to this other world, meeting so many people, and being saved by them. "So we're going to do everything we can to piss you off and stop you in your tracks. It might sound shitty, but that's what warfare is." That was the root of it. "Strategy," "tactics," there were all sorts of names for it and ways to wash off the dirt and legitimize it, but that was the root. I'd do whatever it took to protect those who needed my protection. I did have people to protect and people who had treated me kindly here. After I came to another world, my desire to be believed, my desire to protect others, had allowed me to withstand all the obstacles in my way. I felt so strongly that, yes, it was true, I sometimes did feel pleasure at defeating those trying to harm the ones I was protecting. "Just remember this," I said. "Don't do anything that you aren't prepared to have someone else do to you." That shut him up for a moment. None of these idiots ever considered that possibility. It was a principle of combat to try taking as little damage as possible. But at the same time you needed to prepare for the worst. I was going to treat these naive idealists who only dreamed of victory to a brutal life lesson.

"Hah. Enough bluster from you," dog face snapped. "Do you really expect the ones observing you to send aid?"

"Maybe they consider you so weak we don't require any aid from them to defeat you?" I quickly shot back. It seemed worth inflating my bluff a little, making it sound like the God Hunters didn't even consider this guy worthy of their time. "Should you be carrying on like this? Surrendering now and begging for your life might be the best idea." I was worried for a moment that I was laying it on too thick. This one who assumes the name of god had been a commentator on the waves, just like the one we killed. I wanted him to start worrying that maybe the God Hunters were taking out his audience, even now. That they could do anything they wanted. The more he feared them, the more power he attributed to them, the better it was for us. If he got worried or scared, he might make a mistake. He might create an opening for us to strike.

"Listen to you! Pond scum from some backwater world running your mouth!" dog face barked. It sounded like my taunts had found a target. I used my eyes to signal Ren, Mamoru, Holn, and the others to be ready to take back the carriage vassal weapon. Ren read my intent and took a small step forward—and just that movement was enough to grab dog face's attention. The glare he gave me from beneath his dog mask looked deadly enough to kill. Then he lifted the carriage vassal weapon high up into the air. I tried to think of a way to get it back . . . Then I recalled that the carriage was a vassal of the bow.

"Mamoru, as a hero, order the carriage vassal weapon to increase its resistance," I told him. The method they were using to bind the vassal weapon had to be the same as the one used by the resurrected in our time. This wouldn't have any effect if the weapon was with a chosen holder, but it certainly didn't look like that was the case here. That meant we could order the carriage to resist and hopefully set it free.

"What do you mean?" Mamoru stammered. He didn't know what I was talking about! They probably hadn't encountered any resurrected trying to steal vassal weapons in this time. That meant this fell to me. I lifted my shield . . . and then the one who assumes the name of god suddenly moved at incredible speed.

"I'm not falling for your taunts," dog face said. "I know this is what you want. That's why I'm taking it away from you. And that's not your only punishment!" Shouts went up from multiple people before I could even ready my shield. The one who assumes the name of god closed in so fast that he left afterimages behind. Then he grabbed Melty's collar where she sat on the back of Chick and lifted her off into the air. I cursed. We'd been close to taking him down, but this was completely out of left field. "I'm taking this one as a hostage too!" dog face crowed.

"Melty!" I shouted, the others joining in. Shadow and Eclair leapt forward, but the one who assumes the name of god escaped up into the air, still clutching Melty tightly.

"Oh? Why would you take me hostage?" Melty asked, keeping down her moans and taunting her captor in a tight voice.

"You're exactly the one we want. There's been talk about you," dog face said. "The little vixen, smartest among the slime, who has diplomatic skills." "Vixen" was the name someone had called Melty's mother.

"Hah. I'll take that name as an honor, coming from you," Melty replied, a regal smile on her face. She actually looked proud. For her, maybe being called "vixen" meant she was getting closer to her mother. I actually liked the sound of it too—and that totally disarmed it from having any negative connotations. "Removing me from play isn't going to have any negative impact on Naofumi's political dealings. There are plenty of others who can take my place," Melty said.

"We'll find out the truth of that soon enough," dog face said.

"You've touched upon the anger of all-powerful gods, and now you'll pay the price!"

"All-powerful gods, you say? And yet you can't see the future?" Melty chuckled. "What a joke."

"You scum! You dare mock us!" dog face raged.

"I'm just telling the truth," Melty said. "If you are all-powerful, then you don't need to take hostages. This display of your ineptitude proves you aren't as powerful as you think." Seeing her standing her ground, I realized Melty displayed both the regal nature of the queen and the strength of Trash. "Be honest! Tell us you don't want to die and ask us to stop! Beg us not to kill you! But that won't be enough for Naofumi and the heroes of Siltran to forgive you!" Melty said defiantly. Dog face grunted. "Like Naofumi always says! Only fire if you're ready to get shot!"

"Silence! Say another word and your life is forfeit!" The one who assumes the name of god tossed Melty toward the carriage vassal weapon. She was drawn into the barrier and lifted away. The gemstone on the carriage vassal weapon glowed and changed into the shape of a carriage. Melty was placed inside.

"What are you planning to do to Melty?!" I shouted.

"That all depends on you. Let the ones behind you know! If you want your friend here back, drop the barrier and withdraw or she won't be the only one paying the price! Let's see what your justice is really worth!" The one who assumes the name of god vanished from view, laughing as he disappeared.

"Shit!" I cursed. His speed had been incredible. He took not only the carriage vassal weapon but Melty too. If I had closed in a little more, I might have been able to deploy an Air Strike Shield and save her.

"Zhield Hero!" shouted Shadow.

"Hero Iwatani!" cried Eclair. There was panic in their voices, and confusion at what to do next. "I still wasn't fast enough . . . I need to be faster!"

"Try to calm down," I told them. "He took Melty as a hostage. That means they have no plans to kill her right away, and I doubt he's building a harem like a resurrected."

"I won't allow that!" Eclair shouted, surging to her feet. "Queen Melty stands alongside the heroes as one I must protect, no matter what!"

"That'z right!" Shadow agreed.

"We need to work out where they've taken her and find a way to save her," I said. "Shadow, what do you do again?"

"Recon and infiltration. But I've no idea where to ztart!" Shadow said, exasperated already. "They are like heroez, zipping around."

"I think I can help a little with that," Holn said, pointing at the gemstone in the whip. A faint beam of light was extending out from it. "I think the carriage vassal weapon is telling me where it is."

"Zo I just need to follow thiz light?" Shadow asked.

"That's right, but it won't be that simple," Holn replied. She looked in the direction the light was pointing. It was right toward Siltran. But no, that wasn't it. Even I knew the light was indicating a destination beyond that friendly nation. It almost didn't need to be said.

The final destination of the light was Piensa, the nation the ones who assume the name of god had already taken such an interest in.

"Queen Melty," Eclair said softly.

"How can we get her back?" Shadow asked.

"It seems that the ones who assume the name of god are blaming those they think are behind us for some kind of barrier that's getting in their way," I said. "When we fought them before, they said something about not being able to search for us. It sounds like some function of the 0 series is working in our favor again." It wasn't clear if this was a physical or mental effect. They had come at us with this new approach, however, rather than just using force. They wanted to avoid fighting us head-on. If we could remove any chance of escape and force them to fight, maybe we had a chance at defeating them.

"The carriage seemed to understand the situation, because it changed shape to protect Melty," I recalled. "I don't know how effective it will be, but it's a vassal weapon. We can pray it can do something to help. That's pretty much all we can do right now . . . Anyway, I've no intention of giving up." The carriage vassal weapon was sharing its location with us. There was still hope. We couldn't give up now. "We will take back Melty, obtain the carriage vassal weapon, and fight them head-on. I think the time has come for Piensa to finally be eradicated from this world." We had plenty of heroes on our side. They had some too, but I didn't care. We'd overcome all sorts of odds this far. We had to save Melty.

In that moment, a large shadow dropped down slowly from the sky, accompanied by the sound of heavy wingbeats.

Epilogue: Dragon Slayer

It was a massive Western-style dragon—the same one I had seen when we encountered the Piensa forces. I was immediately on the alert for some kind of attack.

"Heroes of Siltran, Pacifier, and proud guardian dragon," the dragon said. "I do not come seeking violence." The dragon flapped its wings a few more times and landed, then bowed its head low. Then it gradually shifted into the form of a humanoid woman.

"It is you," Holn said, a catch in her voice.

"It has been a while, Holn," the dragon replied.

"Not a meeting I asked for, either. What are you showing up for now?" Holn spat, an annoyed expression on her face. I pointed at the dragon, without saying anything. Holn frowned before finally explaining. "This is a dragon the Bow Hero of Piensa raised . . . a Dragon Emperor."

"To be more precise," the dragon woman said, "I was also, in some part, modified by Holn."

"I'm surprised you're just showing your face like this," Holn said. "You haven't forgotten what you told me when you led Piensa, have you?"

"I'm not here to debate dragons being the ultimate

monster—which they are. But you understand we have more pressing matters to discuss," the dragon said evenly.

"You sound a lot more reasonable than the other Dragon Emperors I've encountered," I commented. I wondered if the title was correct. Either way, I'd rather have this one than something like the one who had been with Takt.

"I have pride as a dragon," the woman replied. "But I have still come to discuss things with you. I hope you would at least hear me out." Now she sounded like the weakest Dragon Emperor. "I wouldn't dream of being arrogant with you either." For some reason, the Piensa Dragon Emperor was looking at me . . . and blushing. A chill ran down my spine. We'd only just met this new dragon, and I was having Demon Dragon flashbacks already.

"Indeed. I'm hoping to maintain a friendly relationship with this Shield Hero too," the Water Dragon said, offering some unsolicited backup. "He has no attack power, so when he strokes your scales, you really do feel it."

"It does?" the dragon woman said. "I would very much like to be stroked."

"Gaelion has said the same thing," Wyndia chimed in. "Getting his scales stroked by the Shield Hero makes him feel really happy." Gaelion was always trying to rub up against me. I hoped he wasn't getting turned on by that! All the more reason to keep him away from me. As for the Demon Dragon . . . she made no attempt to hide her desire for me, but she wasn't rubbing herself over me either.

"Interesting . . . maybe you're a different kind of dragon slayer?" Natalia proposed. "One that dragons like a bit too much?"

"The surveys my descendant and I have conducted actually suggest that most monsters take a liking to him. His encounter rate with monsters is also higher than that for Mamoru," Holn revealed, adding some scientific research to Natalia's suppositions. I wanted to shut this down before things ballooned any further.

"The Bow Hero did say maybe you had a special ability that makes monsters like you," Raphtalia said.

"Raphtalia, even you're getting in on this?" I said.

"Maybe that's why demi-humans like you," Raphtalia said.

"Naofumi is certainly beloved by people other than humans," Ren agreed, looking over at me sympathetically.

"Can I just pack up and run off?" I asked.

"Sorry, everyone . . . Mr. Naofumi is trying to avoid reality again. We're getting off topic as well. Shouldn't we be worrying about Melty?" Raphtalia said.

"That's right," I quickly said. "Forget about me. Focus on Melty." None of this banter mattered at the moment. I had been proving popular with dragons recently, but I didn't swing that way myself. What I wanted to do was be surrounded by countless Raph-chans and Raph species and just drift off to sleep each night.

"Mr. Naofumi, I'm trying to change the subject. Don't make that face," Raphtalia said, cautioning me quietly. Her abilities to read my mind were definitely improving. I was sure of that now.

"Piensa is crawling with our enemies at the moment," I stated. "So what is their Dragon Emperor doing here?"

"Allow me to explain," the female dragon said, finally getting to business. "No more beating around the bush either. I'm begging you, please bring an end to the rampage of Piensa and save my master, the Bow Hero."

"Save him?" I asked. He had come up in conversation a few times, but we hadn't seen anything of the Bow Hero since this fresh chaos started. I thought maybe it was that the Bow Hero and Shield Hero never got along, but Raphtalia had said that he was quite willing to listen. I'd also heard that Piensa had him by the balls, so to speak, so he couldn't defect at the moment even if he wanted to.

"Allow me to apologize for erecting that barrier that prevented your escape," the dragon woman said. "If I hadn't done so, my master would have been killed."

"What's the exact situation with him?" Mamoru asked the Dragon Emperor.

"After it became clear that you had killed one of those who

assume the name of god, the mood of our previously frustrated Piensa royalty swiftly improved, and they started to talk
about unification of the world. At the time, I thought they were
just trying to escape from reality," the Piensa Dragon Emperor
said, seemingly unconcerned about keeping anything back.

To start with, the Piensa royals had failed to achieve their
desired ruling of the world, and the possibility of its realization seemed to be slipping away. The people of the nation, and
the Bow Hero and his party, had drawn the same conclusion.
One day, a mysterious individual had appeared in Piensa, accompanied by vassal weapon holders from other worlds. They
had promised to lend Piensa their strength. That led to the attacks with the deadly weapons on the other nations that had
been considering siding with Siltran. When the Bow Hero had
objected to this, some of his closest friends had been taken as
hostages before he was imprisoned along with them. Her master was turned into a prisoner. The Piensa Dragon Emperor
had been forced to continue to cooperate with those in charge.

She also had no doubts about who was behind it all.

"Is it safe for you to make contact with us now?" I asked.

"I'd say it's pretty dangerous," the dragon woman replied,
"but I determined that my master would give me these exact
orders. We both share the same love for this world." I liked her
reply. In our case, most of the heroes had just been geeking out
about coming into a game they had spent so much time playing.

At least we were all more serious about fighting for this world now. Ren, of course, did it to atone for his past. Itsuki did it to protect the justice that Rishia believed in. Motoyasu . . . for Filo, probably. And myself, I did it to protect this world for Raphtalia and the others. If the ones who assume the name of god or a nation I belonged to had taken those I cared for hostage, and were forcing me to fight those who could resist the real threat to the world . . . I wouldn't have been able to stand it either. Regardless of the risks, I would seek help.

"One of our party was just kidnapped," I told the dragon woman. "I'm presuming you'll help us get her back?"

"I'll help however I can. That's why I'm here," she replied.

"Okay then," I said.

"It seems that the ones who assume the name of god are unable to spy on you, like they can on others. That means, if we work together, we can trick them," the dragon woman said. It sounded like the 0 series was providing a barrier of sorts, which kept the ones who assume the name of god from being able to detect us.

Then the Piensa Dragon Emperor bowed her head in my direction.

"I must admit you really influence me as a Dragon Emperor to obey your every command," she said. "I've never felt this way before." I recalled how the 0 series had an effect that could strip away eternal life as well as being effective against dragons. Gaelion had kept his distance from me just before we came back in time. We'd been talking about stroking his scales. Maybe there was something about me that both scared and attracted dragons.

It was something about the 0 territory, perhaps. The Water Dragon had said he felt impending violence coming from me after incanting magic with "0" in it.

"You said you'll help however you can. Can you be more specific?" I asked.

"I'll give you a secret entrance to Piensa Castle, for a start," the dragon woman replied. "And information on security patrols. I'll give you it all. If they realize what's happening, I can help out in battle. If you can connect me . . . to the terminal of your power . . . I can become . . . stronger . . ."

"Raph!" said Raph-chan. Just as the Piensa Dragon Emperor was reaching unsteadily for me, Raph-chan jumped onto her shoulder and hit her softly in the face with her tail.

"What was . . . I doing . . ." the dragon woman stammered.

"It looked like you were reaching for me," I said. "You weren't trying to absorb me or something, were you?" The Dragon Emperor had that ability. The Demon Dragon could absorb heroes and use their power for herself.

"I'd never do such a thing!" the dragon woman replied. Maybe Raph-chan had been warning her about trying something.

"A terminal . . . yes, there is one here," the Water Dragon confirmed, moving over toward me, a strange look in his eyes.

"Raph!" said Raph-chan, leaping in to whack him too, making him grunt.

"There's definitely a hard-to-resist allure to you, now that you mention it. Who set this up?" the Water Dragon asked.

"That would be me!" came the voice in my head. The moment I heard it, rage boiled up inside me. What had she done to me now?! She was the reason I was now a (sexual) dragon slayer! The next time we met, she was going to pay dearly for this! I wondered why she would even do this. It only meant other dragons were going to mob me! No matter how I raged inside my head, the Demon Dragon's implanted personality didn't reply. It only ever responded to single words and magic-related stuff, so I wasn't really expecting anything, but this had still really pissed me off!

"The one responsible here is the Demon Dragon . . . it seems she's better setting these things up so that I can maintain my rage," I explained, pressing a hand to my forehead.

"Which means if a dragon lends you their power, Mr. Naofumi . . . they can have access to power like the Demon Dragon," Raphtalia asked.

"I think so. What happened with Keel is likely a byproduct of that," I said.

"I fear weaker dragons would be consumed whole," the

dragon woman said. "Such is the strength of the curse I feel
from the Shield Hero." It was my rage . . . my base desire for
power that allured the dragons to me. In any case, it looked
like the Water Dragon and Piensa Dragon Emperor could be
further enhanced by this. "Will you please help? If you help my
master, I'll give you whatever you desire . . . treasure, my body,
even my mind."

"What are you talking about?!" Raphtalia said, concern on
her face.

"It sounds like you want me to possess you," I asked. She
didn't deny it. I wanted her to deny it.

"What is this? Changing bedfellows?" Mamoru asked with
either a poor or deliberate choice of words.

"An interesting situation. I'd very much like to investigate
it. I'd also love to see the Bow Hero's reaction," Holn added,
her curiosity sparking.

"This isn't interesting at all. The one who did this to me is
to blame!" I said.

"Mr. Naofumi, if the Piensa Bow Hero finds out about this,
he's going to be like L'Arc all over again," Raphtalia warned.
That was a nasty example for her to choose. That hadn't been
my fault either. Therese had gone all wacky on her own. In this
case, it was the work of these strange pheromones set up by the
Demon Dragon.

"I've heard that fear feels a bit like love . . . Your presence is definitely appealing to dragons," the Water Dragon said, making things weird again.

"The hero loved by the world!" Filolia laughed. "This is interesting indeed!" No, it wasn't. It wasn't at all. Her sister was waiting behind her. I swore at her not to say anything.

"Can you get this thing off me?" I asked. I wasn't going to feel safe until my auto dragon slaying issue was resolved.

"If I connected and made a few adjustments, that shouldn't be a problem," the Water Dragon said.

"Wait. I'm more suited to this," the dragon woman said. "Is this really a problem a guardian dragon should be using their power to intervene in? I can bring out more of his power."

"You are joking," the Water Dragon replied. The two dragons started bickering, tension crackling in the air between them.

"I'm so glad the Water Dragon has taken a liking to you," Natalia said. She seemed very pleased with herself, like she finally had something to hold over me. "I've never seen him like this before."

"Dafu," said Dafu-chan, equally happy about all this.

"I'll choose . . . the pacifier's dragon, thank you. I can trust him more," I said.

"Yes! My virtue wins the day!" the Water Dragon celebrated. I had no idea what that meant. I continued to bring out the strangest reactions from dragons.

"This can't be . . ." the Piensa Dragon Emperor said,

looking over with jealous eyes. Unfortunately for her, those eyes did nothing for me. In fact, they pissed me off.

"Stop looking at me like that," I told her. "I hate people who make faces like that."

"Yeah, me too," Ren agreed, both of us looking at the Piensa Dragon Emperor. It was like when Bitch was using her wiles to get something. Then Wyndia sidled over and took the Piensa Dragon Emperor's hand. I wondered if any dragon at all would do it for her. This one was trying to become our ally, but she could still put her guard up a little.

"Do you want the Shield Hero to like you?" Wyndia asked. The Piensa Dragon Emperor nodded. "Then I'd stop making faces like that. My dragon, Gaelion, has conducted all sorts of research to keep in the Shield Hero's good books. I can share some tips with you," she offered.

"Wyndia? Let's not cause any more trouble for Naofumi, if we can help it. This might be a Dragon Emperor, but that doesn't mean we can trust her yet," Ren said, dashing over to Wyndia.

"I can do what I like," Wyndia replied, not giving Ren the time of day.

"Water Dragon, hurry up and heal me," I said.

"Okay," the Water Dragon replied. With that, the Water Dragon started to mess around with my shield. The Water Dragon's scales started to glisten.

"Wow . . . this is quite something . . ." the Water Dragon said.

"Ah. The presence is fading a little," the Piensa Dragon Emperor noticed, still looking jealously at the Water Dragon.

"You just need to work hard to make him like you," Wyndia said. "We'll need your strength in our coming battles, so you'll have plenty of chances." Her approach to consolation felt very out of place. She did love dragons and doted on Gaelion. Maybe that was the problem—she wasn't getting her fix since coming to the past. I wished she could make do with the Water Dragon.

"I wish I could send some of this to the Raph-chans," I said.

"Raph?! Raph, raph!" Raph-chan exclaimed. The Raph-chans had helped hold me back when I used the Shield of Rage. Maybe it was flowing into them. They just couldn't turn it into power.

"I'd like to be able to do that too," Ruft said.

"Please don't say that," Raphtalia replied.

"Moving on," I said. "Piensa Dragon Emperor. Whether we save your master or not . . . the sins of Piensa are severe. They've lent aid to those who have kidnapped our friend Melty." Everyone there nodded at my words.

"I agree. There's no justice left in Piensa now. They're trying to sell out this world. Eradicating their noble line is for the best of us all," the Piensa Dragon Emperor said. It sounded like we'd got ourselves an insider. First, we needed to save Melty and the Bow Hero.

Saving Melty meant saving a princess, of course—but now she was a queen.

"Time to take down a nation," I said. "The God Hunter heroes will eradicate Piensa for joining forces with the enemies of this world!"

"Oh, good line!" Filolia cackled, looking over at Mamoru. "The Dark Brave and her allies will help you out! Right, Mamoru?"

"Yeah. I can't sit by any longer—and I'm worried about the Bow Hero. It's time to end this fighting," Mamoru said, sounding fired up himself.

"This reminds me of when we went into Q'ten Lo," Raphtalia said. "You got everyone worked up then too, didn't you, Mr. Naofumi?"

"It was like this, wasn't it?" Ruft said cheerfully. He was actually the very target we had been there to take down.

"Yeah, it was like this," I replied. "I think morale is even higher this time." Everyone was worried about Melty. It wouldn't go like this if I was the one who'd been taken—my lack of attack power probably didn't make me a threat, they'd think. *He'll be fine for a while*, they'd think. "Let's make them really feel it this time!" Getting back to our time was important, but this came first. We needed the carriage vassal weapon and to get to the world of the sword and spear. So we'd take everything back, save the heroes from that world too, and make the ones who assume the name of god pay.

Our intentions were clear. And that was the start of the war.

The Rising of the Shield Hero Vol. 22
(TATE NO YUUSHA NO NARIAGARI Vol.22)
© Aneko Yusagi 2019
First published in Japan in 2019 by KADOKAWA CORPORATION, Tokyo.
English translation rights arranged with KADOKAWA CORPORATION, Tokyo.

ISBN: 978-1-64273-133-0

Written by Aneko Yusagi
Character Design Minami Seira
English Edition Published by One Peace Books 2021

Printed in Canada
1 2 3 4 5 6 7 8 9 10

One Peace Books
43-32 22nd Street STE 204 Long Island City New York 11101
www.onepeacebooks.com